Books by Elizabeth Peters

The Amelia Peabody Series

and

The Vicky Bliss Series

The Jacqueline Kirby Series

and

BORROWER OF THE NIGHT

ELIZABETH PETERS

HARPER

An Imprint of HarperCollins*Publishers*

HARPER

An Imprint of HarperCollins*Publishers*
10 East 53rd Street
New York, New York 10022-5299

Copyright © 1973 by Elizabeth Peters
Excerpt from *The Laughter of Dead Kings* copyright © 2008 by MPM Manor, Inc.
Excerpts copyright © 1973, 1978, 1983, 1987, 1994 by Elizabeth Peters
ISBN 978-0-06-165607-1

First Harper Premium paperback printing: August 2008
First Avon Books paperback printing: September 2000

HarperCollins® and Harper® are registered trademarks of HarperCollins Publishers.

Printed in the United States of America

Visit Harper paperbacks on the World Wide Web at www.harpercollins.com

10 9 8 7 6 5 4 3 2 1

For Betty and George
who don't believe
in ghosts either

FOREWORD

As all lovers of Rothenburg will realize, I have
had the temerity to add Schloss Drachenstein to
the genuine attractions of the town. Like all the
characters in this book, the Counts and Countesses
of Drachenstein are wholly fictitious and bear no
resemblance to any persons living or dead. Equally
fictitious, sad to say, is the legend of the Riemenschneider shrine. Apart from the single aberration,
the sculptor's life and works were as I have described
them.

BORROWER OF THE NIGHT

ONE

WHEN I WAS TEN YEARS OLD, I KNEW I WAS NEVER going to get married. Not only was I six inches taller than any boy in the fifth grade—except Matthew Finch, who was five ten and weighed ninety-eight pounds—but my IQ was as formidable as my height. It was sixty points higher than that of any of the boys—except the aforesaid Matthew Finch. I topped him by only thirty points.

I know—this isn't the right way to start a narrative, if I hope to command the sympathy of the reader. A narrator should at least *try* to sound modest. But believe me, I'm not bragging. The facts are as stated, and they are a handicap, not a cause for conceit. If there is anything worse than being a tall girl, it is being a tall *smart* girl.

For several years my decision didn't give me much pain. I wasn't thinking seriously of marriage in the fifth grade. Then I reached adolescence, and the trouble began. I kept growing up, but I grew in another dimension besides height. The results were appalling. I won't quote my final proportions; they call to mind one of those revolting Bunnies in *Playboy*. I dieted strenuously, but that only made matters worse. I got thin in all the right places and I was still broad where, as the old classic says, a broad should be broad.

Mind you, I am still not bragging. I am not beautiful. I admire people who are slender and fine-boned and aesthetic-looking. The heroine of my adolescent daydreams had a heart-shaped face framed in clouds of smoky black hair. She was a tiny creature with an ivory complexion and a rosebud mouth. When she was enfolded in the hero's brawny arms, her head only reached as high as his heart.

All my genes come from my father's Scandinavian ancestors—big blond men with rosy cheeks and blazing blue eyes. They were about as aesthetic-looking as oxen. That's what I felt like—a big, blond, blue-eyed cow.

The result of this was to make me painfully shy. I suppose that seems funny. Nobody expects a bouncing Brunhild to be self-conscious. But I was. The intelligent, sensitive, poetic boys were terrified of me; and the ones that weren't terrified didn't want to talk about poetry or Prescott. They didn't want to talk at all. Rubbing my bruises, I became a confirmed misandrist. That attitude left me lots of time in which to study. I collected degrees the way some girls collect engagement rings. Then I got a job as a history instructor at a small Midwestern college which, in view of what is to follow, had better be nameless. It was there I met Tony. Tony teaches history too. He's bright; very bright. He is also six feet five inches tall, and, except for his height, he rather resembles Keats in the later stages of consumption.

I met Tony on the occasion of the first departmental faculty meeting. I was late. Being late was a mistake; I hate walking the gauntlet of all those male eyes. There was one other woman present. She looked the way I wanted to look—thin, dark, and intellectual. I smiled hopefully at her and received a fishy stare in return. Most women take an instant dislike to me. I can't say I don't know why.

I spotted Tony amid the crowd because of his height. There were other things worth noticing—big brown eyes, broad shoulders, and black hair that flopped over his forehead and curled around his ears. His face was fine-boned and aesthetic-looking. At that moment, however, it had the same expression that was on all the other male faces, except that of Dr. Bronson, the head of the department. He had interviewed me and had hired me in spite of my measurements. I'm not kidding; it is a common delusion, unshaken by résumés and grades, that a woman with my proportions cannot have anything in her head but air.

I sat down with an awkward thump in the nearest chair, and several men gulped audibly. Dear old Dr. Bronson smiled his weary smile, brushed his silvery hair back from his intellectual forehead, and started the meeting.

It was the usual sort of meeting, with discussions of schedules and committees and so on. After it was over I headed for the door. Tony was there ahead of me.

I don't remember how he got me out of the building and into the Campus Coffee Shoppe, but I have never denied he is a fairly smooth talker. I remember some of our conversation. I hadn't encountered a technique quite like his before.

The first thing he said was,

"Will you marry me?"

"No," I said. "Are you crazy?"

"Haven't you ever heard of love at first sight?"

"I've heard of it. I don't believe in it. And if I did, love and marriage don't necessarily go together. *Au contraire*."

"So beautiful and so cynical," said Tony sadly. "Doesn't my honorable proposal restore your faith in my sex?"

"It merely reinforces my impression that you are crazy."

"Look at it this way." Tony put his elbows on the table. The table wasn't very clean, but neither were Tony's elbows; I deduced that this pose was characteristic. "All my life I've been looking for my ideal woman. I'm pushing thirty, you know; I've had time to think about it. Beauty, brains, and a sense of humor, that's what I want. Now I know you're intelligent or old Bronson wouldn't have hired you. He's above the sins of the flesh, or thinks he is. You are obviously beautiful. Your sense of humor—"

"Ha," I said. "You deduced that from the twinkle in my eye, I suppose."

Tony cocked his head and considered me seriously. A lock of black hair fell over his left eyebrow.

"Is that a twinkle? It looks more like a cold, steely glint. No, I'm willing to take the sense of humor on trust."

"You'd be making a mistake. I am not amused. And even if I were amused, I wouldn't marry you. I'm not going to marry anyone. Ever."

"If you prefer that arrangement," said Tony, with a shrug.

So it went, for most of the winter. The demoralizing thing about Tony was that he wasn't kidding. He really did want to get married. That didn't surprise me; any man with a grain of sense knows that marriage is the only way, these days, to acquire a full-time maid who works twenty-five hours a day, with no time off and no pay except room and board.

Naturally Tony wouldn't admit to these motives. He kept babbling about love. He couldn't help it. His background was hopelessly conventional. He came from a big jolly family out in the Bible Belt, with a fat jolly mother and a tall, thin jolly father—he showed me their pictures, which he kept on his desk. That shows you what he was like. He was crazy about his parents. He even liked his brothers and sisters, of whom there seemed to be an indeterminate number. He had a half-ashamed and inarticulate desire for children of his own. Oh, his ostensible motives were admirable—and his attractions were considerable. To say we were physically compatible is to put it mildly, but that wasn't all; we had a hundred interests in common, from European history to basketball. (He had been the star of his high school team, and so had I.) He shared my passion for medieval sculpture, and he was crazy about old Marx Brothers movies. I couldn't imagine finding anyone I liked better. But I didn't weaken.

"Why not?" Tony demanded one day. It was a

day in January or the beginning of February, and he was getting exasperated. "Damn it, why not? Are you down on marriage just because it's out of fashion? I didn't think you were so conventional!"

"That has nothing to do with it. I'm not against marriage *per se*. I'm against it for me. I'm not going to get married. Why the hell do I have to repeat it every other day? I think I'll make a tape."

"That's ridiculous."

"What, the tape? It would save the wear and tear on my vocal cords. Now listen, Tony—" I put my elbows on the table, and then removed them; I was certainly not going to imitate his vulgar habits. "Your attitude is a perfect illustration of the reason why I don't intend to marry. I state a point of view, and you attack it. You don't listen, you don't try to understand, you just say—"

Tony said it.

"Obscenities will get you nowhere," I said. "My feelings are a fact, not a personal delusion. They are valid for me. What business have you got trying to tell me how I ought to feel? You think you want an intellectual wife, who can discuss your work with you. But it wouldn't last. After awhile you'd start expecting apple pie instead of articles, and then you'd want me to quit work, and if I got promoted and you didn't, you would sulk, and then if we had a baby you wouldn't get up in the middle of the night and change its dirty diapers—"

I stopped, not because I had finished my monologue, but because Tony wasn't listening. His elbows were on the table, his face was hidden in his hands, and he was laughing so hard that the table shook.

Since he wasn't looking, I permitted myself a sour smile. So maybe it did sound funny. But the basic premise was sound. I knocked one of Tony's elbows out from under him so that his chin splashed into his coffee cup, and that ended that discussion.

But it wasn't the end of the argument. I could tell by the speculative gleam in Tony's eye that for the first time he was really thinking about the problem. It was amusing to watch him ponder my hang-up, as he called it, as methodically as he would consider an abstract academic question. At least it was amusing until he came out with his conclusions.

We were at Tony's apartment. He had built a fire in the fireplace and had carefully seated himself in a chair across from the couch where I was sitting. He hadn't touched me all evening, which was enough of a change to make me wary. He sat there for a long time staring at me, and finally he said,

"I've figured it out."

"Oh, have you?"

"Yes. What you need is to be dominated."

"Is that right," I said.

"That tough exterior is a defense," Tony explained. "Underneath, you are looking for a stronger shoulder to lean on. But since you are a superior female, you need to be convinced that the male is even more superior."

"All right," I said, between my teeth. "You may be stronger than I am, you ape, but just try those gorilla tactics on me and you'll get something you—"

"No, no, I'm not talking about anything as crude

as physical domination. I intend to convince you of my intellectual superiority."

"Ha, ha," I said.

"You doubt that I am your intellectual superior," Tony said calmly. "Of course you do. That's your trouble."

I bit back the yell of outrage that was right on the tip of my tongue. He wanted me to lose my temper; that would prove my emotional immaturity.

I leaned back on the couch, crossed my legs, and took a deep breath. Tony's eyes glazed, but he didn't move.

"And how," I inquired, practicing deep breathing, "do you propose to convince me?"

Tony was a funny color. With some effort he dragged his eyes away from my torso and stared at the fire.

"I haven't figured that out yet," he admitted. "But I will."

"Let me know when you do." I fell back onto the couch, hands clasped behind my head. I kicked off one of my shoes. "Did I tell you I expect to have two articles published by the end of the year? How are you coming with the one you started last fall?"

That was too much. Tony growled and lunged. I was ready for him; I slid out from underneath and stood looking fondly down on him as he sprawled awkwardly across the couch.

"Since you are going to dominate me mentally, there's no point in this sort of thing," I said, slipping my foot back into my shoe. "Call me when you're ready to start dominating."

He was ready sooner than I expected.

It was one of those awful March days in the Midwest, when ice and snow and sleet seem doubly outrageous because they follow a few days of mild weather. Slogging along through the slush, I was not in my best mood, even though the evening ahead looked interesting. Tony was about to share one of his finds with me—a man, not a theory of history. Jacob Myers was one of the big wheels in our little town. Actually, he was the only wheel of any size. One of his ancestors had donated the land on which the university was built; the family automobile plant was the leading industry. The public library, the main street, and the park were all named after members of the clan. Having too much money (if that is possible) and a weakness for culture, Myers dispensed fellowships and research grants with a lavish hand. Oddly enough, one of the few faculty members who hadn't profited from this generosity was Tony, though his father and Myers were lodge brothers, or something. I happened to know—though not from Tony—that he had even paid back the money Myers had loaned him to finish graduate school. Myers hadn't liked that. My informant declared the old man used to light his cigars with Tony's checks until Tony threatened to leave the town and the university.

I never said Tony lacked good qualities.

Anyhow, this was the night on which I was destined to meet the great man. And if he was inclined to throw any research money my way, I was fully prepared to accept it.

Tony should have picked me up that night, but that was one of his weapons in our not-so-unarmed cold war: no concessions to femininity, not even common politeness. If I wanted to be liberated, Tony's manner implied, I could damned well be good and liberated. I had no intention of engaging in a vulgar debate on the subject; if he couldn't see for himself that basic courtesy has nothing to do with sexual competition, I was not the girl to point it out. I would have picked *him* up if I had owned a car, on such a stinking wet, dreary night.

With my thoughts running along those lines and my face covered with a thin sheet of ice, I cannot be blamed for greeting him with a snarl instead of a smile. He was as rosy and warm as a nice baby when he opened his door; behind him a cheerful fire crackled on the hearth, and the half-empty bottle on the coffee table indicated that he had been lightening his heavy labors with bourbon. That was his ostensible excuse for not picking me up; he had a dozen books to read and review for the next issue of the university history journal.

He gave me a beaming smile and let me take off my own coat. I threw it, soggy wet as it was, onto the couch. That was wasted effort; I should have thrown it at his notes. He was as neat as a cat about his academic work, and a complete slob otherwise. He pushed the coat off onto the floor and sat calmly down in the damp patch it had left. He started typing.

"I've got two more books to do after this one," he said, pecking away. "Take a load off."

I poured a drink since he hadn't offered me one, and sat down on the floor near the fire. Books were scattered all over the place, where he had presumably flung them after looking them over.

The fire and the bourbon gradually restored my equanimity, and I felt a faint stir of affectionate amusement as I watched poor, unsubtle Tony pecking away at his antique typewriter. He typed with four fingers—two on each hand—and the effort made his tongue stick out between his teeth. His hair was standing on end, there was a black smudge across one cheek, and beads of perspiration bedewed his upper lip. He looked about eighteen, and damned attractive; if I had had the slightest maternal instinct, I'd have gone all soft and marshmallowy inside. I seem, however, to be totally lacking in maternal instincts. It's one of the reasons why I fight marriage. I watched Tony sweat with the kindliest feelings, and with certain hormonal stirrings, but I didn't have the slightest urge to rush over and offer to do his typing for him. I type sixty words a minute. Tony knows that.

"We're supposed to be there in half an hour," I said.

"If you'll keep quiet, we'll make it easily."

"You plan to read two books and type out a review of each in twenty-five minutes?"

"Read?" Tony stopped typing long enough to give me a look of honest indignation. "Nobody reads these things. Don't be silly."

He started typing again.

I picked up the nearest book and glanced at it.

"I see what you mean," I admitted.

All the books were inches thick; I don't know why scholars judge accomplishment by weight instead of content. This one was the heaviest of the lot, and its title, in German, was also ponderous.

"*The Peasants' Revolt: A Discussion of the Events of 1525 in Franconia, and the Effects of the Reformation,*" I translated. "Is it any good?"

"How would I know? I haven't seen that one yet."

Tony went on typing. Casually I began leafing through the book. Scholarly prose is generally poor, and scholarly German prose is worse. But the author had gotten hold of some new material—contemporary letters and diaries. Also, the subject interested me.

In recent years, students have done a lot of complaining about "relevance." No one can quarrel with the basic idea: that education should have something to do with real life and its problems. The trouble comes when you try to define the word. What is relevant? Not history, according to the more radical critics. Who cares what happened in ancient Babylon or medieval England? It's now that counts.

They couldn't be more wrong. Everything has happened before—not once, but over and over again. We may not be able to solve our problems through what are pompously called "the lessons of history," but at least we should be able to recognize the issues and perhaps avoid some of the solutions that have failed in the past. And we can take heart in our own dilemma by realizing that other people in other times have survived worse.

Social upheaval and revolution are old issues, as old as society itself. The Peasants' Revolt, in the southern and western provinces of Germany, is not one of the better-known revolutions, but it has some interesting parallels with our own times. The peasants are always revolting, says the old joke. It's a sick old joke. The peasants had plenty to revolt about. There had been many rebellions, by groups driven to desperation by conditions that make modern slums look like Shangri-La, but in the sixteenth century social discontent and misery found a focus. The focus was a real rebel—a renegade monk who called the Pope bad names and loudly proclaimed the abuses of the Establishment. He even married an ex-nun, whom his bad example had seduced from her vows. His name was Martin Luther.

Although his teachings gave the malcontents a mystique, Luther was against violence. "No insurrection is ever right, whatever the cause." And, in the crude style which was typical of the man at times, "A rebel is not worth answering with arguments, for he does not accept them. The answer for such mouths is a fist that brings blood to the nose."

The autocratic princes of the rebellious provinces agreed with both comments. Many of them approved of Luther's attacks on the Church, since that institution restrained their local powers, but they definitely did not like complaints from their ungrateful subjects. They applied the fist to the nose. The Peasants' Revolt was savagely suppressed by the nobles and the high clergy, many of whom were temporal princes as well as bishops of the church.

Today the province of Franconia is one of the loveliest parts of Germany. Beautiful old towns preserve their medieval walls, their Renaissance houses and Gothic churches. It's hard to imagine these quaint old streets as scenes of violence, and yet this region was the center of the rebellion; blood literally flowed like water down the paved gutters. The city of Würzburg, with its lordly fortress looming over the town, was the seat of a prince-bishop whose subjects rose up and besieged him in his own castle. Another center of revolt was Rothenburg, now the most famous of the medieval cities of Germany.

I visited Rothenburg on a summer tour one year and promptly fell in love with it. Among its numerous attractions is a castle—Schloss Drachenstein, the home of the Counts von und zu Drachenstein. Although I admit to a sneaking weakness for such outmoded relics of romanticism, I was not collecting castles that summer. It was one of those coincidences, which Tony and other romantics like to think of as Fate, that Tony had spent a summer doing the same thing I did. We were both in search of Tilman Riemenschneider.

A sculptor and woodcarver, Riemenschneider was probably Germany's greatest master of the late Gothic. The tomb sculptures and altarpieces he created are concentrated in the area around his home town of Würzburg, where for many years he served as a councilor. At the time of the Peasants' Revolt he was an elderly man, prosperous and honored—a good, respectable member of the Establishment. It wouldn't have been surprising if he had supported the Church which had commissioned many of his works, and shaken his graying locks over the depravity of the rebels. Instead, he joined his fellow councilors in support of the peasants' cause. When the rebellion was suppressed, he ended up in the bishop's dungeon; and although he came out of it alive and lived for six more years, he never again worked with his hands. The altar at Maidbronn, finished in 1525, was his last work.

Yet there were tantalizing references to another work by Riemenschneider, which had vanished during the turmoil of the revolt. A reliquary, or shrine, it incorporated three great jewels that had been "liberated" from the Saracens by a Count of Drachenstein. According to an old chronicle, the shrine had been commissioned by a descendant of this nobleman in the early fifteen hundreds.

Art historians derided this tradition. No trace of the reliquary had ever been found, and there was no mention of it except in the monkish chronicle— a species of literature which is not noted for factual accuracy. I never gave the story a second thought— until that winter afternoon when I found myself translating the letter of a Count of Drachenstein, written at a time when Riemenschneider was a prisoner in the dungeons of the Bishop of Würzburg.

I must tell you, my beloved wife, that the old man remains obdurate. I saw him today, in the prison of the Katzenwickers, where he has lain since the fourth day of July, daily subjected to the question. It would be thought that the fear of outraged God, whom he has so greatly offended, would soften his guilty heart. Yet he refuses to tell me where he has hidden it. This, though it was commissioned by my late noble father, whom God hold in his keeping. It is true that my father promised him payment, as well as the return of the bond he gave for the gems,

*but there can be no payment now, since the wretch
is traitor and rebel. I return to the prison tomorrow, with better hopes. The Lord God will support
the right, as He supported me in the battle.*

I sat there with the fire warm on my back, holding the book with fingers that had gone a little
numb. The room faded from my sight, and the
uneven patter of Tony's typewriter went unheard. I
was seeing another century and hearing other
voices.

The old man.

Riemenschneider was born in 1455. He would be
seventy years old in 1525. He had been imprisoned,
and tortured—"put to the question," as the pretty
euphemism of the day had it.

I glanced at Tony, who was still hunched over his
typing. Without looking up he threw down the
book he had finished, and groped for another. I slid the
remaining volume into his hand. He muttered an
absent word of thanks and went on working; and I
returned to *The Peasants' Revolt*.

There were two more letters from Count Burckhardt of Drachenstein. He had been one of the knights
called up by the Bishop of Würzburg when that worthy's subjects got out of hand. Not all the knights
fought against the peasants. Götz von Berlichingen,
the romantic robber knight known as Götz of the
Iron Hand, had led a group of rebels from Odenwald.
True, he maintained later that he had been forced
into this action, and an imperial court acquitted him
of treason. One is justified in being cynical about
both the avowal and the acquittal.

For Burckhardt von und zu Drachenstein, radical chic had no appeal. He marched out to defend the status quo and the Church. His description of the siege, where he had wielded his battle-ax with bloody effect, made me wince, not so much because of the descriptions of lopped-off heads and split carcasses as because of the tone in which they were couched. He counted bodies the way kids count the stamps in their collections.

The clincher came in the third letter.

Today, my beloved wife, the old man finally broke under the question. I have the thing itself now in my hands. I will make plans to send it home, but this will not be easy, since the countryside is still unsafe. The old man cursed me as I left. I care nothing for that. God will protect his true knight.

The glittering vision that had taken shape in my imagination faded, to be replaced by another picture, equally vivid and far less appealing. My imagination is excellent, and it had plenty of information to work with; in my naïve youth I had visited several torture museums, before it occurred to me that my subsequent nightmares might have some connection with the grisly exhibits. You don't forget things like that—ugly things like thumbscrews and the rack, the iron boot that crushed flesh and bone, the black metal shape of the Maiden, with her sickly archaic smile. I could see the old man in my mind's eye too. There is a self-portrait of Riemenschneider on the altarpiece he did for the church at Creglingen. His face is jowly and a little plump in that carving.

It wouldn't have been plump after a few weeks in the bishop's prison. It would have been emaciated and smeared with filth, like his aging body—marred by festering ratbites and the marks of pincer, awl, and fire. Oh, yes, I could see the whole thing only too clearly, and I could see Burckhardt standing by, cheering the torturers on. One of the great creative artists of his century, gloated over by a lout whose skull was as thick as his armor—who couldn't even write his own name.

I worked myself into such a state of rage and horror that I made a fatal mistake. I didn't feel Tony's breath on the back of my neck until he let it out in a windy gasp.

Clutching the book to my bosom, I turned my head. My forehead hit Tony on the nose. A blow on that appendage hurts; it maddens the victim. Holding his nose with one hand, Tony grabbed with the other. Instinctively I resisted. An undignified struggle ensued. I gave up the book, finally, rather than see it damaged. Tony was mad enough to tear the pages apart.

He was panting when he sat back, clutching his prize and eyeing me warily.

"Don't worry," I said coldly. "You're safe from me."

"Thanks. You female Benedict Arnold, were you going to keep this a secret?"

"Keep what a secret?"

"Don't be cute, it doesn't suit you. I was reading over your shoulder for some time, Vicky. And I know my Riemenschneider as well as you do."

I maintained a haughty silence while he read the

letters again. When he looked up from the book, his eyes were shining.

"Hey," he said, grinning like a boy idiot. "Hey. Do you realize—"

"I realize that we are late. That we are going to be even later. If you want to offend Mr. Myers—"

"All right," Tony said. "All right!"

He got to his feet—always a fascinating process to watch, because of the length of his arms and legs—and glowered down at me.

"All right," he repeated monotonously. "If that's how you're going to be, then that's how—uh—you're going to be. Let's go."

He was still carrying the book when he stormed out the door.

I turned off the lights and made sure the door was locked. I put on my coat. I had seen Tony's overcoat slung over a chair, and I left it there. They say righteous indignation is very warming, and I am nobody's keeper. By the time I got downstairs, I decided I'd better calm Tony. He is the world's most maniacal driver even when he's in a good mood, and the combination of icy streets and Tony's rage could be fatal—to me.

He was in the car, waiting, when I reached the street. That was a relief; I half expected him to drive off and leave me. As I got in I said meekly,

"Okay, Tony, I apologize. Of course I wasn't going to hold out on you. You startled me, that's all."

"Oh, sure," said Tony. But he was mollified; we started off with only a little skid, turning halfway around. Tony straightened the car out and we proceeded at a moderate fifty.

"I know you're thinking what I'm thinking," I went on. "But I also think we're both going off half-cocked. It's pretty vague, isn't it?"

"Oh, sure," said Tony.

He's about as sly as Christopher Robin. His tone and his prompt acquiescence told me all I needed to know about where Tony was going to spend the summer.

I took advantage of his silence to make a few plans of my own. The evidence was far from conclusive. Burckhardt had not been specific about details, which was not surprising; I didn't suppose for a moment that he had penned the letter with his own mailed fist. He was probably semiliterate, like many of his noble contemporaries. No, the letter had been dictated to a secretary or public letter writer, and Burckhardt would naturally avoid names. But the given details fit the case. How many objects of value could there be, belonging to a Count of Drachenstein, that had been "commissioned" from an old man of Würzburg? The letter even mentioned a bond, or surety, given by the old man for jewels such as the legend described.

I winced as Tony narrowly avoided a scuttling pedestrian, and went on thinking. The author of the book had not been concerned with art history or offbeat legends. He had only quoted Burckhardt because, in other parts of the letters, the count had described the fighting. Unless someone knew the legend, he wouldn't notice the vital details, thanks to Burckhardt's caution. But I was reasonably certain that the letters did indeed refer to Riemenschneider's lost masterpiece. Burckhardt mentioned sending "it" home. Even with a strong guard, the trip would be hazardous. It was quite possible that the caravan had been ambushed and the shrine seized and broken up for the sake of the jewels set in its carving. It was also possible . . .

I hadn't made any plans for the summer. If Riemenschneider's shrine still existed, anywhere on the face of the earth, there was one obvious place in which to look for it. And there was nothing to prevent me from looking.

I had reached that point in my meditations when we skidded into a gatepost, bounced off, and continued along a dark, tree-lined drive. We had arrived, only half an hour late.

❀▭❀

I was prepared to dislike Jacob Myers on sight, the way we always hate people who have more money than we do. He was bald and fat. His stomach hung out over his cummerbund. He came up to my chin. He had the mouth of a shark and the eyes of a poet. I felt an immediate rapport—with the shark, as well as the poet.

Myers' house was something of a surprise. I knew his reputation as an art patron and collector, but that didn't mean he had good taste; rich people can afford to buy taste. In size and sheer opulence the house was what I had expected, but the overall impression was unorthodox. The most unexpected objects were juxtaposed and somehow they looked right together. They had only one thing in common. They were all beautiful, from the faded Persian rug on the dining-room floor to the little glazed blue pot on the table. I recognized the pot by its glaze; one of the girls in the college makes them as a hobby, and they sell, in local specialty shops, for about six bucks.

Jake—he told me to call him that—answered the door himself. There was a butler. Jake called him Al, and so did Tony. He looked like a heavyweight boxer and addressed me in tones reminiscent of Sir Laurence Olivier. I was staggering slightly as Jake led us into the living room, bawling out orders for cocktails as we went.

It would take a couple of chapters to describe that living room, so I won't try. There were more Persian rugs—I hated to walk on them—and pictures that could have hung in the Uffizi. There was also a man. He rose from a chair by the hearth as we entered. I had plenty of time to study him as we marched from the door to the fireplace; the room was about sixty feet long.

He was a big man. The breadth of his shoulders and chest made Tony look like an adolescent. He had crisp auburn hair, cut shorter than is fashionable, and his features were more notable for strength than harmony. He radiated animal vitality, plus that indescribable air of—how do I describe it? Competence is the word that comes to mind. He looked like a man who could do anything, and do it well. But maybe I was reading things into his face. I knew him, even before Jake introduced us. He told me to call him George. Everybody was very matey that night—everybody but Tony. He hadn't expected this guest, and didn't bother concealing his lack of enthusiasm.

"Hi, Nolan," he said. "Climbed any more mountains lately?"

"Not since Everest," said George, his smile broadening.

As a put-down, it was pretty good. He *had* climbed Everest. He had also won the amateur tennis singles and sailed the Atlantic in a one-man canoe, or a raft, or some stupid thing. *Sports Illustrated* loved to feature his activities. Certain less naïve publications had described other aspects of his expeditions—the Sherpa who didn't get back down Everest, the animals whose pelts and heads decorated Nolan's walls in defiance of protective laws.

I wondered at first how such disparate personalities as George and Jake Myers had become acquainted. As the conversation proceeded, I realized that it was not business or social interests that made them friends, but a common passion. They were both art collectors, and the rivalry between them added to the appeal of beauty for its own sake. Jake was brutally frank about the rivalry. No sooner had we been served with drinks than he burst out in a childish explosion of spleen. George had beaten him out in acquiring a van der Weyden painting, and the loss rankled.

"How much did you bribe that dealer?" he inquired. "He promised it to me, you know. That was the dirtiest piece of crummy underhanded swindling—"

"Since you stole the Sienese triptych out from under my nose," George interrupted. "This makes us even. Keep cool, Jake; I told you I'd let you have the van der Weyden."

"At a neat profit to yourself."

"Naturally."

Looking back, I can see that what transpired that evening was as inevitable as a chemical formula. If you mix the right amounts of the right chemicals (chemistry was never my forte), you always get nitroglycerin. You don't sometimes get Caesar salad and sometimes Chanel No. Five. Here we had two men, each massively arrogant in his own fashion, who enjoyed their rivalry with the blind passion of nasty little boys; a third man, who was viewed by the other two with varying degrees of good-natured contempt; and little me. Poor Tony had obviously taken a lot from George Nolan; I could tell by the way they looked at each other, and by the barbed comments. Now I am not being a female chauvinist when I maintain that some men get awfully silly in the presence of a woman. They start showing off. Roosters and little boys fight; human males try to put the other guy down in more subtle ways.

George started moving in on me. He did it very well, but I knew his heart wasn't in it; he was only trying to aggravate Tony. Jake saw what was going on, and sat back to watch. He liked Tony and he didn't much care for George; but he loved dissension.

I never said he was a nice guy.

I don't know when I saw the gleam in Tony's eye and realized what he was going to do. It must have been before dinner, because apprehension ruined the meal for me. I was so annoyed with all three men that I munched my way grimly through a magnificent spread, wishing I could get my teeth into somebody's hand. I couldn't figure out any way of stopping Tony, short of falling on the floor in a fit, and that seemed a trifle drastic. George kept needling Tony; there were frequent references to ivory towers and effete scholars and muscles that had grown flabby from too much study. Yet in a way, what happened was my fault. If Tony and I hadn't been feuding . . .

Sure enough, with the dessert, the inevitable name was introduced, by Tony, with all the subtlety of a bulldozer.

"Speaking of sculpture"—which nobody was—"how much would you give for a Riemenschneider?"

George had the face of an actor or a con man, beautifully schooled; but I saw him blink before he readjusted his mask. Then I knew. The guy was a fake. He'd never heard of Riemenschneider, and I felt sure his passion for art was not genuine. For him it was a device to outdo lesser men. As a kid he had probably collected rocks or bottles with the same single-minded fury, chiseling and outbidding other kids in order to get the biggest collection in town.

I would have tripped him up, then and there—and I had thought of a couple of ways in which to do it—but Jake outmaneuvered me.

"Riemenschneider," he rumbled, in his bass bullfrog voice. "Yes—the German woodcarver. Saint Stephen in the Cleveland Museum. God that's a masterpiece. That's really great. Yeah, yeah; there was a theft, couple years ago. The Madonna from Volkach. German government ransomed it."

"Not the government; the editor of *Der Stern*."

"Shut up," Myers said, glaring at Tony. "Twenty-five thousand ransom. That's a lot of money. Yeah, sure, I remember the case. Nothing wrong with my memory. You just stop interrupting me, Tony."

George, for one, had no intention of interrupting. He sat tapping his fingers gently on the table, a faint, knowing smile on his face. But the smile didn't fool me. I couldn't expose his ignorance now; foxy Grandpa had already told him what he needed to know. Myers really did have a fabulous memory. His enthusiasm was genuine, even if it was amplified by the old acquisitive instinct.

"Tony," I said gently, "do you think you ought—"

Jake leaned forward, elbows planted squarely on the table, and squinted at me.

"So you're in on this." His voice was unexpectedly genial. It made a chill run up my spine. "Well, well. That makes it even more interesting. Now don't you interrupt me again, young woman! Let me talk. Let me think. Sure, I know Riemenschneider. I also know it would be virtually impossible to get hold of a major piece. Most of his stuff is in churches or museums. And you wouldn't dangle a minor work in front of my nose. . . ."

He wasn't talking to us. He was thinking aloud. His squinty little black eyes shone like jet. Another chill explored my backbone. The old devil was smart, smart and hard as nails. With one half-hearted question Tony had set a bloodhound on the trail.

Tony, who knew him better than I did, was thinking the same thing. His mouth had dropped open, and there were two parallel lines between his eyebrows. He caught my eye, and his mouth tightened. He looked away.

"You're not a dealer," Myers went on. "Private collectors wouldn't approach you. Which one are you planning to steal, and how do you propose to go about it?"

George laughed. My jaw dropped, in its turn. I shouldn't have been taken aback. I know enough about rabid collectors to realize they will stop at nothing, including homicide, to get what they want. A little matter of robbery doesn't bother them a bit. It's common knowledge that dozens of "lost" art treasures, stolen from the world's great museums, now repose cozily in locked and hidden vaults, where the millionaire owners can gloat over them in secret.

"Damn it, Tony," I burst out. "Why can't you keep your big mouth shut?"

George laughed again, and Jake grinned at me. He looked more like a shark than ever.

"Don't blame him, honey. If you hadn't stuck your two cents in, I wouldn't have paid any attention to Tony. I know he goes off half-cocked all the time. But if there are two of you in this deal—and one of them is a girl like you—"

"Oh—" I began; but before I could get the dear old Anglo-Saxon word out, George interrupted. His face was purple with amusement.

"You're the one who's going off half-cocked, Jake. You know our moral laddy here; he isn't going to steal anything. He's a good boy. No; if I were to hazard a guess—and I always do hazard—I would say that our two experts have stumbled on an unknown work. Or," he added, watching my face, "on a clue to such a work. Isn't there a story . . . ?"

He let the word trail off suggestively.

I was torn between self-reproach and admiration at the guy's technique. He didn't know a bloody thing about the legend of the shrine. He was guessing; but it was inspired guessing, the method of a skilled fortune-teller who uses his victim's facial expressions as a guide to the accuracy of his surmises. And heaven knows my big, round, candid face was as readable as print.

I tried to freeze the face, and I watched Jake, who had responded to the hint as a fish to the lure. His brow wrinkled as he searched his capacious memory. My heart sank. I didn't realize until then how deeply my emotions were involved. It was my discovery, damn it, and nobody was going to take it away from me.

"Nope," Jake said finally. "Seems to me I did read something, once. . . . But I've forgotten. Can't remember everything. Is that it, Tony? Found yourself a clue, boy?"

I felt like sagging with relief. Jake had accepted George's reasoning, and, as a result, he was less excited. A robbery made sense to him. A vague, unspecified clue to an unknown work was not in his line.

His tone maddened Tony, as did George's superior smile. He sat up straight in his chair and looked directly at Jake. His hair was hanging down over one eyebrow, but I must admit he had a kind of dignity.

"Are you interested?" he said. "Yes or no."

"Sure I'm interested."

"That doesn't mean you're going to get it," George said gently. He smiled at me. "It's a matter of pride not to let Jake get things away from me."

"Now wait a minute," I said indignantly. "Who's offering what to whom? It's just as much my idea as Tony's, more so, because I saw the book first, and furthermore—"

Tony let out a yelp, but I didn't need that to know what I had done. I shut up, thankful I hadn't said more. Jake, who was shaking all over, let out a loud "haw-haw."

"I should let you two go on arguing," he said, when he had gotten his mirth under control. "It's not only funny, it could be informative. But the information is apt to help Nolan more than it does me. So shut up, the pair of you. Tell you what I'll do. I don't know what you've got on your minds, or what your plans are, but if either of you turns up with a Riemenschneider, I'll buy it. Fair price, no questions asked. I'll even stake you, if you need money."

"No," Tony said.

"No, thanks," I snapped.

We glared at each other.

The rest of the evening was not notable for the wit and intellectuality of the conversation. I had taken Jake's warning to heart, and so had Tony; since neither of us could control our mouths, it was better not to discuss the subject at all. But it was impossible to think about anything else. By the time we got into the car to go home, I had been suppressing my thoughts long enough. Tony was fumbling with the key and the ignition when I exploded.

"Of all the stupid, conceited, dumb . . . One indefinite comment in an old letter, and you promise him a Riemenschneider! The chances are a thousand to one that it's been destroyed. And even if it hasn't—"

Tony dropped the key. Turning, he grabbed me by the shoulders. He shook me. Then he kissed me. Then he shook me again. Taking unfair advantage of my temporary lack of breath, he said,

"It's all your fault. You got me into this, and by God, I'll get myself out with no help from you. I can read your sneaky underhanded female mind. I know what you're planning. Go ahead. I'll beat you to it. We're starting out fair and square, with the same information."

"Ah," I said. "A challenge. Is that it?"

"That's it."

"It's the dumbest thing I ever heard of. The chances of success for either of us are infinitesimal. Even if we found the thing, it doesn't belong to us. You can't promise Jake—"

"I don't give a damn about Jake. I'm going to find the shrine just to prove to you that you aren't as smart as you think you are."

❀▱❀

Tony and I continued to meet socially, but neither of us mentioned any subject that had the remotest bearing on late Gothic sculpture. This tacit restriction limited conversation considerably. It also cast a pall over our nonvocal activities. I finally figured out why Tony was behaving like a desert anchorite harassed by voluptuous female demons, and I didn't know whether to laugh or sneer. He thought he might babble, under the softening influence of sex. And he might have, at that. I never got the chance to find out. We were both busy.

I wasn't surprised when George started calling me, nor was I particularly worried. If he was more interested in picking my brains than pursuing my body, it made a restful change from my usual dates. He was a wonderful dancer, an epicure, a connoiseur of fine wines, and he spent money like water. He was also witty and amusing. Even his hints about sculpture were thrown out with a grin and a tongue in the cheek, and no expectation of success. But I knew that behind the grin and the charm lay a will of iron. He had announced his intentions of beating both of us to the treasure; and if he lacked Tony's and my special knowledge, he had a lot of other things going for him. Money, for instance, and a high degree of ruthlessness. As a rival for the shrine he was much more dangerous than Tony, and I didn't underestimate him for a second. But that didn't keep me from enjoying the country club and the weekends in New York.

Don't misunderstand those weekends. I spotted George right away; women were very low down on his list of temptations. He wasn't gay, in the usual sense; he just wasn't interested in people at all—people of either sex. Of course Tony, the goop, didn't know that. Men are such suckers for externals; they think a bass voice and a broad chest make a male. We could tell them a few things; but why give away an advantage? Anyhow, George's professed interest in me was just one more irritation for Tony, and George knew it. As the months went on, Tony withdrew altogether. I only saw him at faculty meetings, or in the halls. But I knew what he was doing. And, of course, vice versa. I was hooked, and I had been, from the beginning. The challenge was enough to arouse any red-blooded, six-foot American girl, but that wasn't the only reason I was making plans to head for Germany in June. I was caught by the sheer romance of it. Hidden treasures—lost masterpieces—castles—jewels—and those beautiful melancholy faces only Riemenschneider could carve. To rescue something like that from the dust and darkness of centuries . . .

Furthermore, if that long, lanky male chauvinist thought he could outsmart me, he had another think coming.

TWO

❀▨❀▨❀

THE VIEW FROM THE BUS WINDOW COULDN'T HAVE been more charming—an old town square with a fountain in the middle, a Gothic church on one side, and on the other a tall house whose Wedgwood-blue facade had curves and curlicues as dainty as those of a china shepherdess. As I looked, an airy cascade of soap bubbles floated by, iridescent in the sunlight. Like so many Bavarians, the bus driver was a frustrated comedian. Ever since we left Munich, he had been playing games. He wore funny hats, tooted on horns and whistles, and blew bubbles whenever the bus stopped. His nickname, according to the hostess, was Charlie Brown—a pleasing testimonial to the international appeal of the best of American *Kultur*.

I joined the other passengers in applauding the soap bubbles, and Charlie, wearing a tall black opera hat, acknowledged our appreciation with a burlesque bow as the hostess announced that we would have an hour to spend in Nördlingen before the bus continued on its way.

The passengers filed out and dispersed. Many of them were Americans, taking advantage of one of the cheapest and most convenient tours in Europe. The bus runs from Munich to Frankfort, and its route takes in the greater part of what is called the Romantic Road. From Augsburg, founded by the Romans in 15 B.C., up to Würzburg on the River Main, the road includes castles and ancient towns, imperial cities and beautiful scenery. Nördlingen, Dinkelsbühl, and Rothenburg on the Tauber are the most interesting towns; the bus stops in each.

For ordinary sightseers this is all very well, but one might reasonably inquire what the Hades I was doing on that bus, along with the starry-eyed barefoot American kids and the earnest tourists. I was on my way to Rothenburg; but this might seem a rather roundabout way of getting there.

It isn't as roundabout as it seems. Rail connections are complicated, and being an underpaid serf of an educator I couldn't afford to rent a car. As it was, the trip cleaned out my paltry savings account. I must admit, however, that I had other reasons for taking that bus. I was playing fox and hounds.

My departure from home had been a masterpiece of subterfuge, based on all the spy stories I had ever read. I had not made reservations through a travel bureau. I wrote directly to airlines and hotels, and burned every letter I got back. I left in the middle of the night, wearing a black stretch wig and a friend's coat, and hid out in New York under a false name for two days.

All this was childish fun and games, and possibly pointless. Tony knew where I was going; I felt sure he was heading for the same place, if he wasn't there already. But there was a slim chance that George hadn't figured things out. Hence my cunning maneuvers. I hoped Tony had managed to elude George, though I doubted it. Tony has a very open nature.

However, there was no reason for me to be naïve, just because Tony suffers from that weakness. I took a plane to Munich. There I confused my trail by going east instead of west. I went to Salzburg. Salzburg is a lovely town, and I had always wanted to see it again. Coincidentally, there was a good exhibit of late Gothic art in the city museum. Strolling through its halls, admiring illuminated manuscripts and the paintings of Rueland Freuauf the Elder, I pictured George Nolan skulking after me, completely baffled. There were no works by Riemenschneider in the exhibit. I got back to Munich just in time to catch my bus.

It was a glorious day, warm and sunny. The first part of the trip, via autobahn to Augsburg, was fairly dull, except for Charlie Brown's antics. I spent most of the time peering out the back window to see if any one car stayed constantly behind us. Naturally, none of them did. After we hit the Romantic Road I forgot this nonsense and enjoyed the scenery—the castles perched strategically on hilltops, the churches with their oriental domes, like shiny black radishes, the manicured green fields and little red-roofed villages.

After Nördlingen we stopped again in Dinkelsbühl, whose ancient moat is now a playground for white swans. Then the road began to climb, and as we swung around a curve I saw my goal ahead. It was only visible for a moment; crowning its own high hill, before the lower hills closed in and shut it off—a jumble of turrets and gables and mellow red-brown roofs, enclosed by the stone ramparts of the medieval city wall. Rothenburg is the quintessence of Romance—not the watered-down love stories that pass under that name today, but Romance in the old sense—masked desperadoes lurking in the shadow of a carved archway, to intercept the Duke before he can reach his lady love; conspirators gathered in a raftered tavern room, plotting to restore the Rightful Heir; Cyrano and D'Artagnan, striding out with clanking swords to defend the Honor of the Queen.

I refuse to apologize for that outburst; Rothenburg is that kind of place. The spirit has survived even the cheap gimcrackery of tourism. Over the rooftops I could also see the spires of the church where, on a summer day in 1505, Tilman Riemenschneider had supervised the installation of his altar of the Holy Blood.

The bus joined an ugly jumble of other monsters in a parking lot just inside the walls, and disgorged its passengers. I extracted my suitcases from its belly and started walking. The hostess was summoning taxis for other disembarking passengers, but she didn't offer me one. I wasn't surprised. I look as if I could carry a steamer trunk. I didn't want a taxi anyhow. You can walk clear across Rothenburg in half an hour.

It took me longer, because I kept stopping to admire the sights. The town was just as charming as I remembered. Perhaps the souvenir shops had multiplied—certainly the tourists had—but that was only to be expected. The essential beauty hadn't changed.

The old houses of Rothenburg are tall, six or seven stories in height. The style is like that of the black-and-white Tudor houses of England, with wooden timbering forming complex patterns across the stuccoed facades. The stucco is painted in pastel colors—cream, pale blue, buff. The high roofs taper steeply to the ridgepole; set in the faded rust-red tiles are odd little windows, like half-closed eyes peeping slyly. Some of the houses have oriels with leaded windows and roofs like kobold's caps.

Against the sober antiquity of the houses, flowers blaze like rainbow-colored fires. Everybody in Rothenburg must have a green thumb. Red geraniums spill out of window boxes; white and purple-blue petunias cascade over ledges; emerald-green ivy and vines climb the crumbling walls. From over the shop doors wrought-iron signs, delicate as starched lace, indicate the wares to be found within. Most of the signs are gilded; in the sunlight they shine like webs spun by fabulous spiders.

I went through the marketplace, with its Renaissance *Rathaus* and fifteenth-century fountain, and took Herrngasse across town toward the castle— my home away from home for the next couple of weeks.

I still couldn't get over that piece of luck—that Schloss Drachenstein had been converted into a hotel. It wasn't unusual. Many stately homes and ruined castles have been turned into guest houses by noble families whose bank statements are shorter than their family trees. But that Schloss Drachenstein should be one of the number—that I had a reservation, confirmed by a letter bearing the Drachenstein crest—it was almost too good to be true. I am not superstitious—not much—but I couldn't help regarding that as an omen.

The *Schloss* hadn't even been open to visitors when I was in Rothenburg the first time. I had viewed the tangled weeds of the park through the closed and padlocked gates, which were worth a visit in themselves, being gems of the wrought-iron work for which the region is famous. There were other things to see, so I hadn't lingered, but now I could find my way around without having to ask directions.

The roughly oval plateau on which the town is built juts out, at several points, in long rock spurs. At the westernmost point of one such spur, the first Count of Drachenstein, Meninguad by name, had constructed a massive keep that looked down on the valley, and had protected its eastern side with walls and moats. Over the centuries the castle had grown, and peasants seeking protection from marauders had built their huts under its walls, in the spot that would one day become a prosperous merchant town.

The moat had been filled in long before; but I was surprised, when I reached the park, to discover that the gates I remembered were gone. The weeds had been cropped, and as soon as I passed through the stone gateposts I could see the *Schloss* ahead.

From the guidebook I knew the general plan of Schloss Drachenstein. It was built in the form of an open square enclosing an inner court. An eighteenth-century count, inspired by a visit to Versailles, had torn down one side of the old castle and constructed his version of a château on the foundations. It was not a good idea. The facade, which now faced me, was leprous with decay, and the very roofline seemed to sag. Behind this monstrosity I had a tantalizing glimpse of older walls built of rough brown stone.

The door was a graceless modern replacement, with a bright brass knob. The hinges squeaked, though, when I pushed on it; somewhat cheered by this Gothic note, I went in and found myself in a hall that ran straight through the château from front to back, with doors opening on both sides and a staircase at the far end. There was a desk under the arch of the stairs. Someone was sitting at the desk; I couldn't see clearly after the transition from sunlight to the shadowy interior. As I tramped down the hall I felt self-conscious, as I always do when I have to make an entrance like that. And when I got a good look at the girl behind the desk, I felt even more bovine than I usually do.

Honest to God, she was the image of my adolescent heroines. She had a heart-shaped face, ivory pale, and framed by clouds of dark hair so fine the ends floated out in the still air. Her eyes were big and wide-set, framed by long, curling lashes. Her mouth was a pink-coral masterpiece; her nose was narrow and aristocratic. She was sitting down, but I knew she wasn't tall. She wouldn't be tall. She probably had a figure as petite and fine-boned as her face.

I thought things I prefer not to admit, much less

write down. I said, "*Guten Tag*. I have reserved a room."

"*Guten Tag, gnädige Frau. Ihr Name, bitte?*"

Her voice was a false note in the picture of perfect grace. It was flat and hoarse, and quite expressionless. Her lovely face was blank, too. The big dark eyes regarded me without favor.

I gave her my name, and she nodded stiffly.

"We have your letter. I am sorry to say we cannot offer the luxury to which you Americans are accustomed. The *Schloss* is being renovated and the rooms in the château are all occupied. You requested a chamber in the older portion of the *Schloss*, but—"

"No, that's fine," I said heartily.

My big friendly grin won no response. If anything, the girl's expression became slightly more hostile.

"*Aber*, I forget. Americans like the old, the ruinous, the decayed, do they not? Come, then, and I will show you the room."

She insisted on carrying both my suitcases. As I had expected, she was a tiny little thing, and her refusal to let me touch my heavy bags made me feel like a boor as well as a big lumbering clod. I suspect that was what she had in mind. She didn't seem to like me much. But short of wrestling her for the suitcases, I couldn't do anything but follow meekly.

We went out the back entrance into the central court. The walls forming the other three sides of the court were a marvelous mixture of architectural styles—not surprising in a place that had had nine centuries in which to develop. The wing to my left was of the timber-and-stucco type, like many of the houses in town, but bigger and more elaborate. Scaffolding shielded its face, and there were pieces of lumber and miscellaneous tools scattered around— the renovations of which the girl had spoken, I gathered.

The right wing was a four-story sixteenth-century construction, with richly carved window frames and an ornate Renaissance roofline. But the wall straight ahead was old—old enough to have been standing long before Count Burckhardt's time. Its great doorway had a massive stone lintel with a crumbling bas-relief in the shape of a shield bearing the Drachenstein device—a dragon crouched on a rock.

The courtyard was beautifully tended, and as pretty as a postcard. The grass was a rich, velvety green, and shrubs and flower beds were scattered about. A thick hedge hid the part of the court to my right. From behind its shelter came a murmur of voices. Other guests, I thought—and I wondered whether I knew any of them.

Her shoulders bent under the weight of my bags, the girl led me through the door into the Great Hall of the *Schloss*. It was two stories high, roofed with enormous dark beams. Along one wall was a row of armor, with swords and spears and other deadly weapons hanging on the paneled wall above. A huge stone fireplace filled one corner of the room, which was unfurnished except for a carved chest, big enough to hold a body or three. . . . I wondered why that particular idea had flipped into my mind. Suggestion, no doubt, from the arsenal on the wall.

We went up a flight of stairs to a gallery that ran around three sides of the hall. From this a door opened onto a corridor. On the stairs I tried to take one of the suitcases, and was promptly squelched; but I took no pleasure in the drag of the girl's shoulders as she trudged ahead of me along the corridor into an intersecting passage. It was a relief when we finally reached the room she had selected for me.

The room was lit by a pair of tall windows that opened onto the west side of the castle grounds, a wilderness of tangled bushes and weeds. Also visible were the moldering ruins of a structure older than the *Schloss* itself. It was, I decided, the original keep of the first castle ever built on the plateau; it had to be a thousand years old. I guess Americans are bemused by sheer age; the words dug into my mind and reverberated, awesomely. One thousand years . . . It looked its age. The top floor, or floors, were missing; the ruined walls were as jagged as rotten teeth. Beyond the keep, the ground dropped abruptly, in a series of steep steps, to a wooded and verdant valley half veiled by the mists of afternoon heat.

The view was the only good part of the room. Hilton would have turned faint. The brown stone walls were bare except for a few old paintings, which were so blackened by time that it was hard to see what they were meant to represent. The bed was modern; the pink spread and canopy were new, and their bright cheapness clashed badly with the dignified antiquity of the walls. An ugly green overstuffed chair and a cheap bedside table were also new. They were dwarfed by the dimensions of the room, which contained no other furniture except a flat kitchen-type table, a massive wardrobe which served as a closet, and a bureau with a load of chinaware. I viewed this last item morosely. I used to spend summers on a farm. I also noted, with a pessimistic eye, that the lamp on the bedside table was an oil lamp.

I turned to meet the eye of my guide. She had seen my negative reaction, and it pleased her; but she was rubbing her sore shoulders, and my sense of pity for small things—which includes so many things—overcame my annoyance.

"Lovely," I said. "Delightful, *Fräulein*—er—may I ask your name?"

There was an odd little pause.

"*Ich heisse Drachenstein*," she said finally. "Dinner is at seven, *Fräulein*."

And out she went. She didn't slam the door, but I think she would have done so if her arms hadn't ached. The door was about eight inches thick and correspondingly heavy.

"Drachenstein," I muttered, reaching for my suitcases at last. "Aha!"

She couldn't be the present countess. From what I had learned, that lady was the widow of the former count, who had passed on some years earlier at the biblical age of three score and ten. Daughter? Niece? Poor relation? The last sounded most plausible; she was concierge and porter, and heaven knows what else.

I shrugged and walked over to the bed to start unpacking. Then my eye was caught by one of the dusty paintings which hung opposite the foot of the bed.

For some reason the face—and only the face—had been spared the ravages of time. It stood out from the blurred canvas with luminous intensity. And as the features came into focus, I got the first shock of what was to be a week of shocks.

The face staring back at me, with an unnerving semblance of life, was the face of the girl who had just left. Under the picture, a label read: "Konstanze, Gräfin von und zu Drachenstein. 1505?–1525."

THREE

⊛═⊛═⊛

IT WOULD HAVE BEEN FUN TO THINK I HAD BEEN shown to my room by the family ghost, but after consideration I abandoned the idea. For some reason, the only logical alternative disturbed me almost as much as the ghost theory. Family resemblances like that do crop up, though I had never seen one quite so startlingly close. But it is distasteful to me to think that a random rearrangement of genes can duplicate me, or anyone else, at the whim of whatever power controls such things.

I unpacked, and then kicked off my shoes and lay down on the bed. It was surprisingly comfortable. I didn't mean to doze off, but excitement and travel had tired me out. When I woke up, the sun was declining picturesquely behind the plateau and my stomach was making grumpy noises. It was almost seven. I didn't meet a soul as I retraced my steps, through the Great Hall and across the courtyard. Apparently the rest of the guests had already gone to dinner. I was looking forward to that meal, and not only because of my hunger pangs. I had every expectation of seeing at least one familiar face.

The dining room had been one of the drawing

rooms of the château wing. Its painted ceiling and plastered walls were extravagantly baroque, and not very good baroque. The westering sun, streaming in through floor-to-ceiling windows, freshed the gilt of the smirking naked cupids and cast a rosy glow over the shapes of pulchritudinous pink goddesses. At a table by the window, looking neither cherubic nor pulchritudinous, was the person I had expected to see.

I approached, not with trepidation—because who was he, to resent my presence?—but with curiosity. I wasn't sure how he was going to receive me.

He looked up when I stopped by his chair, and a broad grin split his face. *Then* I felt trepidation. I didn't like the gleam in his eye. He looked smug. I wondered what he knew that I didn't.

"Greetings," I said. "I hope you have been saving a seat at your table."

"*Grüss Gott,*" said Tony. "Let us use the local greeting, please, in order to show our cosmopolitan characters. Sure, I saved you a place. I knew you'd be along. What kept you?"

With a wave of his hand he indicated the chair next to his. I took it, without comment; if he wanted to continue the childish pattern of noncourtesy he had established back home, that was fine with me. I put my elbows on the table and studied him. No doubt about it: jaunty was the word for Tony.

"How long have you been here?" I asked.

"Couple of days."

"You must have made good use of your time. What have you—"

"Quiet," said Tony, scowling. "Not now."

He was trying to look like James Bond again. It's that loose lock of hair on his brow. I didn't laugh out loud because it was expedient to keep on good terms with him, for a time. I turned my head away and glanced around the room.

If the tables in the dining room were any guide, the hotel part of the *Schloss* wasn't large, but it was doing a good business. There were a couple of dozen places laid, four to a table. Most of them were occupied.

"Fill me in on our fellow guests," I said.

"Two American high school teachers," Tony began, indicating a couple at the next table. "A German family from Hamburg—two kids. The honeymoon couple are French; the old miserable married couple are Italian. There are some U.S. Army types from Munich, and a miscellaneous bevy of Danes."

"You've been busy," I said, smiling at him. He looked pleased, the naïve thing.

"The little fat guy who looks like Santa Claus without the beard is a professor," he went on complacently. "What he professes I don't know; he keeps trying to corner me, but I've avoided him so far. The middle-aged female with the face like a horse is English. She's a crony of the old countess's."

"Old countess? Is there a younger one?"

"You must have met her. If she wasn't carrying your suitcases, she was scrubbing your floor. She does all the work around here."

"Her?" I gasped ungrammatically.

"Sure. Irma. The last frail twig on the Drachenstein family tree."

"Irma!" It was some name for a girl who looked like a Persian houri. I was about to express this sentiment—and get some additional insight into Tony's attitude toward her—when a man walked up to the table. He was a stocky young man with brown hair and blue eyes, a deeply tanned face, and an expression as animated as a block of wood. He distributed two brusque nods and a curt *"Abend"* around the table, and sat down.

Now as I have indicated, I find the usual leering male look quite repulsive. I am accustomed, however, to having my presence noted. Tony, who knows me only too well, glanced from me to the newcomer and said, with a nasty grin,

"This is Herr Doktor Blankenhagen, from Frankfurt. Doc, meet Fräulein Doktor Bliss."

The young man half rose, clutching his napkin, and made a stiff bow.

"Doctor of medicine," he said, in heavily accented English.

"Doctor of philosophy," I said, before I could stop myself. "How do you do?"

"Very pleased," said Herr Doktor Blankenhagen, without conviction. He opened a newspaper and retreated behind it.

"Hmmph," I said; and then, before Tony's grin could get any more obnoxious, I went on,

"One more place at the table. Who's that for?"

Tony's grin faded into the limbo of lost smiles. I knew then. I had been half expecting it, but I still didn't like it.

"Hi, there," said George Nolan, making his appearance with theatrical skill, at just the right moment. "Glad you got here, Vicky."

"Hi yourself," I said. "Congratulations on your detective skill. Or did you just follow Tony?"

George laughed, and leaned over to give Tony a friendly smack on the shoulder. Tony swayed.

"Right the second time."

"No problem following him?" I asked sweetly. "Not for a man who has tracked the deadly tiger to its lair, and hunted the Abominable Snowman in his mysterious haunts."

"He went to the Jones Travel Agency," said George, still grinning. "As soon as my gratuity to one of the help produced the name of Rothenburg, I put two and two together."

We both burst out laughing. Tony glowered. Blankenhagen lowered his newspaper, gave us a contemptuous stare in common, and hid behind it again.

The waitress, a stolid blond damsel, came with our soup, and the meal proceeded. Tony sulked in silence, Blankenhagen read his newspaper, and George and I kept up the social amenities. He was a master of the double entendre, and I don't mean just the sexual entendre. He kept dropping hints about sculpture and secret passages in ancient castles. Tony writhed, but I was pleased to see he was learning to control his tongue. Part of George's technique was to probe until he got an angry, unthinking response.

With the dessert came Irma, hot and harassed, but still disgustingly beautiful, to inquire how we had liked the meal. She didn't give a damn, really. It was just part of the job. Tony bounded to his feet the moment she appeared, and even Blankenhagen registered a touch of emotion. I began to wonder about Tony's *joie de vivre*. Maybe it had another cause than the one I had suspected.

When the meal was over, Tony got to his feet and reached for my hand.

"Excuse us," he said firmly. "I want to talk to Vicky alone."

George was amused.

"Help yourself," he said.

We proceeded, in pregnant silence, to the courtyard. Behind the sheltering hedge lay a diminutive garden, its flowers pale pastel in the twilight. Tony sat me down on a bench and stood over me.

"Well?"

"Well what?"

Tony sat down beside me and reached out.

"Oh, come off it," he mumbled. "Don't be that way. No reason why we can't be civil, is there?"

"Civil, is it?" I said, into the hollow between his neck and his right shoulder. "Hmmm . . . I wasn't the one who started this stand-off business, you know."

The succeeding interval lasted a shorter time than one might have expected. All at once Tony took me by the shoulders and pushed me away.

"I can't concentrate," he said in an aggrieved tone. "Why did we start this silly fight in the first place? I haven't been able to think of anything else for months. It's interfering with my social life and my normal emotional development."

"You challenged me," I reminded him. "Want to take back what you said?"

"No!"

"Then we'd better kiss and part. I can't concentrate on any other subject either; and we aren't collaborating, are we?"

"No . . ."

"Only?"

"Only—well, we could compare background notes, couldn't we? Nothing significant, just research. So we can start out even."

"Hmmm," I said. "Why the change of heart?"

"It isn't a change of heart. I'm not asking you to give anything away, and I'm not going to tell you anything important. Only—well, Nolan bugs me. I didn't realize he was so hot on the trail. And if I can't find the thing myself, I'd rather have you get it than Nolan."

I didn't return the compliment. If I couldn't find the shrine, I hoped nobody would. But his suggestion made sense. I didn't have anything that could be called a clue; maybe he did. I had nothing to lose by collaborating.

As it turned out, I didn't gain much. For the most part, Tony's research duplicated mine.

We had both gone back to the old chronicle, which contributed very little except a description of the shrine. If my appetite had needed whetting, that description would have done the trick.

According to the chronicler, the reliquary depicted the Three Kings kneeling before the Child— the *"Anbetung der Könige,"* as the Germans put it.

The subject was popular with European artists in earlier, more devout, eras, so it is not surprising that another version of the *Anbetung*, by Riemenschneider, should exist. This one is a bas-relief, on the side panel of the Altar of the Virgin, which he did for the church at Creglingen, not far from Rothenburg. So when I pictured our shrine I pictured it as he had done it at Creglingen, only in the round instead of in relief. The design was simple and forceful—the Virgin, seated, with two of the kings kneeling before her and the third standing at her right. Of course I knew the Drachenstein shrine wouldn't be quite the same, but the subject was only open to a few variations. Since the old chronicle mentioned angels, I gave my visionary shrine a few of Riemenschneider's typical winged beauties—not chubby dimpled babies, but grave ageless creatures with flowing hair and robes fluttering in the splendor of flight.

The three jewels were a ruby, an emerald, and an enormous baroque pearl.

Tony had looked this up too, but he professed to be more intrigued by the people who had been involved with the shrine back in 1525. (Women are always moved by crass materialistic things such as jewels; men concern themselves with the higher things of life.)

"You had better get the characters straight in your mind," Tony said smugly. "There were three of them. The count, Burckhardt, was a typical knight— and I'm not thinking, like, Sir Galahad. I assume you had the simple wit to write the author of *The Peasants' Revolt*, and ask if there were any other letters from Burckhardt? Oh. You did.

"Burckhardt was a rat. A bloodthirsty, illiterate lout. His repulsive personality is even more apparent in the unpublished letters. I guess that's why they weren't published; they tell more about Burckhardt than about the war. He was obstinate, unimaginative, arrogant—"

"My goodness," I said mildly. "You really are down on the lad."

"Lad, my eye."

"He couldn't have been very old. What was the average life span—about forty? As you say, he was fairly typical. Why the prejudice?"

"Not all of them were hairy Neanderthals. Take Götz von Berlichingen; he supported the peasants."

"Under protest, according to Götz. I don't think he's a good example of a parfit gentle knight. He was a menace on the highways, a robber, looter—"

"At least he had courage. After his hand was shot off, he acquired an iron prosthesis and went on robbing."

"I stayed at his place once."

"Whose place?"

"Götz's," I said, spitting a little on the sibilants. "Schloss Hornburg, on the Neckar. It's a hotel now. They have his iron hand."

"I wish you would stop changing the subject," Tony said unfairly.

"You were the one who brought up Götz."

"And stop calling him Götz, as if he were the boy next door. . . . To return to Burckhardt—he was only heroic when he was up against a bunch of serfs armed with sticks. And did you notice the hypochondria? All those complaints about his bowels!"

"Maybe he had a nervous stomach."

I could have said something really cutting. Tony's prejudice against the valiant knight suggested a transferal of resentment against men of action in general—not mentioning any names. But I didn't even hint at such a possibility. I didn't like Burckhardt either.

"He had one good point," Tony said grudgingly. "He loved his wife. That comes out, even through the stiff formal phrasing. I couldn't find much information on her. All I know is that her name was Konstanze and she was beautiful."

I started. I shouldn't have been surprised. The dates on the portrait in my room would have told me that the woman portrayed had been the lady of our count. But it was—uncomfortable, somehow.

Tony gave me a curious look, but asked no questions. He went on,

"The third character was named Nicolas Duvenvoorde. He was the count's steward, majordomo, or whatever you want to call it. He was Flemish, by his name, and a trusted, efficient servant, to judge by the references to him. Now one of the unpublished letters, if you remember, says the count has sent 'it' to Rothenburg in the care of this steward and an armed escort of five men. The countryside was in disorder; bands of marauding peasants and men at arms marauding after the marauding peasants—"

"Don't be cute," I said. "I'm not one of your giggly girl students."

"Then you tell me what happened next."

"I take it you found no further references to the shrine? Neither did I. But, assuming the caravan started on schedule, there are only two possibilities."

Tony nodded. "Either the shrine arrived in Rothenburg as planned—no reason why not; a group of armed men, on their guard, with their precious burden a secret, had a good chance of getting through—or else they were attacked along the way and the shrine was stolen."

"No reason why not?" I echoed. "But is there any reason to suppose the reverse? If the shrine was stolen, that would explain why it hasn't been heard of since."

"Obviously. But if thieves seized and burned the shrine, what happened to the jewels? Such stones are virtually indestructible, and they have a habit of reappearing. Look at the great historic gems; you can trace them through the centuries, usually by the trail of blood they leave behind them. The fact that the jewels, as well as the shrine, have not been heard of since fifteen hundred twenty-five is suggestive. They must have been hidden—hidden so well that all memory of the hiding place was lost."

"Suppose your hypothetical peasants did the hiding, after they robbed the caravan. The cache could be anywhere in West Germany."

"Or farther. But that isn't likely. A single thief couldn't overpower six armed men. And if there were several thieves, the chance of all of them being killed before they could pass on the secret of the hiding place is remote. Besides, where could they hide it, a group of homeless peasants, so that the hiding place remained undisturbed for four hundred and fifty years? Now this castle . . ."

The massive walls seemed to close in around us. Tony's reasoning wasn't new to me; I had reached the same conclusions, not because we were *en rapport*, but because they were logical conclusions. There were plenty of holes, and weak links, in the chain of reasoning, but at the end of it lay a solid fact: even on the evidence we had, Schloss Drachenstein was worth searching.

I said as much. Tony snorted vulgarly. Like all men, he likes to have his lectures received with little feminine squeals of admiration. So I added tactfully,

"But that's as far as logic took me, Tony. Suppose the shrine *is* here. Where do we look? The castle is enormous. You're so clever at this sort of thing; can't you narrow it down?"

Tony is very susceptible to the grosser forms of flattery. He beamed.

"Obviously the shrine wasn't left out on a shelf, in plain sight. Rothenburg was a real hotbed of radicalism, and although the revolt was officially suppressed before Burckhardt got home, I would think he'd prefer to tuck his valuables away till things were back to normal. Now here's an interesting point that maybe you didn't know. The count and his wife both died that same year, leaving an infant daughter. I don't know how Burckhardt and Konstanze died, but it must have been suddenly. They had no opportunity to pass on the secret. The child was too young to know anything."

"It's plausible. If the shrine exists, it is hidden somewhere in the older section of the *Schloss*.

"I wish I knew the layout of the place a little better. Where do Irma and the old *Gräfin* live? It would be mildly embarrassing to meet one of them while we were ripping up the floor."

"The dowager's rooms are in the tower at the end of our wing." Tony gestured. "I think Irma's room is under the old lady's."

"Nuts. I hoped I was alone in the old wing."

"You're surrounded," Tony said, with mean satisfaction. "Nolan's room is down the hall. I'm next to you, and on your other side is Dr. Blankenhagen, our conversational tablemate. The little fat guy is next to me. That's about all. . . . Oh, yeah, the English female is in the tower too. I told you she was a crony of the *Gräfin*."

"Good God. How can we do any searching? It's like Main Street on Saturday night."

"If you're planning to start ripping up floor boards in the guest rooms, you aren't as logical as you think you are."

I sighed ostentatiously.

"Must I explain my reasoning? I thought it was obvious."

"I've been sharing my humble thinking with you. Go ahead, be obvious."

"Well, isn't the master bedchamber—Burckhardt's own room—the logical place in which to start searching?"

"It might be, if we knew which room was Burckhardt's."

At that moment the moon rose above the wall and turned the little garden into something out of Rostand. I glanced at Tony. He put his arm around me and I leaned back against it.

"I can't fight with you," Tony said.

"You can't fight with anybody. You're too nice a guy. No, none of that. We were reasoning, remember. What we need is a plan of the *Schloss* as it was in the good old days. Or we could ask the *Gräfin* which room was the master bedchamber."

"I'm against that."

"So am I," I agreed amiably. "We don't want to rouse any suspicions. Anyhow, she may not know."

"And until *we* know, I don't see any point in searching the bedrooms. The hiding place won't be obvious; you really would have to rip up floors and tear down the walls."

"Anyhow," I said thoughtfully, "the count's room might not have been the best place to hide something. Didn't they have servants and attendants hanging around all the time?"

"I wouldn't say that. But there are any number of equally likely places: Such as—"

"Don't," I said suddenly. The garden was a magical place, but it was a little uncanny, with the rustling shrubbery and a breeze moving the branches of the trees. "Let's go in. I've had enough atmosphere for tonight. I could stand a glass of plain prosaic beer."

We had our beer, served by Irma, in the room of the château that served as a lounge. The family from Hamburg were playing Skat and the honeymoon couple, in a shadowy corner, were fully occupied with each other. The only person in the room who wasn't distracted by the squeaks and giggles coming from that corner was the English lady, who sat knitting like a robot, without removing her eyes from her needles. George was nowhere to be seen, and I wondered uneasily about the rustling I had heard in the garden.

When the clock struck ten, there was a general exodus. Apparently Rothenburg, like my home town, rolled up the streets at an early hour. That was fine with me. I had other plans for the middle hours of the night.

At the door I was intercepted by the little man whom Tony had identified, somewhat vaguely, as a professor. He introduced himself with a big broad smile.

"*Ich heisse Schmidt.* And you are the American *Professorin, nicht?* What is it that you teach?"

I admitted to being a historian. I was caught off guard by his blunt approach, but it was impossible to resent the little guy. He did look like Santa Claus. Besides, he only came up to my chin. As I have said, I can't be cruel to little people.

"And you, Herr Schmidt?" I asked. "Are you perhaps also a historian"

Herr Schmidt's eyes shifted. All at once he looked like a very sneaky Santa Claus.

"Alas, I am no longer anything. I am, as you say, retired. I enjoy a long vacation. And you, I hope you find Rothenburg pleasant? You are, like me, in the older wing of the *Schloss?* It is charming! Full with atmosphere of the past, very appealing to Americans. But inconvenient, this charm. For example, we must light ourselves to bed. There is no electricity in the old wing."

He picked up a candle, one of a row which stood atop a chest.

"So I noticed," I said drily.

In a mellow moment Tony lit a candle for me and we found ourselves part of a small procession which wound its medieval way across the court. The candle flame flickered in the wind; I had to shield it with my hand. When we entered the Great Hall, the illusion of antiquity was complete. The feeble flames were overpowered by the vast darkness of the room. They woke a dim reflection in the polished surfaces of helmet and breastplate, giving the armored shapes an illusion of life and surreptitious movement.

"I am glad to have company when I cross this room," said Schmidt, scampering for the stairs. "Br-rrr! In candlelight it is too full with atmosphere. I expect to see the countess herself."

"The countess?"

"But yes, have you not heard the legend? The countess walks here, on moonlit nights. Which countess I know not, but she is one of those who has no right to be walking."

He chuckled. I wasn't amused. I had a feeling I knew which countess he meant. Nor was I precisely easy in my mind about Herr Schmidt. If ever a name sounded like an alias . . . And he had been decidedly elusive about his occupation.

In the dim light of the candle, my room looked like an apartment in Castle Dracula. I lit the oil lamp beside the bed, lay down, and tried to read. The smoky light made my eyes ache.

It was a warm night, but the room had a clammy chill which the air from the open window didn't alleviate. I went to the window and looked down into the tangled underbrush beneath. There were no screens in the window; the drop was sheer. To the left was another window—that of Tony's room, I assumed. It was dark, as were all the other windows I could see.

I looked across the grounds at the bulk of the old keep. The jagged walls made a picturesque outline against the moonlit sky. As I stared, something peculiar happened. For a moment a square of wavering yellow light interrupted the blackness of the tower's silhouette. Just for a moment; then it was gone.

I gulped, and told myself to be rational. What I had seen was not a ghost light, but a candle, behind one of the windows of the keep. But why would anyone be in the crumbling ruin at this time of night?

A possible answer wasn't hard to find.

Frowning, I turned from the window and met the enigmatic eyes of the Countess Konstanze.

I lifted the lamp from the table and held it up so that its light fell full on the painted face. It was not one of the world's great portraits. Though the physical features seemed to be accurately represented, the painter had failed to capture a personality. He had been more successful with the pose—the shape of the head and shoulders, the arrogant tilt of the chin suggested a strength of character not implicit in the expressionless face. The resemblance of the sixteenth-century countess to her downtrodden descendant was probably not one of character; but feature by feature the resemblance was uncannily exact.

"If you could only talk," I muttered—and then

made a quick, instinctive gesture of denial. The Gothic atmosphere was thick enough already. A talking portrait would send me screaming out into the night.

I looked at my watch. It was after midnight. The old *Schloss* and its inhabitants should be sleeping soundly by now. I put on a dark sweater, which I had brought for the purpose of nocturnal prowling, and tied a scarf over my light hair. I found my flashlight, and blew out the lamp.

Talk about dark. I hadn't seen anything like it since the old days on the farm. The faint moonlight from the window didn't help much, and when I closed the door of my room behind me the corridor was pitch-black. I didn't want to use the flashlight until it was necessary, so I stood waiting for my eyes to adjust.

A hand touched my shoulder.

I thought of screaming, but my vocal cords didn't cooperate. Before I could get them into operation I heard a voice.

"Hi," it whispered.

"Tony," I whispered back. "You rat."

"Scare you?"

"Scared? Me?"

"I figured you'd be prowling tonight. Couldn't let you go alone. Who knows, you might be nervous."

"Sssh!"

"Come on, let's get away from all these doors."

He found my hand, and I let him lead me until a turn in the corridor brought light—the sickly sheen of the moon filtering through the leaded panes of a window set high above an ascending stair. Tony stopped.

"Those are the tower stairs."

"I was heading for the Great Hall."

"Down this way."

As we shuffled along the dark passageways, my pulse was uncomfortably quick. The castle was too quiet. There weren't even the creaks and squeaks of settling timber. This place had settled centuries ago.

Finally we stepped onto the balcony over the Great Hall. I put one hand on the balustrade and moved back in alarm as it gave slightly. The *Schloss* needed repairs. No doubt there wasn't enough money. The proud old family of the Drachensteins wouldn't have gone into the innkeeping business unless they needed cash. I reminded myself not to lean heavily against that balustrade.

Below, in the Hall, the armored shapes were dim in the gray moonlight. The shadows of tree branches swaying in the night wind slid back and forth across the polished floor. . . .

My scalp prickled. That motion was no swaying shadow. There was something moving at the far end of the Hall—something pale and slim, like a column of foggy light.

The thing came out into the moonlight. I forgot my qualms about the shaky banister, and clutched it with straining fingers.

The figure below had the face of the woman in the portrait. I could see it distinctly in the light from the windows, even to its expression. The eyes were set and staring; the face was as blank as the face on the painted canvas.

The apparition wore a long, light robe, with flowing

sleeves. The feet—if it had feet—were hidden by the folds of the garment, so that it seemed to float instead of walk. Slowly it glided across the floor, the staring eyes raised, the lips slightly parted.

There was a sound behind us. Tony, who had been equally dumbfounded by the apparition, swore out loud when he recognized the man who had joined us on the gallery. Personally, I was glad to see George. The bigger the crowd, the better, so far as I was concerned.

"Did you see it?" Tony demanded. "Or am I crazy?"

"I did see her," George said coolly. "She's gone now."

I turned. The Hall was empty.

Tony ran toward the stairs.

"Go slow," George said, catching his arm. "If you wake people like that too suddenly, it can be dangerous."

"She—she's—sleepwalking, isn't she?" Tony asked.

"What else?"

I didn't say anything. George was right, of course. But I sympathized with Tony. George hadn't seen that infernal portrait.

Then it hit me, and it was my turn to swear. Maybe George hadn't seen the portrait, but Tony had; unless he knew of the uncanny resemblance between the two women, one living and one long dead, he wouldn't have reacted so neurotically to what was—obviously!—a simple case of somnambulism. Tony hadn't told me about all his research, then. I wondered how many other potentially useful facts he was hoarding.

I followed my two heroes down into the Hall.

"I think she went this way," George said, starting toward the east end of the Hall. "You don't happen to have a flashlight, do you, Lawrence?"

Tony did. The light moved around the room, spotlighting the suits of armor and the black mouth of the fireplace.

"Wait a minute," George said. "She couldn't get out this way. The door is locked." He demonstrated, rattling the knob.

"You said she came this way."

"She must have doubled back under the stairs while we were talking. From the gallery that end of the room is not visible. Her room is in the tower, isn't it?"

He led the way without waiting for an answer. At the opposite end of the Hall an open arch disclosed the first steps of a narrow stair.

"We'd better check," Tony muttered. "Make sure the girl doesn't hurt herself, wandering around. . . . Follow me."

The upper floor was a maze of corridors, but Tony threaded a path through them without hesitating once—another proof, if I needed any, that Tony had already explored the *Schloss* thoroughly. So, I reminded myself, we were not collaborating. He didn't have to tell me anything. . . . I wished I knew what George had been doing. I could feel his presence close behind me. For a big man he was very light on his feet.

On the first floor of the tower Tony tried a door. It creaked open. The flashlight showed an unfurnished circular chamber with rags of moldering tapestry on the walls.

"Nobody lives here," said George, peering over my shoulder. "Irma must be on the next floor."

The stairs led up to a narrow landing with a faded strip of carpet across the floor. There was a single door. Tony hesitated, but George marched up to the door and turned the knob. His face changed.

"Lawrence. Look at this."

"What's the matter?"

George grabbed his hand and directed the flashlight beam onto the doorknob. Below it was a large keyhole, with the shaft of an iron key projecting from it. Tony gaped; but I didn't need George's comment to get the point.

"Door's locked. From the outside. Either this is not Irma's room—or that wasn't Irma we saw walking tonight."

FOUR

❀▭❀▭❀

"May I ask what you are doing at my niece's door at one o'clock in the morning?"

The cold, incisive voice came from the darkness of the stairs above us. Tony jumped. The flashlight beam splashed and scattered against the stone arch and then steadied, showing the form of a woman.

She was rather tall, though nowhere near my height. Her hair was snowy white—a beautiful shade that owed its tint to art rather than nature. Her figure was still slender, and her face retained the traces of considerable beauty. Her makeup and her handsome silk dressing gown were immaculate. She had fought time with some success, but the signs of battle were visible; the keen blue eyes were set in folds of waxy, crumpled flesh, and her neck had the petrified scrawniness older women get when they diet too strenuously. I would have known who she was even without the reference to her niece. She looked the way a dowager countess ought to look.

"Good evening, *Gräfin*," George said calmly. "So this is your niece's room. Did you lock her in? And, if so, when?"

He had gall. I have a considerable amount myself,

but I wouldn't have dared to ask that question. To my amazement, the old lady answered it.

"I locked her in at eleven o'clock, as I do every night. What has happened?"

"We saw someone in the Great Hall just now," George said. "It looked like your niece."

"I see." The light was bad, so I wasn't sure; but I rather thought she was smiling. "Let me show you that it cannot have been Irma whom you saw."

She unlocked the door and flung it open. When modest Tony hesitated, she took the flashlight from him and turned it on the bed.

Irma lay curled up under a thin sheet, her cheek pillowed on her hand. She stirred and muttered as the light reached her eyes. Then she sat bolt upright.

"Wake up, Irma," said the *Gräfin*. "It is I."

"Aunt Elfrida?" The girl brushed a lock of curling dark hair from her eyes. Then, seeing other forms in the doorway, she snatched at the sheet and drew it up over her breast. The extra covering wasn't necessary; her nightgown was a hideous, heavy dark cotton that covered her from the base of her neck down as far as I could see.

The countess moved to the bed.

"You have been asleep? You have heard nothing? Seen nothing?"

The seemingly innocuous question had a frightful effect on the girl. Her chin quivered, her mouth lost its shape, and her eyes dilated into staring black circles.

"*Ach, Gott*—what has happened? Is it—has she—"

"No questions," the older woman interrupted. "Sleep again. Sleep."

"Stay with me!"

"There is no need. Sleep, I say."

She moved back, pushing us with her, and closed the door. I had a last glimpse of Irma's face, rigid with terror, and it made me forget what few manners I possess.

"I'll sit with the girl, if you won't," I said. "She needs reassurance, not mysterious silence."

The *Gräfin* locked the door.

"I have not had the pleasure of meeting you, young woman, but I assume you are our newest guest, Dr. Bliss. Is your degree in the field of psychiatry?"

"I don't have to be a psychiatrist to realize—"

Tony stepped heavily on my slippered foot, and the old woman went on.

"My niece's welfare is my business, I believe. As for your search tonight—I have proved to you that it was not Irma you saw. If you are still curious, gentlemen, I suggest you visit Miss Bliss's room—if you have not already made yourselves at home there. At the foot of the bed—conveniently placed for visitors—there hangs a certain portrait. And now, if you will excuse me, I need my rest. Good night."

"Why, that old—" I began.

This time it was George who stepped on my foot. He was shorter than Tony, but he weighed more. I yelled.

"What's all this about a portrait?" George inquired

loudly. The *Gräfin*'s footsteps were still audible above. I didn't care whether she heard me or not.

"Oh, hell," I said. "Double hell. Come on, you guys. I've got a bottle of Scotch in my suitcase, and I think this is the time to break it out."

Shortly thereafter George put down an empty glass and stared owlishly at me and Tony.

"All right, Doctors. Let's hear some high-class intellectual rationalizing. What was it we saw tonight?"

Tony had recovered his cool. There was only one funny thing. He couldn't look at the portrait. He just couldn't stand looking at it. Staring firmly at his glass, he said,

"Either it was the girl, or it was a ghost. If you believe in ghosts—that's what it was. If you don't—someone is putting us on."

George snorted and poured himself another drink, without waiting to be asked.

"Is that the academic brain at work? Your alternatives don't impress me. You think the *Gräfin* lied about locking that door?"

"That doesn't follow. There are any number of possibilities. Maybe she thought she locked it, and didn't. Maybe someone else unlocked it, and locked it again later. Maybe there's another door out of the room."

"Yeah." George looked more cheerful. "That's so. But do you remember what our apparition was wearing?"

"A light robe," I said. "White or pale gray, with full sleeves and a gathered yoke."

"Well, you saw the girl's nightgown—God save

us. I also saw her dressing gown, or housecoat, or whatever you call it. It was lying across the foot of her bed."

"And it, I suppose, was black," said Tony.

"Navy blue," I said. "With small light-colored flowers. Very unflattering, with her coloring. . . . That doesn't prove anything. She could have a closetful of long white robes, and she had plenty of time to change."

Tony stood up.

"This is a waste of time. You think that girl was faking. Well, I don't. Come on, Nolan, let's be off."

George sipped his drink.

"You two kill me," he said conversationally. "Why don't we put our cards on the table?"

"What cards?" I asked. "You know why we are here and vice versa. If I judge your sneaky character accurately, you probably know by now as much as Tony does. But you don't know any more than that; and if you did, you wouldn't tell us. You must be crazy if you think I'm going to give you any information."

George reached for the bottle. I moved it away from his hand. Good Scotch is expensive. Unperturbed, he grinned at me.

"You're quite a girl. If you find the shrine, I might revise my long-seated hostility toward marriage."

"That's big of you. But my hostility is just as deep-seated, if not as long established."

George stood up. Still smiling, he stretched lazily. Muscles rippled all over him.

"I'm noted for getting what I want," he murmured.

Tony, who had been swelling like a turkey, couldn't stand it any longer.

"Play your hot love scenes in private, why don't you?"

"If you'd take the hint and leave, we would," said George.

"Oh, no, we wouldn't," I said. "Out, both of you. I need my beauty sleep. Who knows, I may not find the shrine. Then I would have to rely on sheer sex appeal to catch myself a husband."

"I'm betting on you," said George. He glanced at Tony, who said shortly,

"It's all for none and one for each in this game. We'll see. Come on, Nolan. Good night, Vicky."

❂〓❂

The undercurrents in that conversation set my teeth on edge, and I was still thinking about them the next morning. When I reached the dining room, Tony was the only one at our table. He grunted at me, but didn't look up.

"Where's George?" I asked.

"Been and gone."

"Did you two exchange any meaningful remarks after you left me?"

"Define 'meaningful.'" Tony looked at me. "You know what that crook is planning, don't you? He'll follow us until we find—uh—something, then jump in and grab it."

"Time to worry about that if and when we find it. At the moment we aren't even warm."

"Wrong. The time to worry is now, before Nolan pops out of a dark corner and hits somebody over the head."

"He won't hit me over the head," I said smugly.

"Are you sure?"

Come to think of it, I wasn't at all sure. I wouldn't give Tony the satisfaction of agreeing with him in his assessment of George's scruples, or lack thereof; but I didn't object when Tony proposed that we make a joint expedition out to the old *Wachtturm*. As he said, it wasn't a good place for solitary exploring. A lot of nasty accidents could occur in a crumbling, deserted place like that.

Before we had finished breakfast, Irma came to the table. She was wan and pale, with dark circles under her eyes. On her, even baggy eyes looked good. Tony got to his feet so fast he almost turned his chair over.

"My aunt wishes you—both of you—to have tea with her this afternoon," she said.

"How nice," I said, since Tony was too preoccupied with his tottering chair to be coherent. "What time?"

"Four o'clock." She didn't look at me; she was watching Tony from under those long lashes. His confusion seemed to amuse her; she gave him a small but effective smile before she turned away.

"I suppose," Tony said, capturing the chair and sitting on it, "she's going to bawl us out."

"Who, the *Gräfin*?" There was only one *Gräfin* in that house; it was impossible to think of Irma by her title. The word, with its guttural *r* and flat, hard vowel, suited the old lady.

"Let her complain," I went on. "If she gives me a hard time, I'll report her to the SPCC, or whatever the German equivalent may be."

"Irma's no child," Tony murmured.

"If you want to explore ruins, let's go," I said, rising.

The going was rough. The undergrowth between the castle and the keep was ninety percent brambles. They had the longest thorns I've ever seen on any plant. Tony kept falling into them; I gathered he was still preoccupied with Irma, because after a while he said,

"What makes you think the old lady is hassling Irma? We haven't seen her do anything particularly vicious."

"You don't call that performance last night vicious? The girl is scared to death about something. She works like a drudge, of course, while the old bat sits in her tower drinking tea; but it's more than that."

"Yeah, I know. It's hard to put into words, but there is something between the two of them. . . . I hate to think of handing the shrine over to an old witch like that."

An unwary step took me off the path, such as it was. I stopped, and unwound barbed-wire brambles from my ankle.

"So you're going to hand the shrine over, are you?" I said. "Aside from comments on overconfidence, which I have already made, may I compliment you on your ethics? I assumed you were going to tuck the treasure under your arm and steal away."

"You're getting me confused with Nolan. I think he plans just that. I admit, when I started on this deal I hadn't thought the problem through. I was excited about the hunt itself. Back in Ohio the whole thing was sort of unreal, you know what I mean? I never really thought we'd succeed. It's different now. . . . But I'm sure of one thing. The shrine doesn't belong to us. All we can do is turn it over to the rightful owner. I never had any intention of doing anything else. And don't try to kid me; you never did, either."

"No, but I've been thinking." I unwound the last bramble and stepped back onto the path. "The shrine wouldn't be considered treasure trove, would it? That is strictly defined legally; depending on lo- cal laws, it belongs either to the state or to the state and the finder, half and half. But the shrine belongs to the Drachensteins; that can be proved by means of the documents we've been using. And—listen. The old lady is only a Drachenstein by marriage. If Irma is the count's brother's child, wouldn't she be the heiress?"

"Good point," said Tony, brightening visibly. "We might try to find out about the late count's will. Not that it has any bearing on our search. . . ."

"But it would add to your zeal to think that Irma would enjoy the fruits of your brilliance?"

We had reached the keep and stood beside the high walls. Tony ignored my last remark and its tone of heavy sarcasm.

"Behold the *Wachtturm*," he said, gesturing. "It was built in A.D. eight hundred seven by Count Meninguad von und zu Drachenstein, fondly known to his contemporaries as the Black Devil of the Tau- ber Valley. The keep was abandoned in thirteen hundred eighty-three when the present castle was built. In fifteen hundred five—"

"All right, all right. I've read the guidebook too. Let's go in."

There was no door. Rusted iron hinges, each a couple of feet long, hung futilely from the doorframe. The interior of the first floor was a single circular room, dimly lit by the four narrow slits that pierced the walls. Since said walls were over eight feet thick, the sunlight didn't have much of a chance. The floor was of stone, but so overlaid with dirt that the original surface was virtually invisible.

Tony made a circuit of the walls, peering at the huge stones.

"When they built in those days, they built to last." He spoke in hushed tones, as if something might be listening. "I can't see anything unusual here. Let's go up."

Narrow stairs were cut into the stones of the wall. They were treacherous to climb; each step had a deep trench in the center, worn by generations of feet.

The second floor had been the hall. The windows were a little wider than those below. Across one quadrant of the room lay the remains of a half-wall, or screen, of stone, behind a low dais. The big stone fireplace, with the family arms on its hood, was the only feature in the room, which was littered with chips of fallen stone.

"The count and his lady dined there," Tony muttered, looking at the dais. "Their sleeping quarters were behind the screen. Rushes underfoot, and the dogs fighting over table scraps. . . ."

"Gracious living," I agreed. "According to the guidebook, this place was abandoned long before fifteen hundred twenty-five. It wouldn't be a bad spot to hide something."

Tony shook his head.

"It may have been abandoned as living quarters, but I'll bet it was still in use as a guard tower. Anyhow, if I were the count, I'd prefer to have my valuables closer at hand, so I could keep an eye on them. Way out here—"

He stopped speaking. He was opposite one of the window slits, and a narrow shaft of sunlight lay across the section of the floor at which he was staring.

"What—" But I didn't have to finish the question. I saw them too—footprints, clearly marked in the thick dust. The footprints of a man—a big man.

Tony knelt down. He thumped the floor with his fist, and sneezed as a cloud of dust enveloped his head.

"If anything has been hidden under these boards, I'll eat it," he announced, between sneezes. "Feel them. You'd expect wood so old to be rotten and crumbling, but these boards are practically petrified."

I joined him on the floor. As my fingers touched the rock-hard surface of the wood, I felt weighted down by the sheer overwhelming age of the place.

"They wouldn't have been this hard four hundred years ago," I said.

"That's not what I meant. Look at the construction of the floor. There's only one thickness of wood—each plank is a foot thick, sure, but there's no space for a hiding place in between them. The beams in the ceiling below support these planks."

"How big is the shrine, anyhow?"

"No dimensions were given." Tony went to the wall and thumped ineffectually at the stones. "But I should think it would have to be a meter or so high. Maybe bigger."

Okay, I thought to myself; if you don't want to talk about those footprints, we won't talk about them. And I won't mention the light I saw here last night. For all I knew, it might have been Tony who had carried that light, and this expedition might be a blind, to convince me of the futility of the *Wachtturm* as a hiding place. I watched Tony idiotically bruising his hands on impenetrable stone, and winced. If he had come here alone in the small hours of the night, I had to admire his nerve. The place was sinister enough in broad daylight. I tried to remember how much time had elapsed between my seeing the light, and leaving my room. I couldn't estimate accurately. Tony might have had time to get back from the keep and accost me in the corridor.

Tony turned from the wall.

"These stones look solid to me. We'd have to demolish the place to make sure nothing was hidden here."

"So why are we wasting our time?"

"Let's have a look at the top floor, just in case."

I got to the stairs ahead of him. When I came out onto the next floor, I stopped short, swaying with a sudden attack of vertigo. There was no top floor. The roofless walls were waist high at some points; mostly there was no wall at all, only a sudden drop into the thorny brambles far below. The view across the green valley was sensational, but I didn't linger to look at it. I backed cautiously toward the stairs, and Tony went with me. It was unnecessary to speak; there was no hiding place up there.

When we were out in the sunlight again, Tony drew a deep breath.

"That takes care of that. The *Schloss* is the place for us."

"It's so damned big. Where do we start looking?"

"I think more research is indicated."

"You just want to sit around and read books," I said unreasonably. "I want to *do* something. Even if we don't know where Burckhardt's room was, there are other possibilities. The crypt, for instance—"

"How do you know there is a crypt?"

"There's a chapel."

"Okay, I'll give you the crypt. I still want a detailed plan of the *Schloss*."

"And where do you expect to find it?"

"Two possibilities. The town archives, for one. Also the library, or muniment room of the *Schloss*. There may be other letters or useful documents there too."

"Okay," I said grumpily. "If you're going to be the honest, candid little fellow, I can do no less. You take the archives, I'll take the library. We share any information we find."

"Agreed."

When we reached the courtyard, we found an unexpected duo sitting at one of the tables in the garden. George Nolan and Professor Schmidt were deep in conversation—or rather, Schmidt was talking and George was listening. I thought he looked bored. He brightened when he saw us.

"Exploring, on a hot day like this?" he inquired.

"You know us." I dropped into a chair and smiled affably at him. "Nothing in the *Wachtturm* but dust and decay."

"But I thought Americans admired the old and decayed," said Schmidt.

I was getting a little tired of hearing that sentiment expressed, but I said only, "That place is too old."

"You should see the town. It is not too old. It is very nice."

"I've been here before," I said.

"But not with me," George said. "Let's go sightseeing. Harmless occupation," he added.

"*Gut, gut,*" said Schmidt eagerly. "I know Rothenburg well. There is a *Gasthaus* where we will lunch."

"We have to be back here by four," Tony said, regarding Schmidt unfavorably. "The countess has invited us—"

"But I also! I also have tea with the *Gräfin*. We can easily return by four."

There was no way of ditching him, short of deliberate rudeness. He turned out to be a rather pleasant companion, and an absolute mine of useless information. My half-formed doubts about him faded as the morning passed; he seemed harmless and rather endearing.

Looking like innocent tourists—which three of us certainly were not—we wandered clear across town to the old hospital area, while Schmidt spouted statistics about every building we passed. There are some lovely old buildings in the big hospital court; some of them are now used as a youth hostel. After the rather oppressive antiquity of the *Schloss* and its somber inhabitants, I enjoyed seeing the kids swarming around, weighted down by their backpacks but having a marvelous time anyhow. Sure, most of them were pretty dirty by the time they got halfway across Europe; cleanliness is a luxury when you are short on money and even shorter on time. Like any other mixed group, they had their share of no-goods, but most of them were nice kids seeing the world— pilgrims, of a kind. As we stood there, a pair of them emerged from the unadorned facade of the early Gothic church. I admit it was hard to determine their sex; but with their long locks and faded clothes they didn't look as incongruous as one might have expected.

Outside the hospital stands one of the more formidable of the city gates. George, who was visiting Rothenburg for the first time, seemed fascinated by the fortifications. He nodded approvingly at the sections of wall that stretched out from both sides of the gate.

"They wouldn't stand up against artillery, but I'd hate to attack the place with anything less. A roofed walkway all around for the defenders—arrow slits, I suppose, on the outer wall . . . ?"

"That is correct," Schmidt said. "They are proud of their wall, it is one of the best preserved in Europe."

"Can you walk along it?"

It was a stupid question; we could see at least a dozen people up above, walking or leaning over the wooden rail that fenced the walkway on the town side. But Schmidt answered seriously, "To be sure you can. The walk is kept in repair."

"But not now," Tony said. "Where's this restaurant? I'm starved."

We had an excellent lunch, which included one glass of beer too many for me. Schmidt was glassy-eyed; he had eaten everything he could get his hands on, including a couple of extra platters of heavy dark bread. He announced his intention of taking a nap, and I had to admit it sounded like a good idea.

"I'm going to walk some more," said Tony, with a meaningful glance at me. "See you later."

He intended, of course, to search out the town archives. I really meant to look for the library, to keep my part of our bargain. But it was a hot day, and my stone-walled room was nice and cool, and the bed was soft. I didn't wake up till Tony banged on the door, and I discovered I had just time enough to assume my best bib and tucker for the tea party.

My first sight of the *Gräfin*'s room at the top of the tower took my breath away. It was full of treasures; there was no sign here of the genteel shabbiness that marked the rest of the *Schloss*. An eighteenth-century *Kabinett*, with panels of painted silk, might have been designed by Cuvilliés. Next to it was a writing desk, French by the look of it, that had beautiful brass inlays over its leather surface. The sofa and chairs dated from Ludwig I; crimson brocade seats bore the Drachenstein arms in gold, and the wood was gilded. The *Gräfin* had a weakness for gilt, but she tolerated crasser metals; the massive silver tea service on the table looked like Huguenot craftsmanship. I have seen poorer work behind glass in several museums. The place was rather like a museum, a selection of the best of Schloss Drachenstein. Only the hangings at the window were new. They were expensive looking, made of crimson fabric as heavy as felt, embroidered with— you guessed it—gold threads.

I have been told, by critics, that I have a nasty suspicious mind. The sight of that collection brought out my worst suspicions. If these pieces were representative of the original furnishings of the *Schloss*, then what had happened to the rest of the furniture and ornaments? And why were the surviving goodies all gathered here in the *Gräfin*'s lair? She might at least share them with her niece, to whom they probably belonged legally. I have seen maids' rooms better furnished than Irma's shabby quarters.

I turned from my appraisal to meet the *Gräfin*'s ironical eye. If she knew what I was thinking—and I wouldn't have been surprised to discover that she could read minds—she made no comment. She indicated the tall Englishwoman, who was perched on the sofa beside the tea service.

"My dear friend, Miss Burton."

Miss Burton shook hands with us. Tony's eyes widened when her bony fist clamped over his. Thus warned, and uninhibited by his archaic notions of courtesy, I was able to give Miss Burton a worthy grip when she tried to squash my fingers. She gasped. When she sat down again, her cheekbones were an ugly rust color, and Tony shook his head at me. He was right; we should keep on amicable terms with the *Gräfin* as long as possible, and antagonizing her dear friend wouldn't help. But the two women, who were unappealing separately, gave me the creeps when I saw them together. They only needed a third to qualify for the blasted heath bit in *Macbeth*. Somebody had to keep them in line, and that somebody wouldn't be Tony. He's incapable of talking back to any female over forty. They hypnotize him.

As I expected, Tony was a ready victim for the *Gräfin*. He stammered like a schoolboy when she spoke to him. Irma fluttered around, speechless and servile, offering plates of cookies. George sat and smiled. Schmidt's small dark eyes darted from one face to the next in open curiosity. I was waiting for a chance to ask the *Gräfin* about the *Schloss* library. I had a valid excuse for being interested in historical records, and the less sneaking I had to do, the less chance there was of being caught in a place I had no business being in. But before I found my opening, Miss Burton, who had been eyeing Tony like a hungry tiger, interrupted her friend in the middle of a long speech about the antiquity, nobility, and all-around virtue of the House of Drachenstein.

"Elfrida, I believe this young man is a sensitive. Perhaps we should make use of him tonight."

Tony, who didn't know what the woman meant, and who thought the worst, looked horrified. The *Gräfin* smiled.

"Miss Burton is a student of the occult," she explained.

"Oh. Oh, God," said Tony, looking, if possible,

even more aghast. "Look here—I mean, I'm no sensitive, if that's what you call it. In fact—in fact—"

He looked hopefully at me.

I contemplated the ceiling. I knew his views on spiritualism and the occult; they are profane. He has a morbid passion for ghost stories of all kinds, but only because he can suspend his disbelief for the purpose of entertainment. Torn between the requirements of courtesy and a thorough distaste, Tony looked in vain for rescue. He wasn't going to get any help from me. It was high time he learned to stand up for himself.

"In fact," Tony mumbled servilely, "I'm pretty ignorant about the whole subject."

"Ignorance is not uncommon," said Miss Burton, with a sigh. "Dreadful, when one considers the urgency. . . . But I feel sure, Professor, that you are mediumistic. Look, Elfrida, at his hands . . . his eyes . . . There is a certain delicacy. . . ."

Tony was beet-red.

"But," he croaked.

"Many mediums are unaware of their gift until they try," said Miss Burton, giving him a severe look.

There was a hideous pause. George, shaking with suppressed laughter, gave me a look that invited me to share his amusement. Schmidt was sitting bolt upright, his teacup in one hand, a half-eaten cookie in the other. He caught my eye; and to my surprise, he said seriously, "The *Schloss* is an admirable place for such research, *Fräulein Doktor*. There is a strong residue of psychic matter in a spot where so many have lived and died, loved and hated."

"You are a psychic researcher?" I asked.

"Only as an amateur."

Miss Burton broke in.

"If we can obtain only a moderate degree of co-operation from Professor Lawrence, the least one might expect from a gentleman and a—"

I knew she was going to say it, and I knew I would laugh out loud if she did. It was time for me to be ingratiating; all this was leading up to something, and Schmidt's attitude made me very curious indeed.

"I'm sure Tony will be glad to help," I said, before Miss Burton could say "scholar." "We all will. Don't you need a certain number of people to make up a circle?"

The countess turned to look at me.

"How kind," she murmured.

"Not at all," I murmured back. "I've always been fascinated by the occult."

Tony made an uncouth noise which I ignored. I swept on, "One seldom finds an opportunity to hold a séance in such ideal surroundings. An old castle . . . a very old family . . ."

"The Drachensteins trace their lineage unbroken to the ninth century," said the countess. "In 1525 the original line died out, but the title was assumed by a cousin."

"Died out? What happened to Count Burck-hardt's daughter?"

Tony's question was followed by a silence which gave me time to think of all the things I was going to do to him for letting his big mouth loose again. In my opinion it was too early in the game to let the

Gräfin know the full extent of our knowledge of, and interest in, the family of Graf Burckhardt. But since the damage was done, I decided to make the most of it.

"As a prominent American historian of the Reformation," I said pompously, "Professor Lawrence is particularly interested in the sixteenth century."

"Ah, of course." You couldn't call the gleam in the *Gräfin*'s eye a twinkle, but she was definitely amused. I found that expression even less attractive than her normal look. "No doubt you, too, are a prominent historian of the Reformation, Miss Bliss? It is a pleasure to find foreign scholars so well informed about our local history.

"As for Graf Burckhardt, he did indeed leave an infant daughter. She was taken into the family of her second cousin, who became Graf Georg. She later married his eldest son."

So that, I thought, was the physical link between Konstanze and Irma, who was the direct descendant of Graf George and his wife. Funny thing, genetics. . . .

"You said fifteen hundred twenty-five?" Tony tried to look casual. "That was the time of the Peasants' Revolt. Was Graf Burckhardt killed in the fighting?"

"How strange that you should not know that, with your interest in the family," the *Gräfin* said. "No, he was not, although he fought valiantly in Würzburg for his liege, the bishop. He died of a virulent fever, it is said, soon after his return home."

George leaned forward in his chair.

"What happened to Burckhardt's wife?"

The *Gräfin* grinned at him. It was a full-fledged grin, not a smile, and it was a singularly ugly expression.

"Of course you would be interested in her—after last night."

Miss Burton gasped.

"Elfrida! Why didn't you tell me? Has the countess returned again?"

FIVE

❁▱❁▱❁

I HAD FORGOTTEN ABOUT IRMA. SHE ATTRACTED MY attention by dropping the tray she was holding. It made a splendid crash. We swung around, as one man—to use a male chauvinist formula—and when I saw the girl's face, I leaped out of my chair. I thought she was going to faint. All my half-formed suspicions about the relationship between aunt and niece came into focus, and without stopping to think I said rudely,

"If you're talking about Konstanze, she hasn't returned, and she isn't about to. The dead don't come back. Anyone who believes that rot is weak in the head."

Miss Burton's nostrils flared. "You said you believed!"

"I said I was interested. I am willing to admit the possibility of contacting those who have passed beyond. . . ." That was an exaggeration, but I didn't want to be excluded from the seance. ". . . but ghosts, clanking chains in the halls? Ha, ha, ha."

My laugh was a bit artificial, but it affected Irma as I hoped it would. A faint touch of color came back to her cheeks, and for the first time since I'd met her she looked at me with something less than active dislike. I didn't blame the girl for resenting me; to her, I represented the freedom and independence she conspicuously lacked. I didn't resent *her*, even if she did have all the physical qualities *I* lacked. I felt sorry for her, and whether she cared for me or not, I wasn't going to stand around and let the two witches bully her. Not with that kind of half-baked stupidity, anyhow.

Tony had also been studying Irma with concern. He chimed in. "I agree. I'm willing to go along with your theories up to a point, ladies, but let's not get distracted by fairy tales."

"Do you call Konstanze's portrait a fairy tale?" The *Gräfin* had stopped grinning. She wasn't used to back talk from inferiors, and it angered her.

"These chance resemblances are fascinating, genetically," Tony said smoothly. "I remember once seeing a row of portraits in a French château. Two of the faces might have belonged to identical twins. But one man wore medieval armor, and the other the uniform of Napoleon's Guards."

Irma had forgotten my kindly intervention. She was staring at Tony the way what's-her-name must have looked at Saint George, when he killed the dragon. Tony's chest expanded to twice its normal size. He was so busy exchanging amorous glances with Irma he didn't notice the *Gräfin*; but I did, and an unpremeditated shiver ran down my back.

"How fascinating," she said, through clenched teeth. "You are indeed a confirmed skeptic, Professor Lawrence. Some day you might like to visit our crypt. I think you will find it interesting, in spite of your rational explanations."

"Oh, there is a crypt?" For a moment Tony forgot to leer at Irma. This was his opening.

"Yes, there is a crypt. Ask me for the keys whenever you like. I do not allow casual guests to go there, but in your case . . ."

"Perhaps I may also take advantage of your generosity, *Gräfin*," I said. "Is there a library in the *Schloss*? I am something of an expert on old books and manuscripts. If you have never had the library examined by someone who knows books you may discover there are objects of value that could be sold."

"How kind you are." The old bat gave me one of those smiles that make nervous people want to hide under the nearest piece of furniture. "I fear we have already disposed of most of our treasures. But of course you are welcome to look. Let me give you the keys now."

I accepted the keys, and with them my *congé*, as Emily Post might say. The exodus was a mass affair; the tea party had not been a social success. It was primarily my fault, and I was delighted to take the responsibility. But I wasn't sure the good guys had come out ahead.

At least we had the keys to the library. I tossed them, jingling, as we went down the stairs. George patted me on the back.

"Nice work, Vicky. But you're wasting your time."

"Hush your mouth," said Tony, with some vague idea that he was speaking a kind of code. Schmidt, who was ahead of me, turned to give us a bewildered look.

"You will inspect the library?" he asked.

"Yes. Why not?"

"Oh, of course, of course. I only meant to ask—I too am an antiquarian. An amateur, of course!"

"Of course," I said. We had reached the corridor leading to our rooms, and I gave the little man a very hard stare. He beamed ingratiatingly.

"It would be a privilege to assist you," he said.

"She has an assistant," Tony said. "Me."

"Then as a favor to an old man?"

I didn't see how I could refuse without giving the whole business an aura of secrecy, which was the last thing I wanted. In the unlikely event that I found a useful clue, I believed myself capable of distracting Schmidt's attention from it.

"Sure," I said. "The more the merrier. How about you, George?"

"No, thanks. It's not in the library. I've already looked."

He ought to have been on the stage. He didn't even look back as he walked off down the corridor, humming softly to himself.

"It?" said Schmidt, with a frown.

"Crazy American," said Tony wildly. "You know how they are."

"If he doesn't," I said, sighing, "he's finding out now. Come on. Where is the blasted library, anyhow?"

It was on the same floor as the Great Hall, off a corridor to the south. When the door swung open, I couldn't hold back a groan. The room had once been handsome. The fireplace was of marble, with stiff Gothic figures of saints supporting the mantel;

there wasn't a nose or chin left among the holy crew, and the stone was pitted, as if by acid. Tapestries covered the walls, but they were cobwebby masses of decay; behind them, small things scuttled and squeaked, disturbed by our entry. The bookshelves sagged; the books were crumbling piles of leather and paper.

At some time, the library had been stripped of most of its contents. The remaining volumes were either valueless or decayed beyond hope of repair.

Then, by the dust-coated windows, I saw something that looked more interesting. It was a tall cupboard, or *Schrank*, black with age, but still sound. It was locked. I tried the keys the countess had given me, and found one that worked.

The *Schrank* contained several books, a metal box, and a roll of parchments. I took the last object first and carried it to a table. Tony and Schmidt looked on as I unrolled it.

The parchments were all plans of the castle and its grounds. They were very old.

I let the sheets roll themselves up again, and twisted them out of Tony's clutching hand.

"Naughty, naughty," I said gaily. "We don't care about these old things, do we? Nothing valuable here. Let's see what else there is."

The books were three in number—heavy volumes, bound in leather, with metal clasps and studs. I wondered why they had not been sold with the other valuables, for they could be considered rare books. When I tried to open one, I understood. Hardly a page remained legible. Water, mildew, worms and rats had all taken their toll.

"Amazing," said Tony, breathing heavily over my shoulder.

"Rather peculiar volumes to find here," I agreed, picking up the next book. It was in equally poor condition.

"What is it?" Schmidt asked.

"You might call them books of philosophical speculation. In their day, they verged on the heretical. I'm surprised to find them here because the Counts of Drachenstein don't strike me as intellectuals. This is Trithemius; this one is Albert of Cologne, better known as Albertus Magnus—"

"The great magician!" Schmidt exclaimed. "Fascinating! May I please—"

I handed him the book. He glanced at it, and shook his head.

"I cannot make it out. You two perhaps understand?"

"I read medieval Latin," Tony said. Schmidt let him have the volume, and he opened it.

I was too distracted to indulge in my usual bragging. Of course I read Latin, classical and medieval, as well as most of the European languages. I had a feeling Schmidt did, too. Whatever his other talents, he had no gift for dissimulation. In other words, he was a lousy liar. When he said he couldn't read the book, his eyes shifted and he changed color, the way Matthew Finch did back in fifth grade when he was trying to psych the teacher.

I left Tony deep in the heresies of Trithemius, and turned to the object that interested me most. If papers could survive for four centuries, it would be in just such a metal box.

The box was locked, but the key proved to be on the countess's ring. I tackled lock and top cautiously; air, admitted to a formerly sealed container, can be destructive to items within. But it was clear that this box had been opened in the recent past. The lock had been oiled, and the lid lifted easily.

After a minute I turned to Schmidt, who was hovering.

"Nothing much," I said, as casually as I was able. "A couple of old diaries and some account lists."

Tony's head came up. His nose was quivering.

"I'll have a close look at them some other time," I said, before he could speak. "Must be almost time for dinner. Shall we?"

I hated to put that box back in the *Schrank*. I didn't trust Schmidt as far as I could throw him. Not nearly as far—I could have thrown him quite a distance. His shifty looks and inconsistent behavior were not proof of guilt; but whether he was witting or ignorant, my safest attitude was one of indifference to anything I found. I felt sure the metal box had once contained the letters which had been reprinted in *The Peasants' Revolt*. Therefore someone had already searched its contents. And the box was as safe in the *Schrank*, under lock and key, as it was anywhere.

❀▭❀

Having reached that conclusion, I was able to meet George's smiling curiosity at dinner with relative calm. We fenced through the meal, with innuendoes falling thick and fast, and Tony glaring, and Blankenhagen watching all three of us as if he suspected our sanity. We had reached the coffee stage when Irma came to the table. As soon as I looked at her, I knew something was up.

"My aunt asks that you spend an hour with her this evening," she said, addressing Tony.

"This evening? Sure . . . Is there any particular . . . I mean, why does she . . . ?"

The girl's face got even paler.

"I cannot say, *Herr Professor.* It is not for me . . . She asks the others to come also. *Fräulein,* Herr Nolan, and you, Herr Doktor Blankenhagen."

Blankenhagen was watching her curiously.

"The *Gräfin* has not honored me before," he said. "I think this is not a social occasion. I will come; but I too ask you, why?"

The repetition of the question was too much for Irma. She shook her head speechlessly and turned away.

"I think I know why," I said coyly, as Blankenhagen, still on his feet, stared after her slim form.

"So do I," said Tony, with a dismal groan.

We were correct in our assumption; but I was surprised when Irma led us to one of the guest rooms instead of the *Gräfin*'s aerie in the tower. The room was the one occupied by Schmidt. He stood modestly to one side while Miss Burton bustled about, arranging the setting for a séance. A heavy round table had been pulled out into the center of the room and a pack of alphabet cards was arranged in a circle on its top. In the center of the circle, looking as menacing and squatty as a toad, was a planchette.

The *Gräfin* was seated in a high carved chair.

Hands folded in her lap, face and hair lacquered into mask-hardness, she had the air of a high priestess waiting for a ceremony. Seeing our surprise, she condescended to explain.

"Herr Schmidt kindly allows us to use his room. It has a particularly interesting aura."

If Schmidt had any misgivings about the proceedings, he didn't show them; beaming, bobbing up and down on his toes, rubbing his hands together, he seemed quite pleased about the whole thing. It was the first time I had seen his room, and as I studied it I could understand why it might be appropriate for a séance. It was by far the largest of the guest rooms, and was the only one still furnished with antiques. The walls retained their paneling—dark, worm-eaten wood, atmospheric as all get out. The windows were heavily draped.

I caught Tony's eye, and knew what he was thinking as surely as if he had spoken aloud. Was this the master bedchamber, the room once occupied by Count Burckhardt himself? Some of the furniture might have belonged to him—the great canopied bed with its carved dragon posts, for instance.

George cleared his throat.

"Ladies, I want to warn you that I'm not a believer."

"So long as your attitude is not positively hostile . . ." said Miss Burton.

"No." George looked sober. "I've seen a few things in my travels. . . . Well, what about it, Doctor?"

Blankenhagen's face was a sight for skeptics. If he had been able to voice his real feelings, they would have come out in a howl of outraged rationalism.

But something made him strangle his protests, and when I saw Irma, standing white-faced in a corner, I thought I knew what the something was.

"I remain," said Blankenhagen, after a moment.

We took our places at the table. I sat between George and Tony. The two Germans flanked Irma.

"Miss Burton prefers to sit to one side, in order to take notes," said the *Gräfin*, as Tony, always the little gent, glanced inquiringly at that lady before seating himself.

"And you?"

"I never participate," said the *Gräfin*, with an unpleasant smile.

Miss Burton extinguished the lamps, leaving only a single candle at the end of the table.

"Now," she said, "put only the tips of your fingers upon the edges of the planchette. You all understand the procedure? If we are able to make contact, the discarnate will spell out its answers to our questions, using the alphabet cards. Do not resist the movement of the planchette. And let me ask the questions."

She sat down behind Tony, holding a pencil and a pad of paper. His shadow hid all of her except her hands. They looked like the claws of a scavenger bird as they clutched the writing implements with feverish intensity. I wondered what sick desire had driven Miss Burton to spiritualism. The best psychic investigators approach the subject in a spirit of genuine inquiry and endeavor to maintain scientific controls. Not Miss Burton; the bony, clawlike hands betrayed her. The room had an "aura," all right—not the psychic residue of past centuries, but the projected emotions of the living. The flickering candlelight left people's bodies in darkness, casting ugly shadows on faces that seemed to hover disembodied in air.

The room grew very silent. A rustle of the draperies, at a sudden breath of wind, made us all jump. Gradually the stillness spread again. I found myself staring dreamily at the bright shape of the candle flame. It took some effort to wrench my eyes away; the whole business was a perfect example of hypnotic technique, and it was damnably effective. The silence was not the absence of sound; it was a positive force that seemed to grow and strengthen. Silence, concentration, and a single point of moving light in darkness. . . . Yes, very effective. It was hard to keep my mind critical and controlled.

A prickle ran down my back. The planchette had moved.

I lifted my hands until my fingertips barely brushed the planchette. So far as I could determine, the others had done the same. I could have sworn no one in the circle was exerting enough pressure on the planchette to move it.

It moved again. Rocking unsteadily, it shifted toward the side of the circle.

Miss Burton's voice was hoarse with excitement.

"Is there a spirit present?"

At opposite sides of the circle of alphabet cards were two cards bearing the words "yes" and "no." The planchette sidled across the table and nudged the "yes" card.

Someone gave a little gasp.

"Quiet!" hissed Miss Burton. "Do you wish to communicate with someone here?"

The planchette edged coyly away, and then, with a swoop, again pushed the "yes" card.

"What is your name?"

The diabolical little wooden triangle teetered out into the center of the table. It hesitated. Then it moved purposefully around the alphabet cards.

"K-O-N——"

My elbows ached. I watched the animated chunk of wood with horrid fascination as it bobbed and dipped around the "N" card, scraping back and forth in painful little jerks. I realized that I was mentally describing its actions with words I would have used for a living creature. It seemed to be alive, to be directed by a guiding intelligence.

After an uncanny suggestion of struggle, the planchette slid slowly toward the "no" card. "No"— then "no" again—then it gave a violent heave—*upward*, against six sets of fingertips. It fell over and lay still. I felt as if something had died.

"What the hell," George began.

"Hush," said Miss Burton solemnly. "There is conflict—a hostile entity. . . ."

The candle needed trimming. The room was noticeably darker. The other faces were dim white blurs. I rubbed my elbows, and wondered how much practice it would take to manipulate a planchette unobstrusively. It could be done. It had been done, in thousands of fake séances. Maybe it didn't require practice. I mused, ignorantly, on the eccentricities of the subconscious.

"This is a very strange thing," Schmidt began, and then gasped. "Look—the young countess!"

Irma had fallen back in her chair, arms dangling at her sides. I could hear her breathing in low, deep sighs. It was a horrible sound.

Blankenhagen got to his feet.

"Don't touch her!" Miss Burton's voice stopped the doctor as he reached for Irma's wrist. "She is in trance. If you try to waken her, it could be disastrous. Let me handle this. Irma—can you hear me?"

There was no answer. The doctor looked from Miss Burton to the unconscious girl. Miss Burton took a deep breath and said distinctly, "Who are you?"

For a few seconds there was only silence. Then, from the sleeping girl's mouth, came a voice speaking a strange garble of words. It sounded like German, but it was a form of the language I had never heard. Or . . . had I? It sounded vaguely familiar.

Then, for the first time, my hair literally bristled. I had heard the language before, when a visiting professor of Germanic literature read some of the *Meistergesang* of the sixteenth century in their original form. Irma was speaking *Frühneuhochdeutsch*— the earliest form of modern German, the language used by Martin Luther and his contemporaries.

Miss Burton scribbled like a maniac, taking the speech down in phonetic symbols. Her cold-blooded competence was repulsive.

The voice—I couldn't think of it as Irma's— stopped.

"Why have you come?" Miss Burton asked.

This time, prepared, I caught some of the answer. I didn't like what I heard. Tony understood, too; his breath caught angrily, and he pushed his chair back.

"This has gone far enough," he began, and was cut short by the scream that ripped from Irma's throat. The next words were horribly clear.

"*Das Feuer! Das Feuer!*" She shrieked, and slid sideways out of her chair.

Blankenhagen caught her before she hit the floor.

That broke up the séance. Miss Burton moved about lighting candles. Her eyes glittered. Blankenhagen knelt by Irma, and the rest of us huddled in a group near the door.

"What did it mean?" George hissed. "That last word?"

"Fire," said Tony uneasily. "Fire."

"What fire?" George demanded. "Is she trying to tell us the *Schloss* is going to burn?"

"How should I know?"

Miss Burton came back to the table.

"Did anyone recognize the language?" she asked briskly.

I gave her a hostile, unbelieving stare, which didn't disturb her in the slightest, and turned to Blankenhagen.

"How is Irma?"

"She recovers," the doctor said shortly.

"She will feel no ill effects, except for great weariness," Miss Burton said complacently. "I have seen deep trance before. My dear Elfrida, how fortunate. You told me the girl was susceptible, but I had no idea!"

The countess hadn't moved from her chair. She didn't look at Irma.

"Now, the language," Miss Burton went on. "A form of German, I believe. Professor Lawrence?"

"Not now!" Tony said angrily.

"Professor Schmidt? Really, this is too important—"

Schmidt was too shaken to argue. I felt a touch of sympathy for the little guy when I saw his twitching face; he was like a man who goes out hunting for a lost pussycat, and meets a tiger. With a despairing shrug he took the paper Miss Burton thrust at him.

"Yes, yes," he muttered. "It is the early form of modern High German. 'I am the Gräfin Konstanze von Drachenstein; from the sunny land of Spain I came, to die in this place of cold winters and colder hearts.'"

"Lousy prose," George said critically.

Schmidt hurried on.

"Then, it is something like this: 'There is danger everywhere. I cannot rest. I cannot sleep, here in the cold of eternity. Let me see the sun again, let me feel warmth, breathe the air. Give me life. She has so much; let her share life and breath with me. Let me have—'"

The sobbing cry might have been the ghost's own addition to Schmidt's translation. It was Irma's voice, though. Supported by Blankenhagen, she had raised herself to a sitting position. As we turned, guilty and surprised, she slumped back with closed eyes.

"Idiot," said the doctor furiously. "It is criminal, what you do! To put such insane ideas into the girl's mind—"

"It is you who are insane, to deny the evidence of

your own senses!" Miss Burton was as angry as Blankenhagen. Two febrile spots of color burned on her sallow cheeks. "You heard her; you must know it was not Irma who said those words. Possession by the spirits of the dead is a well-documented fact; only a bigoted scientist would deny—"

"*Herr Gott in Himmel*," bellowed Blankenhagen. "Will no one stop that cursed woman's mouth?"

He surged to his feet, lifting Irma as if she were a child. Miss Burton's color faded; she fell back a step as the irate doctor advanced on her. I decided it was time to intervene.

"I'll stop it," I said. "If she says another word, I'll gag her. Come on, Doctor. You'd better get Irma out of here."

Miss Burton gave me a long, measuring look, and decided I was not only willing to carry out my threat, but capable of enforcing it. The *Gräfin* smiled like Andersen's Snow Queen. George was smiling too, but he looked rather thoughtful. Tony didn't say a word; he just moved up behind me and put a steadying hand on my shoulder. Of the whole group, the one who was most upset was little Herr Schmidt. His face was puckered like that of a baby about to cry.

"*Furchtbar*," he muttered. "I am ashamed; I did not know she heard. I did not realize—"

George gave him a slap on the back.

"Don't kick yourself, Schmidt. It wasn't your fault. Well, ladies, I guess it's time to break up the party. Thanks for an interesting evening. Not much fun, but interesting."

The light touch was inapropos. Blankenhagen

bared his teeth at George and stamped toward the door. I started to follow, since it was clear that the *Gräfin* didn't intend to go with her stricken niece, but Tony's hand held me back.

"Wait a minute," he said. "*Gräfin*, you once said I might explore any part of the *Schloss*. I want the keys to the crypt, please."

"The crypt?" The *Gräfin* laughed musically. "You are thinking of going there now? I admire your courage, *mein Herr*, it is an uncanny spot by night, even for a skeptic. But if you are determined, come to my room and I will give you the keys."

I caught up with Blankenhagen in the hall.

"I'll show you where Irma's room is," I said. "You may need some help."

His rocky face relaxed a little.

"You are good," he said formally.

The only thing he needed me for was to undress Irma and put her to bed. I wondered at his modesty; a doctor shouldn't be embarrassed about female bodies, even bodies as gorgeous as Irma's. Then it occurred to me that maybe he was thinking of her as something other than a patient.

The girl didn't stir as I wrestled her into one of her hideous nightgowns and tucked her in. She was a little thing; it wasn't hard for me to handle her. But I didn't like the flaccidity of her muscles, or the depth of her trance. As soon as I had her in bed, Blankenhagen took over. After a few minutes she began to mutter and stir.

In the silence I heard footsteps outside—Tony and the old witch, going after the keys. The footsteps didn't stop, they went on up the stairs. The cold-blooded female hadn't even looked in.

I moved closer to the bed and took Irma's hand, which was groping desperately, as if in search of something. Blankenhagen gave me a faint smile of approval. I felt absurdly complimented. The smile made him look almost handsome.

Finally Irma's eyes opened, and I gave a sigh of relief. Blankenhagen leaned over her, murmuring in German—repeated reassurances, comforting and semi-hypnotic. The technique seemed to work; her face remained calm. Then she turned her head and saw me.

"It is the *Fräulein Doktor*, come to sit with you," said Blankenhagen quietly. "She will stay—all night, if you wish . . . ?"

The question was meant for me as well as for Irma. I answered with a prompt affirmative, and patted the kid's hand.

Gently but decisively it was withdrawn.

"Thank you. You are good. But I would like my aunt."

"But—" the doctor began.

"My aunt! I must have her, she alone can help me. . . . *Herr Doktor*, please!"

Her voice rose. I recognized the sign of incipient hysteria as well as Blankenhagen did. Our eyes met, and he shrugged.

"Yes, of course you shall have her. I will fetch her."

Irma's eyes closed.

"I'll get the *Gräfin*," I said in a low voice. "You'd better stay here. If Irma changes her mind I'll come, any time."

"*Sehr gut.*" He got up from his chair with an anxious glance at the girl, who lay unmoving. He opened the door for me, and as I was about to go out he moved with a quick grace I hadn't expected in such a stocky, solid man. He kissed my hand.

"You are a good woman," said Blankenhagen, in a burst of Germanic sentimentality. "I thank you for your help . . . I apologize for what I thought . . ."

I didn't know what he had been thinking about me, and I didn't particularly want to know. He was still holding my hand—his hands were big and warm and hard—when Tony appeared on the stairs that led to the next floor. He stopped, with a corny theatrical start, when he saw us. Blankenhagen released my hand, and Tony came on down slowly, his eyes fixed on me.

"Got the keys?" I inquired.

"Huh? Yeah. How's Irma?"

"Not good. She wants Auntie. God knows why."

Auntie chose that moment to make her appearance. I think she heard me. She gave me a mocking, ice-blue stare, and spoke to Blankenhagen.

"I will stay with my niece tonight. Thank you, Doctor."

"But I—"

"I will call you if there is need. But I think you may sleep undisturbed. I know how to deal with this. It has happened before."

The door closed on our staring faces, but not before we had seen Irma's face turn toward the old woman, and heard her breathless greeting.

Blankenhagen made a movement toward the closed door, but I grabbed his arm.

"Better not," I said. "She'll throw you out of the hotel if you interfere. She has the right."

"And I have none," Blankenhagen muttered.

"No," Tony agreed. He glanced at me. The glance was friendly; he had concluded that the doctor was falling for Irma and was therefore safe from my predatory clutches. "Better go to bed. See you all in the morning."

I observed the awkward angle of the arm Tony was hiding behind his back, and I remembered why I had come to Rothenburg. I had not come to rescue oppressed damsels. Let the boys take care of that.

"Go to bed, while you explore the crypt?" I demanded. "You've got the keys behind your back right now. I'm coming with you."

"The crypt?" Blankenhagen repeated. "Why in the devil's name do you want to go there?"

"Why not?" I said flippantly. "Maybe we'll meet Konstanze. That's where she—er—lives, isn't it?"

"I should not go with you," Blankenhagen muttered. "If I am needed—"

"You weren't invited to come," Tony said indignantly.

"I invited myself," said the doctor, with an unexpected gleam of sardonic humor. "I do not know what you are doing, but if I were in your shoes, I would not mind a companion. There are forces abroad in this place which are not good, though they are not supernatural. For safety it is best to travel in groups."

"I agree," I said, before Tony could object. "The countess won't call you, Doctor; she made that pretty clear."

Blankenhagen nodded.

"Come, then. I understand none of this; but some of it I must understand if I am to help that girl. She has need of help, I think."

We went down the stairs, through the Hall, and out into the night-shrouded court. There was enough moonlight to let us see the arched door of the chapel in the north wing. Tony's first key fit the lock.

The interior was a blaze of tarnished gilt in the rays of Tony's flashlight. I blinked, and mentally discarded one possible hiding place. The chapel had been redecorated in the baroque period; twisted marble columns, sunbursts of gold plaster, and stucco cherubs by the cartload filled the long, narrow room. The remodelers would have found any treasure here.

"The entrance to the crypt should be near the altar," I said.

Blankenhagen hesitated.

"I am wondering—should we not wait until daylight?"

"You aren't scared, are you?" Tony grinned weakly.

"The dead are dead," said Blankenhagen.

In broad daylight it might have sounded sententious. In the baroque gloom, with the memory of the séance fresh in our minds, it had the ring of a credo.

"Thanks for reminding me," said Tony. "This way."

The entrance was behind the altar. It was barred by a grilled iron gate, which yielded to Tony's second key. He turned the flashlight down into the black pit of the stairs, and he wasn't the only one who hesitated just a bit before starting to descend.

The crypt extended the full length of the chapel. Rough square stone pillars supported the vaulted roof. There was none of the dampness I had expected, but the air had a musty smell that struck at the nostrils, and the imagination.

Across the floor, row on row, lay the tombstones of the Drachensteins. Those nearest the stair were simple marble or bronze slabs, with a name and a date: Graf Conrad von u. zu Drachenstein, 1804–1888; Gräfin Elisabeth, *seine Frau*, 1812–1884.

"That must be Irma's father," said Tony, pointing to a bronze plaque bearing the dates 1886–1952. "He was succeeded by his younger brother."

"They are a long-lived family," said Blankenhagen thoughtfully.

We moved forward.

Graf Wolfgang. Gräfin Berthe. 1756–1814. 1705–1770.

As we approached the far end of the crypt, the simple stones were replaced by more elaborate ones. Tony flashed his light on a sculptured form clad in armor, with hands clasped on its breast and the remains of a four-footed beast under its feet.

"The first of the effigies," he said in a low voice. "We're getting there."

Against the wall we found the sixteenth-century markers.

Graf Harald von und zu Drachenstein, Burckhardt's father, looked in gray marble much as he might have looked in life. His face, framed in stiff stone ringlets, was stern and dignified. The hardness of stone suited his harsh features. His left hand rested on his sword, and his right held the banner of his house, with its crest of a dragon on a stone. Beside him lay his countess, her face set in a pious simper, her hands palm to palm under her chin. The ample folds of her best court gown were frozen for all eternity.

Tony moved to the next monument. Upon it also lay a knight in armor, encircled by a long epitaph in twisted Gothic script. It had been carelessly carved. The letters were not deeply incised. But there was no traffic or weather here to wear them down. Tony translated the essential data.

"Graf Burckhardt von und zu Drachenstein. *Geboren* fourteen hundred ninety-five. *Tot* fifteen hundred twenty-five."

"Thirty years old," I said.

There was an empty space next to Count Burckhardt, presumably because the old family had died out with him. The stones of the cadet line began beyond the next pillar.

Tony returned to Burckhardt's effigy and waved his flashlight wildly about.

"What is it?" Blankenhagen asked. "What do you search for?"

"Don't you see? All the counts have their wives laid out beside them—in rows, when they wore them out too fast. There's room for her there by his side. Where is the Countess Konstanze?"

SIX

THE COUNTESS KONSTANZE WAS DEFINITELY NOT IN the crypt. Tony checked every stone, stalking up and down the dim aisles like an avenging fury. Blankenhagen saw some of the implications; when we finally left the chapel, he burst out,

"What is the meaning of this folly? Do you suggest that because this dead woman is not in the crypt, she is . . . *Ach, Gott!* You are encouraging this madness! No wonder the child believes . . . What does she believe?"

Tony scowled malevolently at a smirking plaster cherub, and then slammed and locked the door of the chapel.

"Three guesses," he said. "And I'll bet you're right the first time."

We crossed the moonlit court in a silence that could be felt. No one spoke till we reached our rooms.

"*Gute Nacht*," said Blankenhagen stiffly.

"Hah," said Tony.

I waited till I heard the other doors close. Then I waited a little longer. I had no intention of going to bed. Sleep would have been difficult, after our bizarre

discovery, and anyhow I had work to do. The dead
countess was turning out to be as distracting as the
two living females of the Drachenstein blood; I was
spending too much time on them, and not enough
on the shrine. But I carefully avoided Konstanze's
painted gaze as I found my flashlight and slipped
out the door. My journey along the dark halls was
not a pleasant experience. I went straight to the library and opened the *Schrank*.

The roll of maps was gone.

Locks and keys were no hindrance to the unknown creature that walked the halls of the *Schloss*
by night. I had the *Gräfin's* set of keys to the *Schrank*
and the library. There might be other sets of keys;
but in the midnight hush of the room I found myself remembering ghoulish legends instead of facts.
"Open, locks, to the dead man's hand . . ." How did
the poem go? The necromantic night-light, made of
the severed hand of an executed murderer whose
fingertips bore candles concocted of human fat, was
popularly supposed to open barred doors, and induce slumber on the inhabitants of a house. Not a
happy thought . . . Tony had told me that story, blast
him.

I snatched up the metal box, which was where I
had left it, and retreated precipitately. I didn't draw
a deep breath until I was back in my own room with
the door locked. (I was aware of the illogic of this,
but I locked the door anyhow.) Then I sat down at
the table with my prize.

The papers in the box appeared to be undisturbed. The one on top, bearing a blob of red seal-
ing wax, was the one I had left there. It was a deed of

sale, referring to fields in the valley once owned by an eighteenth-century count.

The papers were a miscellaneous lot, ranging in age from the nineteenth century back to the fifteenth, including household lists, the moldy diary of an early countess, and the like. I went through them methodically; one never knows what unexpected source may provide a clue. But it was not until I got near the bottom of the box that I hit pay dirt.

It was part of a letter, in a beautiful Latin hand, and something about the delicacy of the strokes suggested a woman's writing. I knew, with a queer sense of fatality, who had written it.

Rats or mice had gnawed the parchment. There was a big hole right through the center of the sheet. The damage had occurred before the letters were put in the metal box, of course. I wondered absently where they had been, until they were gathered together by a historically minded Drachenstein. The ink was faded; the language was difficult. But I understood enough.

"I have returned from the chapel," the scrap began, "where I gave thanks to Christ and his Blessed Mother and to Saint George, patron of our house, who preserved you from harm in the battle. My dear lord, I implore you to care for your health, which is so precious to me. I gave a receipt for a remedy for the stomach. . . ."

The receipt was forever lost; the ink faded out at this point. I suspected that modern pharmacy hadn't lost much, but it was strangely touching to see evidence of the countess's housewifely concern. After a fold in the parchment the writing regained legibility.

"I pray also that God will soften the obduracy of that wretch who tries to keep from you what is yours, thus sinning doubly, since he hinders your carrying out your sainted father's will, and prevents Holy Church from claiming its own. . . ."

I couldn't stand it any longer. I turned the sheet over and at the bottom found the name I knew would be there:

"Your wife, Konstanze von Drachenstein."

The letter contained nothing more except domestic details, and questions about—Tony had not exaggerated—Burckhardt's bowels. I scrabbled through the remaining documents in the box. At the very bottom I found two more fragments.

It was obvious why these scraps had not been given to the author of *The Peasants' Revolt*. Not only were they void of details about the rebellion, but they were in bad condition. The first one I had found was the best preserved. The other two were only scraps, each bearing a few disconnected sentences.

". . . send this by the hand of our loyal steward Nicolas," said one of the two. "I beg your return. The Bishop came again today, to ask when the shrine will come to him. God knows I do not oppose him, for this was the desire of your blessed father. But I feel he regards me with coldness. . . ."

I'll bet he did, I thought. A sixteenth-century chauvinist cleric, and a woman who was both foreigner and scholar. The impeccable Latin was evidence of the countess's intelligence. No doubt she had been educated by a family priest, as a few rare women were in those days. I thought I knew who had owned the volume of Trithemius in the *Schrank*.

I picked up the last scrap of parchment. It was written in a hasty scrawl that was very unlike the neatness of the earlier letters. I deduced that it was, in date, the last of the three.

". . . anxious. No news has come since you wrote you were sending it here, in the care of Nicolas the steward. It is too long, he should have arrived a week since. In God's name, my husband, come home. The Bishop . . ."

The rest was gone, presumably into the interior of an ancient rat. I sat there staring at the dusty little bit of paper that had knocked my theories into a cocked hat.

Our second possibility had been the right one. The shrine had never reached Rothenburg. The caravan must have been ambushed after all—the steward killed, the shrine stolen. I felt tired enough to die. I tossed the papers haphazardly into the box and staggered to my bed.

❀▭❀

I woke next morning to golden sunlight, the singing of birds, and a balmy breeze from the open window. I felt terrible. After a second I remembered why.

I was late to breakfast, but Tony was still there. After one look at me, he shoved a cup of coffee in my direction and remarked, "You look like hell. What's the matter, did our little expedition last night scare you that much?"

"It didn't scare me at all. But it was odd, not to find her there."

"It kept me awake for a while," Tony admitted. "Konstanze may not be haunting Irma, but she's beginning to haunt me. If it weren't for the shrine, I'd be tempted . . ."

"To pack up and leave? Go ahead. The shrine isn't here."

I told him about the letters.

"The roll of maps is gone too," I concluded glumly. "I don't suppose you took them? Okay, okay, I was just asking. I'm upset."

"Things are getting confused, aren't they? Sorry you came? Willing to admit this is too much for your poor little female brain?"

I sneered at him over the coffee cup, and he grinned.

"Then start using those brains you keep bragging about. You haven't been thinking, you've been re-acting intuitively and emotionally. The letters are only negative evidence. Our reasoning still stands. Why haven't the jewels turned up, unless the shrine is hidden somewhere?"

"Oh, I had no intention of giving up. I haven't even begun to search yet. I just wanted to give you an excuse to cop out."

"I'm staying, whether the shrine is here or not."

I stared at him in surprise. His voice was grave and his face sober.

"That girl needs help," he went on. "I don't know why the old lady hates her so, but she's slowly driv-ing her crazy. I can't walk out on a situation like that."

"Sucker," I said. "Softhearted chump. Easy mark."

"Uh-huh," Tony agreed. "I talked to Blankenhagen at breakfast. He thinks Irma needs to get away from this place. She ought to be amused and distracted. So I told him you'd take her shopping this morning. Isn't that the universal panacea for disturbed females?"

"You have your nerve promising my services. I have other things to do this morning. I'm going to—"

"Take Irma shopping. Don't put it that way; tell her you need her to show you the best stores. You're a paying guest; the old lady can't object if you ask for Irma's services."

"Huh," I said.

"I knew you would. Sucker, chump . . . We're meeting Blankenhagen at the Architect's House for lunch. One o'clock."

"And you, my knight in shining armor? Are you coming along to carry our parcels?"

"Not me. I have other things to do this morning. I'm going back to the archives. I'll meet you at one."

But Tony didn't appear at the Architect's House at one, or at two, or at two thirty, when our party rose to leave.

The excursion had done Irma good, and it hadn't hurt me either. This nonsense about shopping being good therapy doesn't apply to *me*, actually, but . . . I bought a loden cloak. I love cloaks, they are one of the few items of dress that look better on tall people than on cute little short people. My cloak wasn't gray or dark green, like most of the loden material;

it was creamy white, trimmed with bands of red and green, and fastened at the throat with big silver buttons. It was divine.

I also bought a carved wooden reproduction of a Gothic saint, and didn't even wonder how I was going to get it in my suitcase. It was three feet high. I also bought . . . Well, we could have used Tony as a carrier. But I wistfully declined peasant blouses trimmed with lace, and rose-printed dirndl dresses with white aprons, and stuff like that. I love it, but on me it looks the way a pinafore would look on Tony.

One particularly charming dress, which had a laced black velvet bodice embroidered with tiny white rosebuds and green leaves, made my mouth water. I showed it to Irma.

"Why don't you try it on? It would look gorgeous on you."

Irma and I had gotten quite matey by then—two girls together, and all that. It was nice to see the kid smile for a change. At my question the smile disappeared, and she shook her head.

"No, no, this is for tourists. The money is far too much."

Tactfully I dropped the subject and we made our way toward the restaurant. The rest of Irma's wardrobe was as hideous as her nightgowns; that day she was wearing another high-necked dark print that hung like a burlap bag from her shoulders. I had never seen her in one of the pretty peasant dresses of the region, which are common street wear in southern Germany, and which would have suited her petite beauty.

As Irma sparkled and giggled at Blankenhagen, I continued to wonder why she was so broke. The hotel was making money. The prices were outrageous, as I had cause to know. The countess had spoken of selling books; Irma said furniture and objects d'art, even the iron gates, had gone under the dealer's hammer. Were taxes and running expenses so high that two women, living frugally, could barely eke out a living? Judging from the objects I had seen—most of them in Elfrida's quarters—the stuff that had been sold was of prime quality, worth a considerable amount.

As the time wore on and no Tony came loping into the courtyard dining room, with its vine-hung balconies, worry replaced my curiosity about the Drachenstein finances. I kept telling myself it was absurd to worry; what could happen to him in broad daylight, in the law-abiding streets of Rothenburg? But it wasn't like him to forget an appointment. I was increasingly silent and distracted, and Blankenhagen started casting me significant glances, raising and lowering his eyebrows and making other signals. He didn't care whether Tony was missing or not, he just wanted to entertain Irma.

Finally, as we were leaving, I saw Tony in the doorway. My whole body sagged with relief. I hadn't realized how uptight I was. So, naturally, I was furious with him.

"Where the—" I began, as we went toward him. And then I shut up, because I had gotten a good look at his face.

"Sorry for being late," Tony mumbled. "I got . . . I got interested"—he choked oddly—"in something.

I forgot the time. No, thanks, I'll grab a sandwich someplace. I'm . . . not hungry."

"The scholarly habit," said Irma, smiling at him. "It must be very difficult for a wife."

She was pretty obtuse, that girl. There was Tony, looking like a sick dog, and she thought he was just an absentminded professor. But when she blushed and batted those long lashes at him, he revived enough to blush back. Irma was certainly responding nicely to treatment, I thought. Maybe a girl that resilient didn't need quite as much TLC as she had been getting lately.

We got back to the *Schloss* without incident, except for Tony running into trees and buildings and knocking down an occasional pedestrian. Irma decided he was faint with hunger, and after she had deposited him tenderly in a chair in the garden, she bustled off to get him sandwiches and beer.

When she had gone, Blankenhagen turned on Tony.

"Now what is bothering you? You behave like a creature from a horror film. Is it so hard for you to be normal, for that child's sake?"

"Sorry." Tony stared dismally at us. "I'm stunned. I just found out what happened to the Countess Konstanze."

"Well?" the doctor said, less angrily.

"She was burned to death as a witch. Down there in the main square of Rothenburg, on the afternoon of October twenty-third, fifteen hundred twenty-five."

"*Herr Gott.*" Blankenhagen dropped into a chair.

I decided I might as well sit down, since everyone

else was. I shared the general feeling of shock. The damned woman had become too real; it was like hearing of the ghastly death of an old acquaintance.

"The trial records are in the town archives." Tony produced the notebook without which no aspiring scholar goes anywhere. "The evidence was conclusive—if you believe in witchcraft."

"But . . . witchcraft!" Blankenhagen shouted. "This was the beginning of the Renaissance . . ."

"The persecutions were at their height just then. Five years after the countess was killed they burned thirty-five witches in a single day, in Cologne. The mania gripped every country in Europe. By the time America was settled, the worst was over, but we had our Salem trials, and that was a century after Konstanze."

Blankenhagen muttered something in a language that was neither German nor English. Tony gave him a surprised look, and translated.

" 'It is setting a high value upon our opinions to roast men alive on account of them.' Nobody ever said a truer word. But Montaigne came along too late for Konstanze, and the *Essays* were only the opening wedge of rationalism. If you think people are ever rational."

"So that is why she is not in the crypt with her husband."

"You bet your sweet life that's why. She was accused of murdering him."

"You said witchcraft. . . ."

"Same thing." Tony turned pages. "She cursed him to death. The count fell ill the day after he got back from Würzburg. At first they thought he had the plague or something. Here's part of the testimony of the old woman who had nursed the count in infancy, and who tended him during his illness.

"'On the Friday my lord was stronger and we dared hope for his life. My lady shed tears of joy. She had watched by his bed day and night, allowing no one else to take her place. . . .'"

"What's wrong with that?" I asked.

"Wait. It gets worse. She goes on: 'On the Friday at night I sat with my lord again. I was afflicted with a strange heaviness of the eyes.'"

"So she was tired," I said. "An old woman, sitting up night after night . . ."

"Sure, sure. But the judge said it was undoubtedly the countess's black magic at work. Then, says the nurse, 'When I woke I saw my lord standing by the bed. His face was strangely colored and his eyes turned in his head. He was dressed in hose and shirt only, with the embroidered belt my lady had made for him. When in my affright I spoke to him, he laughed a fearful laugh and looked not to know me. I ran to fetch my lady and she came from her room all heavy with sleep, her black hair about her face. When he saw her, my lord went mad. He felt at his belt as if for his dagger, but it was lacking, and when he so found, he threw himself at her throat and would have strangled her. I could not move him, but my cries brought the two men-at-arms who slept in the next chamber, and together we dragged my lord from his lady's throat and put him into his bed, where he fell into a swoon. The next day he was in great pain and took no nourishment save a cup of broth. In the evening the painful torments of the first days suddenly returned. He lay in agony, his body torn by spasms, until at midnight his soul left him.'"

"How ignorant they were!" exclaimed Blankenhagen.

"What do you suppose was wrong with him?" I asked.

Blankenhagen shrugged.

"It might be any number of natural illnesses."

"That wasn't all," said Tony, turning to another page of his notebook. "The countess's maid, or tiring woman, tied the noose around her neck. She was even more verbose than the other witness, so I'll synopsize. It seems that the week before the count returned she had to obey a call of nature in the middle of the night, and went to the privy—oh, yes, Doctor, they had them—near her mistress's room. She was still in the darkness of the hall when she saw the countess's door open and Konstanze standing there with a candle in her hand. Then—I'll have to give you her own words, or you'll lose the atmosphere—'There appeared from nothingness a Tall Man clothed all in black, with only darkness where his face should be. He went to my lady and caught her in his arms, and the folds of his black cloak wrapped her round like two great wings. He was seven feet tall, my Lord Bishop, and I heard the click of his hooves upon the floor of the hall. . . .'"

Tony closed his notebook.

"At that point the wench fell down in a fit, frothing at the mouth."

"No doubt." Blankenhagen shook his head disgustedly. "The superstitions of the time encouraged hysteria."

"Oh, God," I said, suddenly sick. "Remember what Irma said at the séance? *Das Feuer . . .*"

Blankenhagen surged to his feet with an angry exclamation.

"Enough of this morbidity! If that poor girl hears a word of this frightful story—"

"She already knows it," I said. "At least I would prefer to think that, rather than admit the alternative."

I was right, of course, but it wasn't the most tactful thing I could have said. Blankenhagen cursed splendidly in German, using a few expressions I had never encountered before, and went storming off through the shrubbery.

"I don't blame him," I groaned. "I'm beginning to lose my nerve too. You know something, Tony? This isn't fun anymore."

"What's wrong with you?"

"I'm just trying to sound like a heroine," I said meekly. "I know I'm the wrong size, but I figured I could try to sound sort of imbecilic and clinging and scared. . . ."

"Ho ho," said Tony, baring his teeth. "Who says you're the heroine?"

"All right, I'll let Irma be the heroine. But there are times when I think she qualifies for another role."

It was Tony's turn to swear. He wasn't as inventive as Blankenhagen, but he was louder, and finally

he stalked off, leaving me alone with my thoughts—
which were not good company.

❈▭❈

I was beginning to look forward to mealtime at the
Schloss. A girl my size needs her nourishment, but
that wasn't the only reason. In the dining room I met
friends and enemies and assorted suspects; I could
study Irma to see how far she was from a nervous
breakdown. Mealtime was when the *Gräfin* sent
forth her invitations. Oh, yes, mealtime was fun
time, all right.

Dinner that night was comparatively dull. Irma
looked pretty good, and there was no word from the
Gräfin, not even an invitation to a small intimate
exorcism. Blankenhagen was still sulking; he practically bit my head off when I made a casual remark
about the weather. Tony was just as mean. He was
seething about something, and I gathered that the
something involved George Nolan, from the way
Tony ignored him. George was in a splendid mood.
He babbled on, quite entertainingly, about Veit
Stoss and Tilman Riemenschneider and other German sculptors. I got to the point where I thought if
I heard Riemenschneider's name pronounced just
once more I would rise up and smite George over
the head with my plate. To make the gloom complete, it started to rain, which ended my plans for a
stroll through the quaint old streets of Rothenburg
after dark.

When we adjourned to the lounge, I managed to
take Tony aside.

"What ails you? Somebody hurt your feelings?"

"It's that Nolan," said Tony, adding a few qualifying adjectives. "Do you know what that rat said to me today? This afternoon I met him in the Hall, and do you know what he said?"

"No," I said. "But maybe you will tell me what he said."

"He said—" Tony choked. "He said he didn't like the way things were going around here. He said he suspected there was dirty work afoot. He said"—I really thought for a minute Tony was strangling—"he said he was willing to forget our differences and combine forces, because I needed—I needed a man of action in on this caper!"

"Well, now, that was thoughtful," I said; and then, because Tony really was mad, I changed the subject. "I talked to Irma today. Guess what she said to me. She said—"

"Cut it out," Tony growled.

"She's the Drachenstein heir," I said. "The castle and its contents belong to her. The old lady has the right to live here as long as she likes, but the place is Irma's."

"It sure is, from the kitchen to the scullery." As I hoped, Tony was sufficiently distracted by this information to forget his wrath. "Oh ho and aha. That is interesting."

"I thought so," I said. And then George turned back, with a jovial question about our plans for the evening, and I led Tony away before he lost his temper again.

To my relief, Miss Burton wasn't in the lounge that night. I couldn't have faced her. Tony went to the piano and started to pound out a weird medley of tunes, from rock and roll to Gilbert and Sullivan. He plays by ear, and he doesn't play too badly; but the piano almost defeated him. I don't know when, if ever, it had been tuned.

Seeing Schmidt reading a newspaper on the sofa, I headed for him. My attempts to pump him were singularly unsuccessful.

"I took my degree at Leipzig," he admitted finally. "But that was many years ago, my child, long before you were born. Ah, how charmingly the professor plays Beethoven. A friendly tribute to Germany."

The sounds coming from the piano would have made Beethoven spin in his crypt, but I didn't have the heart to hassle Schmidt anymore. There was a pinched gray look around his mouth, and when I asked after his health, as tactfully as possible—I can be tactful when I feel like it—he shook his head.

"I have, they tell me, a slight condition of the heart. It is not serious; but the events of these last days have not been soothing for me. If you will excuse me, I think I will seek my bed."

Tony made his excuses not long after that. I eluded George, who wanted to chat about our mutual friend Tilman R., and followed Tony. When he said good-night, at the door of his room, my suspicions were confirmed. I knew that sweet innocent smile of his. We had agreed to share information, but only up to a point.

Sure enough, a couple of hours later I heard his door open. I almost didn't hear it. After everyone else had gone to bed I turned out my light, propped my door open about half an inch, and sat down on the floor next to the crack.

The rain had stopped by that time, and the moon poured cold silver light through the open window. The slow drip of moisture from the leaves was as soothing as a lullaby. My eyelids got heavy. . . .

What with sleepiness and stiffness, it took me a couple of minutes to get limbered up and follow Tony. I had planned to bounce out at him, figuring I owed him a scare or two, but on second thought I decided I would follow the sneaky little rascal and see what he was up to.

By the time I reached the gallery above the Great Hall, Tony was halfway down the stairs. I waited in the shadows; I could see all right, thanks to the moonlight, but the Hall was an eerie place. If I hadn't known it was Tony up ahead, the shadowy figure gliding down the stairs would have scared hell out of me. At any rate, the countess wasn't walking tonight. There was a flash of reflected light from the row of armored figures against the wall, but no movement except for Tony.

Tony walked out into a patch of moonlight that lay quivering across the floor. He looked as uneasy as I felt; he kept glancing over his shoulder at the shadowy area under the stairs. I couldn't move without his seeing me, so I stayed put, but I didn't like my location. Almost half the area of the Hall was hidden from my sight by the gallery. If Tony went back under the stairs I might lose him.

One of the suits of armor got down off its pedestal and started walking toward Tony.

SEVEN

❁═❁═❁

A RATIONALIST IS AT A DISADVANTAGE WHEN EVENTS
are irrational. One of the count's contemporaries
would have howled with terror and bolted. Tony
wasted several vital seconds trying to tell himself
that what he saw wasn't really happening.

I could see the armor quite clearly in the moonlight. It was armed *cap-à-pie*, and the metal plates
clanked musically with each stiff stride. The visor
was closed. I saw the right arm go up; the fan-shaped
piece of steel at the elbow spread like a peacock's
tail. The mailed hand held a long dagger.

At long last, Tony moved. He moved backward,
and I didn't blame him a bit. Unfortunately, his retreat took him into the hidden area under the stairs,
and when the armor followed him I couldn't see either of them. I heard a clank, and a howl from Tony,
and deduced, through a haze of horror and disbelief, that the idiot had swung at the armor, which
was a damned silly thing to do. . . .

The whole episode didn't take very long. Even so,
my paralysis was inexcusable, and what I did next
was even worse. Instead of rushing down the stairs
to Tony's rescue, I ran the other way.

I could claim I was going for help; and, in fact, some vaguely sensible instinct led me to the doctor's door. I banged on the door with both fists and yelled. The door was locked, or I would have rushed in. Finally Blankenhagen answered me. I shouted something—it was incoherent, but forceful. Then I got a grip on myself. I turned and ran back.

I had a flashlight, which I had completely forgotten in all the hullaballoo. By its light I located Tony. He was flat on his back on the floor under the stairs—his eyes closed, his face white, and blood all over his shirt.

Maybe I'm not the type for a heroine, but then I behaved like the worst stereotype of the feeble female. I flopped down on the floor beside Tony, held his hand, and insisted that he wake up. I think I cried. I was sure he was dead, and it was all my fault; I had talked him into this crazy escapade, I had jeered at him and dared him.

Blankenhagen had to push me out of the way to get at Tony. I sat on the floor sniveling while the doctor, fully dressed, poked interestedly at Tony's shoulder.

"You took long enough," I said nastily. "A fine doctor you are. Do you have to put on a tie while somebody is bleeding to death?"

"Be still," said Blankenhagen coldly. "He is not dead."

As if to prove it, Tony opened his eyes.

"Well," I said, hastily wiping my face on my sleeve. "Are you with us again? That was a dumb thing to do, Tony."

I don't think Tony heard me, which is probably

just as well. His eyes focused on something behind me. I turned. There was George, wearing a dressing gown. His shanks were bare, and as hairy as a gorilla's.

"What happened?" he asked.

Poor Tony considered the question.

"You wouldn't believe it," he mumbled.

George turned to Blankenhagen.

"What's wrong with him, Doc?"

"He hit his head falling," said Blankenhagen, with a ruthless jab at a spot over Tony's left ear. "He has also been stabbed," the doctor went on reluctantly. "It is only a scratch, very shallow. Herr Lawrence, it is time you spoke. What has happened?"

I tried to imagine what Blankenhagen's face would look like if Tony said, "I was attacked by a suit of armor."

"I was attacked by a suit of armor," muttered Tony.

Blankenhagen's face took on exactly the expression I had visualized. Tony was in no mood to accept skepticism. He sat up and thrust out a dramatically stiffened arm.

"You don't believe me? Then tell me what's happened to that set of armor?"

The pedestal was undeniably empty. We were close enough to read the identifying label. It said, "Armor of Graf Burckhardt von Drachenstein, *ca.* 1525."

"That's what happened," I said. "I saw the whole thing."

Tony gaped at me. George said calmly,

"I thought maybe you were the one who slugged him."

"Well, of all the—You think I was in that armor?"

"You're too tall," George said, with the same maddening coolness. "So am I," he added.

"Hah, that is right." Blankenhagen looked relieved as the conversation took a rational turn. "I have noticed, with old suits of armor, how small these ancestors of ours were. Diet, of course, and unhealthy living . . ."

Poor Tony collapsed again. He hit the back of his head, groaned, and swore.

"While you're standing around arguing about medieval diet I'm slowly bleeding to death, and Schmidt is getting away. I know you don't care about me, but—"

"Schmidt, of course!" exclaimed the doctor. "He is not here."

"Oh, damn," said Tony.

"Come on, get up." I lent him a strong right arm. "You can't be much hurt or you wouldn't be so talkative. Schmidt is the only one of us who could fit into that armor. Let's go get him."

George was already halfway up the stairs.

Blankenhagen followed, leaving me to support Tony's tottering footsteps. When we reached Schmidt's room we found another crisis in process. The fat little man was lying on his bed and the doctor was bending over him.

"I found him in the doorway," George said. "Looks like a heart attack."

"He said he had a bad heart," I said.

"Maybe we were wrong about him," Tony said, leaning heavily on my shoulder. "A man with a weak ticker couldn't go tearing around in armor. If he heard that racket Vicky made and came running out . . ."

Schmidt's eyes opened. Involuntarily I stepped back and Tony, deprived of my support, swayed wildly. Schmidt's face was transformed by the most vivid expression of terror I have ever seen.

"*Ruhig sein, Herr Professor*," said Blankenhagen soothingly. "You are better now."

"But he . . ." Schmidt mumbled, "Herr Lawrence. He is not . . . dead."

Tony was not a reassuring sight; the cut, though shallow, had bled copiously, and his shirt front was a bloody mess. With his hair standing on end and his face white under the dust that smeared one side of it, he was enough to alarm anyone, much less a man who had just had a heart attack. George stepped in front of him.

"Of course he isn't dead, he's in great shape. You're the one we're concerned about, Schmidt; did you hear something that alarmed you?"

Schmidt's shriveled eyelids drooped.

"A scream," he said with difficulty. "Someone screamed. . . ."

His eyes followed George, who was wandering around the room.

"That will do," Blankenhagen said. "He must rest now."

The doctor followed us to the door.

"It is not serious," he said in a low voice. "A faint, shock—not his heart. He will be recovered in the morning. Lawrence, go to bed. A bit of plaster on that cut, that is all you need."

George and I escorted Tony to his room and put him to bed. The doctor's diagnosis was correct; once I had mopped off the blood I could see the cut was nothing to worry about. I slapped some Mercurochrome and a couple of Band-Aids on it.

George had settled himself in a chair with a cigarette and Tony's bottle of bourbon. When I had finished being Florence Nightingale he offered me a drink, which I was glad to accept. Tony demanded his share, pointing out that it was his bottle.

George shook his head.

"Can't risk it. Concussion and alcohol—very dangerous, old man. That was quite a crack on the head."

He helped himself to a second drink and smiled cheerfully at Tony.

"If it wasn't Schmidt in the armor, who was it?" I asked, sensing that the conversation was about to deteriorate into an exchange of pejorative comments.

"Who says it wasn't Schmidt?" Tony grumbled.

"If it was, what did he do with the armor? It wasn't under the bed or in the closet. I looked."

"Who else could have squeezed into that hardware?"

"It wasn't me, old son. I'd stick out both ends."

"Blankenhagen?" I suggested. "He's muscular, but not tall. How big was the armor, anyhow?"

"I don't remember. I'd have noticed if it had been unusually outsized, but a few inches more or less . . . How long does it take to get out of a suit of armor? I never tried."

"More to the point, how long does it take to get *into* a suit of armor? I don't suppose our mysterious comedian stands on a pedestal fully accoutered every night. . . ."

"It wouldn't surprise me if he did," Tony grumbled. "Maybe he likes dressing up in armor. Some people think they are Napoleon or Jesus Christ. Some people think they are pineapples."

"Pineapples?" I repeated. "That's a weird one. I never heard of that. Where did you—"

"Will you stick to the subject?" Tony shouted. "I gather that in your incoherent fashion you are trying to ascertain whether the comedian had time to climb into his armor after I left my room. I don't think he did. So he was down there waiting for me—or for somebody. . . ."

"You," I said hastily. "I'd rather have him waiting for you. . . . When you went creeping off to bed at ten o'clock, I knew you were planning to prowl tonight."

"He could safely assume one or the other of us would be along," Tony said, eyeing me malevolently. "We haven't missed a night so far."

"You've gotten him into the armor," remarked George, who had been following this exchange with a broad grin. "What about getting him out of it? Would Schmidt have time—"

"Forget about time," I said wearily. "I lost track completely. Nobody has a respectable alibi."

"I can't understand why you're so vague," Tony said critically. "You must have been on the gallery, if you were following me. Why didn't you pay attention? Wasn't the action exciting enough to hold your interest?"

I felt myself blushing.

"All right, so I lost my head. When you backed up into the area under the stairs I couldn't see you anymore. What did happen down there? I heard a funny clanking sound. You didn't hit that thing with your bare fist, did you?"

It was Tony's turn to redden.

"I wasn't thinking straight either," he admitted, trying to hide his scraped knuckles.

"Left hook or right jab?" George asked with interest.

"Oh, shut up," Tony growled. "The whole thing was confusing. I guess I can't blame you for not seeing what happened. I don't remember myself. I did swing at the damned thing. Felt like I broke my arm. After that everything went black."

"We'll forget the whole thing," I said magnanimously. "You'd better get some sleep, Tony. We'll all be more sensible in the morning."

"Right." George got to his feet. "Tony, old boy, I'll be sitting up the rest of the night, with my door open. Don't worry about a thing. I won't let anyone get to you."

I pushed George bodily out the door.

❀═❀

I didn't sleep well that night. I guess Tony didn't either; he was up early. I had been sort of hanging around. I figured he might need some help, and that he would be as reluctant to ask for it as I was to offer it directly. As soon as I heard his door open I stepped casually into the hall. He had gotten into his clothes without assistance, but he looked as if he had not enjoyed the process; he held his left arm at an awkward angle, and his face was all bony points and gray hollows.

He gave me a look of solid dislike, and I dropped the arm I was about to offer him.

"Where's Nolan?" he asked brusquely.

"In his room, I guess. Why?"

"I want to talk to him."

"Can I come?" I asked meekly.

"Sure, why not? If I'm going to eat crow, I might as well have an audience."

Intrigued, I trailed along after him. George answered the door right away; alert and bright-eyed, stylishly dressed in brown slacks and a fresh white sport shirt, he was a sight for sore eyes. He hauled Tony over the threshold and deposited him in a chair.

"God, you look terrible," he remarked. "Didn't I tell you not to worry? I sat up most of the night, didn't see a thing. Never need more than three, four hours sleep. . . . What's on your mind, Tony?"

"You made me an offer yesterday. I'm ready to take you up on it."

"Now I wonder," said George thoughtfully, "why you changed your mind."

"Good God," Tony said querulously. "After last night, how can you wonder? It may be you or Vicky who gets the ax next time. Worst of all, it might be me again. We foreigners ought to form a protective alliance. I don't intend to take you by the hand and lead you to the shrine. But I'm willing to share some of my brilliant deductions in exchange for some help."

"Great." George stood there beaming, all tanned and white-toothed. "You do the thinking, I do the dirty work. Is that it?"

"Approximately."

"Then let's get at it, whatever it is."

"After breakfast." Tony rose with a theatrical groan. He avoided my eye, and I wondered what low-down scheme he had in mind now.

During breakfast Tony was honored by a personal call of condolence from the *Gräfin*. She pressed him back in his chair when he started to rise, and he sat back with a thud. Quite by accident, of course, she had her hand on his injured shoulder.

"I am so sorry for your terrible experience," she said, smiling like a wolf. "I hope it has not made you decide to leave us."

"On the contrary. I wouldn't leave a bunch of helpless women alone in this place. Unless, *Gräfin*, you intend to call the police?"

"Do you honestly think, Professor, that the police can give the kind of help we need?"

She walked away, giving him no time to retort.

"Get her," I said. "Now she's a believer."

"Oh, she doesn't believe in the supernatural, Tony said disgustedly. "Didn't you watch her at the séance? She's using the ghost theory for her own ends, and God knows what they are."

"I know I'm not supposed to be thinking," George said. "But I'll throw in this little tidbit as my contribution to general goodwill. Irma is the heiress. This place and everything in it belongs to her."

The only new thing about that tidbit was that George was aware of it. But until then I hadn't considered the corollary.

"What happens if Irma dies?" I asked.

"I didn't think it would be smart to ask that. But I guess the old lady would inherit everything. Which isn't much—just this old pile of stones and a lot of work. Every object of value has already been sold. . . ."

He stopped. None of us finished the sentence aloud. We didn't have to.

Except the shrine.

"The old lady couldn't possibly know," Tony began.

"Wanna bet?" I said.

"No. Well, Nolan, let's get going—if you're still game. What I'm proposing to do is not only socially unacceptable, it is probably against several laws I can't call precisely to mind at the moment."

"I've broken a number of laws in my time," said George—with perfect truth, I felt sure.

It was Sunday. The workmen who had been remodeling the south wing were gone for the day. Tony loaded George down with tools and led the way to the chapel. When we reached the stairs to the crypt, George stopped.

"What are we going to do down there?" he asked suspiciously.

"Just a spot of tomb desecration," Tony answered.

George dropped a crowbar. He gave Tony a funny look, but bent to retrieve the tool without comment.

When we reached the tomb of Count Harald,

Tony knelt down and shone his flashlight along the cracks between the tombstone, with its carved effigy, and the stone floor.

"When I was here before I noticed something different about this tomb. Look. The stones on the other tombs are cemented into place." He opened a pocket knife and illustrated on the next tomb, that of Count Burckhardt. The knife blade ran along the crack without penetrating, leaving a trail of fine white powder. "But Harald's stone . . ." The blade of the knife disappeared, sinking deep into the black line between the tombstone and the next slab.

"Looks as if someone has had it up, once upon a time," George agreed. His eyes glowed like a cat's in the dim light. "I don't envy them the job. That stone weighs hundreds of pounds."

"That's why I enlisted you," Tony said affably. "With my bad arm I can't lift a pillow."

George glowered at him, and then burst out laughing.

"All right, old boy. I asked for it."

Tony did enjoy the next hour. Reclining comfortably, with his back up against the stone feet of Count Burckhardt, he watched George sweat. I didn't help much. George had the necessary muscle, and he knew what he was doing—first the crowbar, then a series of wedges to prop the slowly rising stone. Finally he had it tilted back like the lid of a box, with about three feet between its lifted edge and the floor.

George sat down and lit a cigarette.

"I don't think we should risk raising it any more,"

he wheezed. "There's nothing to brace it on the other side if the angle gets too steep. Now what?"

"Now I take over."

Tony crawled to the edge of the hole. I was already peering in. I couldn't see anything, though; it was too dark down there.

Besides shoving in wedges, at George's orders, I had spent the time kicking myself. I should have noticed that crack. Here we were looking for a hiding place, and this was one of the right size. This could be it. I was so excited I forgot to breathe. I even forgot George Nolan, big and brawny and thoroughly unscrupulous, standing over me.

Tony turned his flashlight down into the crypt. But no flash of refracted light from huge jewels dazzled our eyes. No gilded wings glimmered and shone. There seemed to be nothing in the vault but a wooden coffin bound with strips of rusted metal. It rested on the bottom of a hole that was faced and floored with stone. The top of the coffin was about two feet below floor level. It was pushed to one end of the vault, so that there was an empty space at the bottom. Tony turned his light in that direction.

A moment later I was backing hastily away on hands and knees like a puppy that has encountered a porcupine. George stared at me and bent down to look for himself.

"Nolan, go get Blankenhagen," said Tony, in a funny croak.

George stepped back.

"For that? Believe me, old man, *he* doesn't need—"

"He doesn't, but I do." Tony lay down on the floor and closed his eyes.

George peered into the hole again, shrugged, and went to the stairs. When he was out of sight Tony scrambled to his feet.

"Better you than me," I muttered, as he slid into the pit and bent down, out of sight, below the lifted slab. For a while I could see only agitated but controlled movement as he worked. Then he poked his head out. He was in his shirt sleeves.

"Don't look if you'd rather not," he said, eyeing me.

"Don't be insulting," I said, breathing slowly through my nose. "It was just the air down there that got me—made me dizzy for a minute."

Tony lifted a dark bundle out of the hole and deposited it gently on the chapel floor. It was his jacket, rolled around something that bulged in peculiar places. Tony climbed out beside the bundle and started to open it. I spoke without premeditation.

"It isn't—it isn't the old count, is it?"

"No, he's still resting peacefully in his coffin. At least I hope he is. This is a little something extra."

He folded his jacket back. I braced myself, but there was no need. Disconnected and jumbled, the bones suggested an anthropological exhibit rather than a human being who had died in agony. But I knew I would not easily forget my first sight of the huddled shape, with its fleshless face turned up as if gasping for the air that had been denied it.

The skull was yellow but intact. A wisp of rusty hair hung over one side. There were other objects in the pile besides bones: bits of tarnished metal, a blackened silver ornament, some scraps of rotting cloth. And under a handful of ribs . . .

Then I heard footsteps echoing on the floor above and saw George appear at the top of the stairs, a featureless silhouette against the light. Blankenhagen followed him down.

"So you got it out," George said.

"I felt better after you left," Tony said blandly. "*Grüss Gott*, Doctor. Maybe you can tell us what to do with this."

Blankenhagen knelt and began to finger the exhibits.

"He has been dead too long to profit from my services," he said drily.

"He?" Tony's nose quivered with curiosity.

"Definitely male. The occipital ridges . . ." Blankenhagen's index finger pointed. "Also, the configuration of the pelvis is unmistakable." He lost himself in professional meditation for a time. "Yes. A male of mature years, but probably under forty. The third molars are present, but not badly worn; the ilium and ischium—"

"I'll take your word for it," Tony interrupted. "No way of telling how he died?"

"That would depend on where you found this."

Blankenhagen lifted a dagger and balanced it on his palm. The blade was dark and rusted, the hilt elaborately carved.

"It was lying among the ribs."

"Ah, hmmm." Blankenhagen sorted ribs. Then he held one up. "Yes, it is possible to see the mark of the blade. It passed along the inner surface. It would then presumably have pierced the heart."

He dropped the brittle ivory bone back onto the jacket and wiped his hands on his knees.

"A murder?" George said interestedly. "Who's the victim? Silly question, I guess, after all this time."

"Oh, no," said Tony, in a lazy drawl I knew very well. "No doubt about his identity. This was the steward of Count Burckhardt. His name was Nicolas Duvenvoorde."

He picked up the tarnished ornament.

"This was a clasp or badge worn on the doublet. You can see the Drachenstein arms, and, if you strain your eyes, the initials N. D. Maybe it was a present from the count, for meritorious service. The scraps of clothing are right for the period, and suitable for a man of respectable but non-noble rank. There's a pair of leather boots down there, too. They are pretty moldy, so I didn't bring them up, but here are the spurs that went with them. Traveling costume, that's what he was wearing." He produced some bits of leather, which did indeed have a mildewed look. "This was a pouch, which was worn at the belt. These coins were probably inside it. Here's a thirty-kreuzer bit from Würzburg, dated fifteen hundred thirteen, and an imperial florin with a head of Charles the Fifth and a date of fifteen hundred twenty-three. And the last bit of evidence, if we need one, is the dagger itself. On the hilt is the dragon and stone, the Drachenstein crest. The workmanship is too fancy for a servant's weapon. This curlicue under the crest seems to be Burckhardt's personal mark. You can see the same design on his tomb."

He turned the flashlight beam to the right, where it illumined the shield at the shoulder of the reclining knight on the next stone.

"In fact," Tony concluded, "we can not only identify the victim, but we can hazard a good guess as to the murderer."

There was a brief, impressed silence, during which Tony vainly tried to look modest.

"By God," George exclaimed, "I have to hand it to you, Tony. That's a damned good piece of detective work."

"Seconded," I said briefly.

Tony smirked.

"Oh, well, anyone could have done it. Anyone who knew his history and had a logical mind, trained in deductive techniques—"

I interrupted. I hope I am a good sport, but I do not care for blatant egotism.

"Now that we've got him, what are we going to do with him?"

"We must notify the *Gräfin*," Blankenhagen said stiffly. Now that the first excitement was over and his curiosity had been satisfied, he had relapsed into his normal state of cold disapproval. "I do not know what her wishes will be; if it were I, I should call on the good father from Rothenburg."

"A brief ceremony of exorcism might not hurt," Tony said obscurely. He rose to his feet. "Ow. I'm as stiff as he is. I'll go see the *Gräfin*. After all, the poor devil was a faithful family retainer. They ought to be able to spare him a few feet down here in the vault."

"I will remain here," Blankenhagen said. "When you return with the *Gräfin*, bring a sheet or blanket."

"I'll stay," George offered. "Why don't you interview the old lady, Doctor? Tony ought to be in bed—he's probably strained that arm. And frankly, I'd rather face a whole cemetery of dead bodies than Elfrida."

"I am not on good terms with the *Gräfin*," Blankenhagen said. "Perhaps you can think of an acceptable excuse for your breach of hospitality and good taste here; I certainly cannot, and I see no reason why I should face her indignation when she hears what you have done. But I agree Lawrence should go to bed. I will look at his injury later."

We left him standing over the bones with bowed head. He could have been praying, but I didn't think so.

"It wasn't there," I said to Tony, who was leaning pathetically on my arm.

"It isn't there now, anyhow."

"That was a bright idea, though," I said generously. "Where do we look next?"

Tony shook his head.

"I've used up my hunches. Without a plan of the *Schloss*, I'm lost. I wish we could find those missing maps."

His voice rose a little on the last sentence, and George turned around.

"Maps? Blankenhagen has some."

"What kind of maps?"

"Old ones, on parchment, in a big roll. He was

looking at them when I knocked on his door. He told me to wait outside, and when he came out the maps were gone."

"Blankenhagen." Tony smacked himself on the forehead. "He must be involved in this thing somehow. . . . Nolan, I've got to have those maps. Did he lock his door?"

"Yes, he did. But I think your key will open it. The locks in this place are simple, cheap deals."

"Okay. Then you go—"

"No," I said. "Tony is going to beddy-by. George, you get the *Gräfin* and take her straight down to the crypt. Make sure she and Blankenhagen stay there for a while. I'll get the maps."

"I'll get the maps if you interview the *Gräfin*," George offered.

"What are you so nervous about? I thought you were accustomed to breaking laws with devil-may-care insouciance. I admit what we did was outrageous—"

"Unbelievable," George agreed heartily. "Why did we do it?"

We both looked at Tony.

"I was mad," said Tony simply. "Not crazy mad—angry. I hate being stabbed."

"I'll tell the old lady that," said George. "I am sure she'll understand. Damn it, I don't like this partnership. I get all the dirty jobs."

"Then we'll dissolve the partnership," Tony said. He looked a little ashamed as George gave him a reproachful look, but he continued, "I didn't say we were going to share all our clues. You worked like a Trojan today, and I appreciate it; but without me you wouldn't have found Nicolas. So far, I think we're quits."

"Big deal. I didn't want Nicolas anyhow. What am I supposed to do with him?"

He left, grumbling, and I went on my errand. George was right about the keys. Tony's key fit Blankenhagen's door. All the keys probably fit all the doors, which was not a comforting thought.

Blankenhagen hadn't bothered to hide the maps very well. They were on top of his wardrobe, quite visible to anyone with my inches. I grabbed them and left.

Tony sat up when I came in.

"Got them? Good work."

"Lie down." I slid the roll of parchment under his bed. "Blankenhagen is on his way up. I just got out in time."

There was a knock at the door. Tony flopped back onto his pillow.

"All settled," George announced briskly. He pushed Blankenhagen into the room and followed him, rubbing his hands together with the air of a man who has just finished a painful session at the dentist's. "The *Gräfin* was quite reasonable. The minister will be up later, and they'll probably have some kind of service, today or tomorrow. She won't have the lad in the family vault, though. Says, with all due respect for Tony's deductions, that she can't accept the identification as certain, and anyhow, the crypt is reserved for Drachensteins. They'll bury him in the town cemetery. Lord knows what they'll put on the tombstone."

"Good," said Tony, closing his eyes as Blankenhagen

started poking at his shoulder. "What excuse did you give her for our tomb robbing?"

"Funny thing," said George thoughtfully. "She didn't ask."

"You have done yourself no injury," Blankenhagen said, tucking in an edge of bandage. "But remain quiet and do not raise any more tombstones. Such childishness."

He stalked to the door and went out. George followed, with a rather wistful glance at me.

"Maybe we ought to keep him in the club," I said.

"Generosity does not become you. Somebody is behind all these kookie manifestations here, and until I find out who it is—"

"You don't seriously suspect George, do you? He hasn't had time to arrange all the things that have happened."

"I know. I'd like to suspect him, but he doesn't fit. Herr Schmidt is a better bet. How is he, by the way?"

"Okay, I guess. He's up and around, anyhow. He wouldn't even go to the hospital for a checkup, as Blankenhagen suggested."

"Very interesting. Maybe he faked his faint. He told you his degree is from Leipzig? Convenient that it's in the East Zone, where official inquiries aren't easy for us amateurs to make. And of all the suspicious names—it's as bad as Smith."

"I think the countess is our man—pardon me, woman."

"She's almost too perfect," Tony objected. "Probably she has a heart of gold under that frosty exterior. I can't see her galloping around in a suit of armor, either."

"Don't be fooled by that air of languid dignity. She's as hard as nails. She detests Irma; she's a natural bully, and you must admit Irma asks to be trampled on. Also, the *Gräfin* is the only one to profit if, for instance, Irma fell down the stairs while she was sleepwalking."

"She could encourage, if not actually induce, the sleepwalking," Tony agreed. "She's got that girl mesmerized. But the profit motive doesn't amount to much if this"—he waved a hand around the poorly equipped room—"is all Irma's inheritance."

"Unless she knows about the shrine."

"Right." We stared at one another in silence. Finally Tony said,

"We don't want to face it, do we? But it would be naïve of us to assume that we're the only ones who could have spotted the original clues. Anyone who read that book and who knew Riemenschneider's life story could have reached the same conclusions we did. And don't forget the *Gräfin* may have other information. She could have removed significant family papers from that collection before we saw it."

"But she hasn't found the shrine yet. Or has she?"

"No. She wouldn't tolerate our messing around if she had. Hasn't it struck you how cooperative the old witch has been? Keys to the crypt, keys to the library, no embarrassing questions about our nocturnal wanderings or even about our outlandish performance this morning. Her restraint is completely out of character, unless—"

"Unless she is hoping we can find the shrine for her. She may know that it exists; but if she doesn't know where it is hidden, she might think that we, with our training, stand a better chance of finding it than she would. Has it occurred to you—"

"That we had better guard our backs if we do locate the shrine? Yes, dear, it occurred to me with a vengeance when that homicidal armor came at me."

"I don't think you were in any danger from the armor," I said callously. "You won't be in danger until you locate the prize. That was just fun and games, to spur you on. You always think better when you get mad."

"Fun and games," Tony muttered. "Somebody has a sick sense of humor."

"Definitely," I agreed, thinking of Irma and the séance.

"Enough of this," Tony said. "We haven't enough evidence to make sensible deductions about the living villain. Let's get back to the dead villain. You do see, I trust, what our discovery this morning has to do with the problem of the shrine?"

"I haven't had time to think about it. But—my Lord, yes. In that letter of Konstanze's she said the shrine, and the steward, had not arrived. Now we know he did arrive. And stayed here."

"Indeed he did. Now," said Tony patronizingly, "go on. What was old Nicolas doing down there with the count's dagger between his ribs?"

"Hmm. How about this? The steward was not a faithful hound after all. He stole the shrine for him-

self, sneaked into the castle—which he knew
well—at the dead of night. He was about to hide the
shrine in the old count's tomb when Burckhardt
wandered in—to pray, or pay his respects, or something. Seized by rage at the sight of his double-dealing
servant, and the shrine—which he assumed had been
lost on the way from Rothenburg—Burckhardt
stabbed Nicolas, tumbled him into the ready-made
grave, and hid the shrine himself. Then he got sick—
wait, wait! Remember the testimony of the nurse?
The murder must have happened that very night.
Burckhardt was already ill, ill and delirious. That's
why he never told anyone where he put the shrine.
It's still hidden!"

"Not bad."

"Not bad! What else could have happened?"

"You have fallen in love with your own theory,"
said Tony severely. "A dangerous fault in a scholar. I
can think of at least one other possibility. The count
himself came home with the caravan and the shrine.
He and the faithful steward hid it, at dead of night,
as you so quaintly put it, in the old count's tomb.
Konstanze didn't know a thing about this. Later the
count got to worrying about the safety of the hiding
place, and went down, with the steward, to move the
shrine. They hid it somewhere else, and then the count
stabbed the steward, etcetera, etcetera."

"I don't mind making the count the villain," I
said. "I never liked him anyway. But you have a
slight credibility gap, bud. Why should Burckhardt
hide his own property and kill his faithful retainer?"

"Remember what was supposed to happen to the

shrine? Count Harald's will left it to the church. The countess is definite about that in her letters, and she agrees that it should be done. Suppose Burckhardt didn't agree. The jewels were worth a pile, you know. Maybe he needed money. He wouldn't let anyone, especially his pious wife, know he wanted the shrine for himself. When the faithful steward realized what Burckhardt had in mind, he threatened to expose him, and Burckhardt murdered him. That way Konstanze never would know where the shrine was hidden, and Burckhardt wouldn't be about to tell her."

"Plausible," I admitted. "But all the theories are plausible. You're the one who used to lecture me about the difference between possibility and proof; judging by some of the articles I read in the journals, a lot of historians don't know the difference. We have no proof, Tony. We can't even be sure that the shrine was ever here, in the castle, much less in that vault."

"Oh, yes, we can." Tony was so proud of himself he swelled up like a toad. Reaching into his pocket, he carefully withdrew a small object.

I looked at it as he held it up to the light, and my stomach got a queer queasy feeling. The object was a wing, carved of wood and lightly gilded. In form it was the sort of thing that might have been broken off a phoenix, or a golden bird in flight; but there was a quality about it that eliminated these possibilities and defined it as what it was—

"An angel's wing," I whispered.

EIGHT
❀▆❀▆❀

I HELD THE PIECE OF WOOD IN BOTH CUPPED HANDS.
I didn't speak because, to tell the truth, I was afraid
my voice wouldn't be steady. I mean, that wing really
got to me, and not just because it confirmed an almost abandoned hope. For the first time I visualized
the thing we were after, not as a prize or a treasure,
but as a work of art. I was seeing golden angels.

When I had suppressed this surprising burst of
sentiment, I said with affected coolness,

"Game and set to you, Tony. You're 'way ahead.
But you haven't won the match yet." Reluctantly I
put the carved wood down on the table. My hand
felt oddly empty. "Do you realize this is the first
solid piece of evidence we've found?"

"We've been distracted by side issues. I still am,"
Tony admitted. "I can't get that woman out of my
mind. I keep seeing her—a girl with Irma's face—
standing in the flames and screaming."

"Stop it."

"Sorry. But—"

"Of course she haunts us," I snapped. "Who
wouldn't be disturbed by a gruesome story like hers?
If it weren't for her resemblance to Irma, though . . ."

I let the words trail off, and Tony looked curiously at me.

"What?"

"It's gone. I almost had an idea there, for a minute. . . . Let's stick to the important question. We know now that the shrine did reach Rothenburg. It has to be here somewhere. Let's have a look at those maps."

We spread them out on the bed. They had been rolled for so many years it was hard to hold them open; they had a tendency to snap back on our hands like teeth. I leaned on two of the corners while Tony flattened the other side.

"Okay," he said, after studying them for a moment. "This top plan concerns the remodeling of the east wing in seventeen hundred fifty-two. We needn't worry about that. If there had been anything there, the workmen would have found it."

I put the parchment down on the floor. The sheet underneath was yellower and the writing more faded.

"Here we have a general layout done in—early seventeenth century, wouldn't you say? There's no date. It's not detailed enough to be of any use. Same for this . . ."

I added two more rolls to the one on the floor.

"Now here," said Tony, looking with satisfaction at the next maps, "we get to red meat. These are plans of the *Schloss* as it was in the early fifteen-thirties. I'll bet they were done by Burckhardt's successor when he took over the title."

"What a mess," I said.

"The new count was no draftsman," Tony agreed. "And the parchment needs cleaning. But you can make out most of it. Ignore the east wing, which was later demolished. Here's the wing we are presently occupying—this line of rooms. The master bedchamber . . . is the one now inhabited by Schmidt."

"I suspected as much."

"Oh, you know everything, don't you?"

"I said 'suspected.' How come Schmidt rated that particular room? Tony, maybe he's already found the shrine!"

"Think it through," Tony said, with maddening superiority. "Schmidt is still here, poking and prying and acting suspicious. If he had found the shrine he wouldn't stick around. Do we then conclude that the shrine is not, after all, concealed somewhere in the chamber that belonged to Burckhardt?"

"We might if we were sure of two things."

"One, that Schmidt is a good hunter; two, that Schmidt *is* a hunter, not a weird but innocent bystander. All right, we don't conclude anything. The room next to his is mine now. According to the plan, it was once two smaller chambers occupied by servants of the noble pair. The next room— yours— belonged to the countess."

"How modern," I said, with a flippancy I did not feel. I wasn't sure I wanted to have Konstanze that close to me.

"It was unusual for them to have had separate bedchambers." Tony squinted at the dirty parchment. "Well, the legend is clear. Maybe she used it as boudoir or dressing room. Maybe she liked to sleep with the window open and Burckhardt liked it closed. Maybe he snored. Maybe—"

"Surely her room would be right next to his. If not . . ."

Tony grinned.

"They didn't have our hang-ups about sex. I can see the count stamping down the corridor between rows of genuflecting servants on his way to spend the night with the countess. . . . But one of the noble gentlemen was more sensitive—or maybe he was susceptible to drafts. See this line?"

"Between the count and countess's rooms?"

"Through the wall. I think it's a passageway. Maybe blocked up now."

"That's all we lacked—a secret passage."

"Nothing unusual about it. This isn't Cleveland, Ohio; we're in medieval Europe here. The place is probably riddled with secret passages. When you have walls ten feet thick, you can do all sorts of interesting things. I wish this parchment weren't so filthy; I can't make out all the fine lines. But this looks like another passage, from the library to one of the guest chambers. The count probably put his questionable acquaintances in that room, so he could eavesdrop on their conversations."

"What's this?" I pointed to a drawing of something that looked like a thick chimney.

"It would appear to be the count's concept of an elevation drawing of the tower. Note that there seems to be a hidden stairway in the outer wall."

"In the tower, eh? Then Irma could have gotten out of her room even with the door locked."

"Maybe," Tony said shortly. He lifted the last parchment and stared at the bedspread. "That seems to be all."

"Seems to me it's enough."

"No, there's something missing. We have two sheets covering the first and second floors of the *Schloss*. Where's the plan of the cellars?"

"Right on. There must be a subterranean level, for storage and cooking. Maybe a dungeon or two. The count had to deal with crimes on his own premises; there weren't any policemen. And I'd expect a well. If the defenders had to retreat within the castle walls, they were gone geese without a water supply—"

Someone banged on the door, interrupting my discourse. I kicked the whole collection of maps hastily under the bed.

"Come in," Tony said.

It was George.

"The *Gräfin* asked me to tell you that the services are this afternoon."

"How come so fast?" asked Tony.

"How should I know? Maybe she doesn't want him lying around."

"And we're expected to attend the obsequies?" I asked.

George smiled.

"I wouldn't miss it for the world."

❧ ⟡ ❧

I had assumed the service would be held at the Jakobskirche, where Riemenschneider's altar is the chief attraction, but I was mistaken. I should have known better. There is no more space for the dead inside the town walls. So, following directions, Tony and I crossed the town and went out through the Roedertor to the new cemetery. It really is new; I couldn't find any graves earlier than 1720.

For reasons known only to himself, Tony insisted on arriving early, so we wandered around the cemetery for a while. It is a pretty place—if you like cemeteries—well tended, and pretty well filled. A high stone wall encloses it; like the city of the living, it is bright with flowers. We saw several *Hausfrauen*, with green plastic watering cans, tending the begonias and the miniature pink rose trees which had been planted on the graves.

The others began to arrive. Miss Burton accompanied the *Gräfin*. She would come, I thought; dead bodies are just her thing. Blankenhagen was also present, watching Irma with more than professional interest. George watched everybody.

We filed solemnly into the little church and took seats—all of us except Tony. He marched up the aisle and accosted the pastor, a slight, dreamy-looking little bald man. I couldn't hear what they said, but I saw some object pass from Tony's pocket to that of the pastor. He disappeared, and Tony joined me. He was looking smug, but I had no time to question him before the coffin was carried in and the service began. It was short and ambiguous, in keeping with the state of the remains. When it was over, we straggled out into the cemetery behind the two young Rothenburgers who carried the wooden coffin. In a short time only a mound of fresh earth remained to show where the bones had been laid. It looked raw and stark in contrast to the ivy and flower-covered plots around it. No one would plant roses on Nicolas' grave.

The *Gräfin* turned away. Miss Burton joined her, and they went off together. Irma suggested a visit to a café, and Blankenhagen was so pleased at her good spirits he neglected to intimate that our presence was not wanted. So we went to The Golden Star, and drank beer, and made conversation. Irma was looking gorgeous. She giggled and flirted, turning from Blankenhagen to Tony with impartial goodwill. I noticed she didn't bat her eyelashes at George.

As we were leaving the café I grabbed Tony and dragged him to the rear. He struggled some.

"I want to talk to you," I said. "If you can tear yourself away from Cinderella for a minute."

"She gets prettier all the time," said Tony, watching the threesome which was now some distance ahead.

I wasn't jealous. I merely felt he ought to face facts.

"Yes, she does, and I wonder why? How come she's so relaxed and pleased with life these days?"

"Maybe she's in love," said Tony fatuously.

"And maybe she's pleased because her plans are working."

It took the romantic jerk several seconds to see what I meant.

"Irma?" he exclaimed, so loudly that I slapped my hand over his mouth. He pulled it off and continued, just as indignantly, but in a lower voice.

"You're crazy jealous. How could she manipulate all our ghosts?"

"I will pass over your gratuitous and uncouth insult," I said, "and point out a few solid facts. The profit motive applies just as well to Irma as it does to her aunt. So far as opportunity goes, she has the best of anyone. You saw the hidden stairs on the plans; she could have gotten out of her room and left the door locked. As for the armor, it would take a short man to wear it—*or a woman*. But the really damning fact is the séance. Unless you believe in possession—which I do not—how do you explain her reference to the fire? She's lived here all her life, she could have found out about Konstanze's death the same way you did."

"I don't buy the motive," Tony said, but he was disturbed. "This is a damned roundabout way to get at a hidden treasure. She is the only one who could search openly for the shrine. Why all the ghosties and ghoulies? It's a crazy way to act."

"Maybe she is crazy. Maybe she has motives we don't understand because we don't know enough about the situation."

"So what do we do now?"

"What we do is, you tell me about that mysterious envelope you slipped the minister."

"Nothing to tell," Tony said.

"Let us apply logic," I said sarcastically. "You want someone to believe you kept something out of the steward's belongings because there was important information in it—papers, maybe, in the pouch—though how you expect anyone to believe papers would survive . . . You think someone will try to dig up the . . . When, tonight?"

"That is the most ridiculous series of non sequiturs I've ever heard!"

"What time do we meet?"

It was about midnight when we took up our vigil in the cemetery. We had some difficulty finding a place that wasn't already occupied. It was behind a low wall, shadowed by two funereal trees. We could have been closer to the steward's grave, but I refused to move. I have few superstitions, but I try to avoid lying on graves when I possibly can.

After we were settled I glanced uneasily at the sky. The moon was almost full, but the sky to the west was overcast, and from time to time clouds obscured the moon and left the graveyard quite dark. The night was warm, but damp lingered in the earth under the tree, and the blanket I had brought was useful.

Tony keeps insisting, with maddening monotony, that what happened was not his fault. Now I don't hold him accountable for meteorological phenomena. The dark cloud that hid the moon around 2 A.M. was more or less unexpected and undeniably uncontrollable. But the fact remains that if he had been paying attention . . . I'm perfectly willing to admit I wasn't paying attention either. All I want him to do is shoulder half the blame.

It was not until we heard the creak of hinges that we realized what was going on. Even then things might have worked out if Tony had kept his head. Instead of moving slowly and quietly, he leaped to his feet, planting a knee in my stomach in the process. I grunted.

The scuffle was warning enough for the grave robber. I had only a glimpse of a dark form leaving the grounds at impressive speed. Tony started in pursuit and lost valuable time by falling into the hole that had been excavated. When he realized where he was, he got out with considerable alacrity. The moon was still hidden, and he cursed it fluently, without noticeable results.

I had caught up with him by that time, having recovered my breath while he was floundering around in the open grave.

"Hurry," I yelled. "Street outside is lighted . . . we can see . . ."

We couldn't see our quarry, but we could hear him. Cemeteries are notoriously quiet places, especially in the middle of the night. From the sounds, the man seemed to be heading for the gate on Ansbacher Strasse.

As we had already ascertained, the gate was locked. I didn't expect it to detain our agile adversary for long, however. He was over the gate before we reached the spot. Our progress had been frustratingly slow; even if I had had no qualms about stepping on graves, the stones were close together and the paths were winding. We got over the gate, in our turn, leaving a piece of my slacks on the spikes.

The street outside curves and is lined with trees. There was no one in sight. Assuming that the grave robber would head for the inner city, and the *Schloss*, we took that direction. As we neared the open area in front of the city gate, we were finally rewarded by a glimpse of the man we were after. One glimpse was enough for Tony, who staggered and stopped, for a vital couple of seconds, before he got a grip on his nerves and began running again.

I couldn't blame him for hesitating. The figure was that of a tall Black Man, enveloped in a cloak that swooped out around his body like giant dark wings. The head appeared to be a featureless lump.

The monstrosity disappeared under the stone arch of the Roedertor. I admit, without shame, that I felt a healthy reluctance as we followed, running into darkness and into the enclosing walls that had been designed to hold back entire armies.

If you have never seen a medieval city gate you may picture it as a pair of wooden doors, plus a portcullis or two. Not so. This particular gate, which is more properly called a bastion, consists of a series of massive walls and narrow passages, designed so that a defending force could clobber the attackers at several points. Once past the first gate, an invader found himself in a circular area hemmed in by high stone walls with enclosed galleries, from which various missiles could be propelled onto his head. The only way out of this area was over a moat, whose drawbridge could of course be raised. Beyond the drawbridge a high tower defended the inner part of the bastion.

The gates are gone nowadays, and the drawbridge has been replaced by solid pavement. All the same, my shoulders hunched apprehensively as we entered the circular court. Pounding along the brick-paved street that crosses the moat and goes through the narrow tunnel under the tower, I felt a wave of sympathy for the soldier who had had to attack the place—not for the arrogant knight, safely encased in steel, but for the conscripted peasant in his leather jerkin, clutching his pike in a sweaty hand and hoping to God he'd never have to use it. I half expected an arrow to whistle over my head and rattle on the pavement. It was the sort of humorous gesture our adversary seemed to enjoy.

We got through the tunnel without incident, however, and came to a baffled halt in the street beyond the bastion. The tall houses of the old city loomed dark and silent on either side. We hadn't made enough noise to awaken the inhabitants, since we were both wearing rubber-soled sneakers. The loudest sound was Tony's heavy breathing.

I was pretty sure we had lost our man. There were a dozen hiding places in that crowded, narrow way, half a dozen alleyways and side streets he might have taken. Yet I still felt vulnerable and exposed, as if someone were watching me.

I glanced up over my shoulder. The town walls were shadowy bulwarks, cutting off the sky. A single lonely streetlight did little to lighten their darkness.

Up above, on the balustraded walkway, something moved. It looked like a black sleeve, flapping.

I clutched at Tony, who was staring stupidly down the Schmeidgasse. He let out a yelp.

"For God's sake, don't do that!"

"He's up there," I gasped. "On the wall. Tony—I think he waved at me."

"You would think that," Tony said bitterly. He pulled away from me and ran toward the flight of stone stairs that led up to the ramparts.

There may be worse places in which to pursue a crazy grave robber, but offhand I can't think of many. The stairs are composed of the same rough brownish stone that constitutes the walls. They are steep, narrow, and very uneven. The walkway is stone-floored too; it is actually the top of the rampart, with a thin outer wall on one side. On the other side, only a waist-high wooden railing stands between the wall-walker and the paved street twenty feet below. There are lights at infrequent intervals; they are suspended from the houses that face the wall across a wide alley, and they do not illumine the stone underfoot, which is rough and full of unexpected dips and bumps. Tony took the stairs three at a time and went roaring down the narrow walkway like a mad bull.

I went after him, though I would have preferred not to do so. The pursuit was pointless now, and potentially dangerous. Our quarry could easily elude us; the fact that he had not already done so in the Schmeidgasse made me highly suspicious of his present route. But there is no arguing with Tony when he gets in one of his rages; I couldn't even get close enough to talk to him, much less reason with him. So I followed. I had left him in the lurch once before, and I didn't enjoy the memory of that moment of cowardice.

It's a wonder we both didn't break our necks. I kept stumbling; once I caught my foot in a concavity and ricocheted off the railing with a force that made that insufficient barricade quiver. Tony was some distance ahead, running like an Olympic champ. He kept vanishing and reappearing as the stretches of darkness between the streetlights swallowed and then disgorged his fleeting form. The effect was quite unnerving.

The worst places were the towers that break the wall at intervals. The walkway goes through them, and the enclosed chambers are extremely dark. Preoccupied as I was by more vital matters, I couldn't help noticing the stench as we passed through these tower rooms, and I wondered what primitive instinct moves some members of the so-called human race to relieve themselves in every secluded corner, as dogs do.

All at once I heard a rackety din ahead. We had been running noiselessly till then; I recognized the new sound and a chill stiffened my knees. I ran faster, but it was useless; I couldn't catch up with Tony. He had already reached the wooden flooring.

That was the cause of the rumbling noise—heavy feet, no longer on stone, but on thin wooden planks. One stretch of the walkway had this surface underfoot; I suppose it replaced a broken section of stone. I glanced over the railing to my right and saw that my memory of the topography was accurate. The alley was gone; steep tiled roofs crowded up to the very rail. And that meant we were approaching a critical spot.

The walls of Rothenburg have many towers, but only six or seven main gateways. We had ascended at one of these gateways and were now approaching the next, at a rate that spelled trouble. The inner chambers of the towers are brightly lighted compared with the complicated inner structure of the bastions. Still running, I tried to remember how the next one was designed. It was the Spitalstor, if my memory served me, and it was a wonderful place for an ambush.

In a desperate burst of speed I closed up on Tony, who was getting winded. I was close enough to see what happened, but not close enough to prevent it.

The rock missed his head. It must have meant to miss it, because it was as big as a skull and it came whizzing out of the pitch-black entrance to the Spitalstor when Tony was less than six feet away. It landed on his bad shoulder, and it knocked him flat.

I had no intention of vaulting over Tony's prostrate body to continue the chase. No, indeed. But I wouldn't have been able to in any case. Tony fell on me. It was becoming a habit.

Tony was out cold, but he was breathing okay. I untangled myself and lifted his head onto my lap. He sat up with a start.

"Damn it," he shouted, "why aren't you chasing that guy?"

There was a brief silence, fraught with emotion.

"I ought to let your head bounce off the floor," I said, finally.

"Damn, damn damn. To fall for a hoary old trick like that. . . . Damn."

"If you're restraining your language on my account, don't," I said, helping him up. "Can you make it back to the *Schloss*? No point hanging around here."

"Oh, sure. The principal damage is to my inflated ego."

That was an exaggeration. He was feeling poorly, and our progress was slow. With Tony leaning heavily on me, I began to feel my own age, and I was looking forward to going to bed. But when we reached the *Schloss* it was evident that I was still some distance from that indulgence. Our corridor was wide awake. The first person we saw was George, and the sight of his flushed, grim face told us something serious had happened.

"What's up?" Tony asked.

"Schmidt. He's dead."

"Dead!" Tony tried to enter Schmidt's room, but George's arm barred the door.

"Don't go in yet."

"Why not?"

"I've seen a lot of dead men," said George, "but I never saw one who looked like that."

"Stop talking like The Monk," I said sharply. "What happened?"

George fumbled in his pocket and located a cigarette and matches. He looked at them blankly, as if he had forgotten what to do with them.

"I heard him scream," he said. "What a sound . . . The *Gräfin* heard it too. She was in the hall when I came out of my room. I went through Schmidt's door like a bulldozer. It wasn't locked. Schmidt was sitting up in bed facing the window. The lamp by the bed was lit. He didn't look at us, not even when the door crashed open. He was looking at the window. He never looked at us at all. He just kept staring . . . at the window. Then he keeled over."

George was perspiring. His shirt clung to his broad chest.

All eyes turned toward the windows, which were open to admit the night air.

I pushed George aside. Without looking at the

motionless form on the bed, I crossed the room, and leaned out the window. The distance between it and the window of Tony's room was a good twenty feet. To the left, at an even greater distance, were the windows of the neighboring guest chamber. There were no windowsills. The outer panes were flush with the stones of the wall. Below was a stretch of blank wall reaching down to the foundations.

I craned my neck and looked up toward the sloping eaves of the roof. A very tall man, standing on the window ledge, might have been able to touch the edge of the roof with his fingertips. I might have done it myself. I'd have hated to try.

"Unless somebody has suckers on his hands and feet, like the Human Fly, there's no way out here," I reported, withdrawing my head.

"But that's impossible. I tell you I was in the corridor within seconds of the time I heard him scream. Nobody could have come out that door without my seeing him."

"And I," said a cool voice, "was in the corridor when Herr Schmidt cried out. No one left his room."

The speaker was the *Gräfin*. Blankenhagen was with her. He was fully dressed, of course; I wondered what kind of emergency it would take to get Blankenhagen out of his room without his pants. He bent over Schmidt. Then he flew into violent action, stripping the clothes from the little man's chest and fumbling in his bag for a hypodermic.

"The man is not dead. Telephone to the hospital. We must have an ambulance as quickly as possible. Run!"

The *Gräfin* obeyed. She didn't run, but she moved fast. The rest of us stared blankly at one another.

"You said he was dead." I looked accusingly at George.

"I thought he was." George was badly shaken. "He sure looked dead. I couldn't help—"

"Nobody's blaming you," I said, more mildly. "Doctor, can we do anything?"

"You can go," said Blankenhagen, without looking up. "All of you. Out of here."

So we left. But I sat in my room with the door open till the ambulance arrived and took Schmidt away. The doctor went with him. Then I closed and locked my door and, remembering the interchangeable keys of the *Schloss*, I wedged a chair under the handle.

I was glad Schmidt wasn't dead. I rather liked the old guy, despite the fact that I would not have been willing to stake my life on his honesty. In fact, I had been willing to consider him a prime suspect. His earlier attack hadn't put me off the scent; the suggestion of invalidism was a good alibi in a case where the villain displayed such startling agility. But this attack couldn't have been faked. Unless . . .

I had already considered the idea that there were two villains. Tony's encounter with the armor was particularly significant. Blankenhagen had suggested that Tony had hit his head when he fell, but I had seen that neat round lump behind his ear, and the word that came to my mind was "blackjack." If someone had been waiting for Tony in the darkness under the stairs, and had knocked him out, it would explain a lot of things.

It began to look more and more like Blankenhagen. If Schmidt's heart attack tonight was a fake, only the doctor could back him up in his pretense. Yet in that case would Blankenhagen risk taking Schmidt to a hospital, with a whole staff of doctors and interns?

It looked less like Blankenhagen.

I took a sheet of paper and a pencil, thinking maybe things would be clearer if I wrote them down, the way the detective always does in a mystery story. I wrote down Schmidt's name, and that of the doctor. I couldn't think of anything else to write.

Even if Schmidt's heart attack was genuine, he could be one of the conspirators. However, he had not been the black figure we had pursued that night; he was far too short. The Black Man had had ample time to reach the *Schloss* while we were limping along the streets.

So then what? George's crazy story implied that Schmidt had faced someone, or something, that had scared him almost to death. How had the intruder reached Schmidt and escaped without being seen? And what had the hypothetical villain done to frighten the old man so badly?

Suppose someone had dangled an object from the roof in front of Schmidt's window—an object so horrifying that the mere sight of it swimming in space had been enough to paralyze Schmidt's weak heart.

I scowled and drew doodles over the rest of the paper. I couldn't think of anything that scary. A grinning skull? A phosphorescent phantom?

Schmidt was a grown man. He might be startled, but no homemade phantom could frighten a man to that extent.

How about a Black Man crawling up the wall like a bat?

I threw my pencil on the table so hard the point broke, and stood up. Just for that, I told my undisciplined imagination, you and I are going exploring.

The heavy cupboard that served as my closet was pushed into the corner I wanted to examine. It was ten feet high and four feet wide and seemed to be built of concrete. My first shove didn't even rock it. After I had greased a track under the feet with a candle, and strained every muscle in my back, it began to yield. There are some advantages to being big, I guess.

Finally I had the cupboard moved out at an angle. I squeezed in behind.

The whole room had once been wood-paneled, but now only a few rotting fragments remained, in areas like this, which were normally concealed by furniture. I lifted my lamp in one hand and ran my fingers over the stones. They felt like stones. I rapped tentatively on one of them, and scraped my knuckles. I put the lamp on the floor, sat down beside it, and made a profane remark.

And there it was. As simple as that. I had been looking at the stones which were on my eye level, and that would have been over the head of a stocky medieval male. The doorway was so low that even Burckhardt would have had to bend over in order to pass through. I could see the outlines clearly, where the mortar was missing. In earlier times, of course, tapestries and/or paneling had covered the door.

It yielded a trifle when I pushed against it, but it refused to open. I looked in vain for a bar or catch. Then the answer came to me. I was in the countess's room. The active party in the nocturnal get-togethers would be coming into the room, not leaving it. In those days a lady was supposed to act like a lady.

A wooden coat hanger proved strong enough to act as a lever. The door opened with a protesting squeal of rusted hinges. I told myself that next day I would squander a few marks on a can of oil. The creaking doors of Schloss Drachenstein were beginning to get on my nerves.

I lifted up the lamp and held it through the opening. I couldn't see much—only the top of a flight of stairs going down.

There were only four stairs. Then the passage leveled out. I had wondered how a passage could run between the rooms of the count and countess without blocking the windows of Tony's room. Now I understood. It was below the window level.

When I reached the end of the passage I found a variation where I had expected a repetition of the arrangement outside my own room—that is to say, steps leading up to the count's chamber. The steps were there, but at the foot of them was a narrow opening just wide enough to admit a human body, through which the stairs went on down.

I stood on one side of the hole and meditated. I was awfully tired, and the stale air was giving me a headache. I didn't expect to find a hiding place in these walls; they were too accessible, if not to servants, then to the innocent inhabitant of the countess's room. Burckhardt wouldn't hide the shrine in any place where Konstanze might have found it. So what was I after?

It was no use. Even fatigue doesn't deaden my insatiable curiosity. With a sigh I stepped over the gap in the floor and mounted the stairs that led up.

They ended in the outlines of a door, which yielded, as mine had done, to the leverage of my handy coat hanger. It only opened an inch or so, though, and then it stuck. I put my flashlight and one eye up against the opening and saw a blank wooden surface beyond. I poked at it with my coat hanger. Nothing happened.

I knew where I was: outside Schmidt's room. The paneling was blocking the door. There must be a way of opening the panel, but it was no use trying from this side. So I descended the stairs and instead of stepping into the passage I squeezed through the hole and followed the steps on down.

They went down for quite a distance. The walls closed in on me like the shaft of a mine. I kept feeling a weight hanging over my head—several tons of assorted walls, roofs, and floors. The air was stifling.

At the bottom of the stairs was another passage. I followed it doggedly, my flashlight trained on the floor ahead, my head pulled in like a turtle's, to avoid the low ceiling. I went slowly because I didn't want to fall into a hole like the one up above.

The obstruction I encountered was not a hole. At first sight it was an amorphous shape that filled the entire width of the corridor. In the dust-haunted beam of the flashlight it seemed to move. But when I advanced resolutely upon it, I realized that the illusion of movement had been caused by reflected light dancing off a metal surface. I had found Count Burckhardt's missing armor.

NINE

❀▭❀▭❀

THERE WAS NO ONE IN THE ARMOR NOW. IT WAS dismembered, helmet and greaves lying across the hollow breastplate. Behind it, the corridor ended in a wall of wood. In its surface was an ordinary door handle, made of iron, and a closed bolt. I pushed the bolt back. It moved sweetly, without the usual screech of rusted metal. When I looked at my fingertips I saw why. They were covered with a thin coating of oil.

I turned the door handle and stepped out into the Great Hall.

The western windows were dull gray squares, but the rosy light of dawn was beginning to show in the east. The room didn't look haunted or eerie now; it was only melancholy in its faded grandeur. Pale light lay like dust on the scarred paneling; silence filled the space which had once rung with the songs of the minnesingers and the Latin of a vanished nobility.

As I had anticipated, the door was located in the area under the stairs, where Tony had been attacked. I didn't let the door close; I had locked my own door from the inside, so I would have to return by the secret passage.

I examined the outside of the door. There was no latch or hinge visible. The panel fitted so closely against the others that only someone who knew it was there could have found it. Finally I found a carved flower that yielded to pressure and then turned on a pivot. As it moved, so did the inner handle. I played with the flower till I was sure I knew how to operate it, and then turned reluctantly back into the hot, airless passageway.

❈⚌❈

My tablemates were all in their places when I went down for breakfast next morning. Blankenhagen looked as if he hadn't slept.

"How is Herr Schmidt?" I asked.

"Still critical." The doctor looked from me to George to Tony, and it was obvious he wouldn't have given ten *Pfennige* for the lot of us. "There will be no visitors. None."

"Then you ought to take yourself off the case," said George, answering the implication rather than the words.

Blankenhagen thought it over.

"You are right. It is correct. I will give orders that I may not be admitted."

I couldn't help laughing.

"Cut it out," I said. "I'm sure Schmidt is safe from you."

Blankenhagen eyed me with moderate approval. Apparently he took my comment as a personal compliment, which was not how I meant it. I meant he was too smart to harm Schmidt under such carefully guarded conditions when he was already under suspicion. However, seeing the doctor's rare and attractive smile, I decided not to explain myself.

"He hasn't said anything?" George asked carelessly.

"He cannot be questioned. The criminal—if there is a criminal—is safe for the time being."

"Aren't you being rather melodramatic?" I asked. "With an attack so severe, Schmidt must have experienced great pain. He might well scream, or cry out. Everything indicates he was alone in the room."

My reasoning did not convince anyone. George laughed and Tony shook his head. Blankenhagen's face assumed its normal scowl.

"I would accept that idea willingly were it not for the other strange events which have happened here. Have you heard of what transpired at the church last night? It is all over the town this morning."

"No, what?" I asked, spilling coffee into Tony's lap. It was still fairly hot; anguish replaced the guilt written on Tony's ingenuous countenance. I handed him my napkin and said to Blankenhagen, "Something happened at the church?"

"Hurrumph," said Blankenhagen, eyeing Tony suspiciously. "In the churchyard, to be precise. Desecration of graves."

"Graves?" said Tony.

I was out of coffee, so I interrupted him before he could go on to explain that he thought only one grave had been damaged.

"What do you mean, desecrated? Dirty words written on the tombstones?"

"That, yes. Stones and crosses overturned, one

grave opened." He gave us a critical stare, but by now we were all registering proper shock and surprise. "Interesting, is it not, that the opened grave should be that of the steward?"

He left the table, stamping a little. George looked from me to Tony and started to speak. Tony stood up.

"Let's go for a walk."

"It's raining," said George.

"I didn't mean you."

Rothenburg looked thoroughly medieval in the rain. There were few pedestrians, and the old gabled houses leaned together like gossipy ladies. I knew Tony wanted to get away so we could talk freely, but his first remark took me by surprise.

"The blanket," he said, groaning.

"The what? Oh, that. It wasn't marked. Just an ordinary cheap blanket."

Tony looked relieved.

"Smart," he said.

"Your conversation is very oblique today," I complained. "You are now referring to the Black Man? Yes, it was smart of him to attack several graves. The town authorities will be looking for an ordinary sickie. He didn't fool Blankenhagen, though."

"Blankenhagen is too damned bright for his own good."

"You are suggesting that he did the desecrating himself?"

"He could have."

"The man we saw was too tall. And don't tell me we were misled by the costume and the general air of brimstone. I think Blankenhagen is okay."

"You would."

"George is tall enough, but he has an alibi, if you believe the *Gräfin*."

"Nobody has a good-enough alibi for anything," Tony said sweepingly—but I could see his point. "Remember what is at stake, in terms of cold hard cash. The value of the shrine is literally incalculable— a hundred thousand, two hundred, maybe half a million bucks. That's a lot of dough, even for a man who considers African safaris and original Rembrandts among the necessities of life. I know Nolan is rich—so he says. How do I know how much he's got and how much more he may fancy he needs? The day after he suggested an alliance I got stabbed. Not seriously, just badly enough to make me require help. No, I don't accept the *Gräfin*'s word, or anybody else's."

"Tony . . . Are you sure any person is behind all this?"

"Don't tell me you, of all people, are going over to the spiritualists."

"A scholar is supposed to keep an open mind. All our instincts are against a supernormal explanation, but instincts aren't logic. How do we know?"

"Well." Tony brushed raindrops off his face and thought. "For one thing, this business is too corny to be supernatural."

"Corny?"

"So far we have had a séance, with spirit possession, a White Lady walking by night, a perambulating suit of armor, a diabolical character in a black cloak, and even a semi-dead man with a look of stark staring horror. It isn't even good horror fiction;

it's straight out of *The Mysteries of Udolpho*. By some straining of the brain I could believe in ghosts; but I can't believe in a ghost that acts like *Terror Comics*."

"Thanks. I just wanted someone to talk me out of it. It is corny. Do you suppose that's a clue—to the way the criminal's mind works?"

"No. The obvious interpretation is that the criminal is as corny as his plot—a retarded adolescent who is naïve enough to believe people will be intimidated by his pulp-fiction ghosts. But he may be just the opposite—a sophisticate with a sardonic sense of humor, who is smart enough to know that people are intimidated by pulp-fiction ghosts. Or he may have practical down-to-earth motives for all the things he's done, motives that escape us now, but that—"

A large raindrop tobogganed off his nose and fell straight down his throat. Cut off in full eloquence, Tony gargled and clutched at his Adam's apple. I laughed.

Maybe it was the laugh, or maybe I overdid my attempt to boost his ego. Anyhow, Tony got very defensive and mean. He had not suggested going out because he wanted to walk in the rain with me. He had an errand. It led us to the telephone-telegraph office, and the rat wouldn't tell me what he intended to do there.

In view of the rain he consented to let me enter the office, but he sat me in a corner and I couldn't hear a word of his conversation with the girl behind the counter. The conference took some time and ended with the dispatch of several cables. When we left the office together the rain had stopped, although the skies were still gray. Naturally I didn't ask any questions. I have my pride.

We found a *Bierstube* on a back street, and ordered beer.

"Look," said Tony abruptly. "I've been thinking."

I made encouraging noises. More ego-boosting was obviously in order if I wanted to get anything out of him.

"You were saying the other day that we seem to be obsessed with ancient history instead of concentrating on the shrine. It's true. I can't get these people out of my mind—Burckhardt, Nicolas, Konstanze. But there's some method in this particular madness. Our reconstruction of what happened in the crypt that night in fifteen hundred twenty-five is not just antiquarian hobbying. It has helped us in our search. We know now that the shrine was in Count Harald's tomb at one time. We don't know whether it was Burckhardt or the steward who put it there, but that's not important. What matters is who took it out. And we know it wasn't Nicolas."

I was inclined to agree with that.

"Burckhardt was on the loose that night; it's almost certain that he murdered Nicolas. So he must have been the one who disposed of the shrine. Therefore we can make a few deductions as to where he may have hidden it."

Tony summoned the waitress and ordered more beer.

"The hiding place can't be too obscure," he continued. "Burckhardt wasn't a man of great subtlety, and I don't imagine he intended to find a permanent hiding place. Only his sudden death prevented him from disposing of the shrine."

"I'll bet he didn't plan to give it to the church."

"It's a safe bet. Why hide it, if that was his intention? Now there aren't that many places where it could have been hidden. I've made a list. Maybe you can think of some more."

Tony pulled out his notebook.

"The crypt is one place. I don't see why the old boy should have removed the treasure from one tomb only to put it in another, but it won't take long to check. I'll examine the other tombs this afternoon. The chapel was remodeled in the eighteenth century, so that's out. You've looked at the library, and didn't find anything. Burckhardt wouldn't choose his wife's room, or the servants' quarters, or any of the public rooms such as the kitchen, scullery, etcetera. It seems to me that the best possibilities are Burckhardt's room and the cellars. I'm going to check the cellars first because of the fact that the plan of that part of the *Schloss* is missing. Does this make any sense to you?"

"It does. But I can think of one other place."

"Where?"

"The *Wachtturm*."

"We looked there."

"Not thoroughly. Another point. The *Schloss* seems to be riddled with secret passages. Maybe there is one from the crypt to the tower. Or the crypt to—almost anywhere. I can't see Burckhardt carrying an object the size of the shrine through the public corridors on that fateful night."

"It's a point. Well, we won't find anything sitting here drinking beer."

He stood up and the waitress swooped down on him with the bill. I stayed put.

"Do I understand you are inviting me to join you in your investigations?" I inquired.

"Understand whatever you like." Tony hesitated. Then he blurted, "I don't want you poking around in those lonesome places by yourself. You're dumb enough to go exploring on your own, even after what has been happening. If I have to take you with me to keep you out of mischief, that's what I'm prepared to do."

"Oh," I said. "You're so sweet to little helpless me. I don't know how to thank you. I'm just all a-twitter. . . ."

"I'll even put up with your smart-aleck remarks," Tony said shortly. "Come on."

I had been trying to decide whether to tell him about the secret passage and my discovery of the missing armor. I decided not to.

A little later, dressed in working clothes and equipped with flashlights, we descended into the crypt. After an hour of eyestrain and general wear and tear, Tony rose stiffly to his feet.

"If any other stone has been moved within the past five hundred years I'll—well, I don't think it has. Have you got a cigarette?"

We sat against a pillar and rested for a short time. But before his cigarette was half finished, Tony stood up.

"I can't sit, I'm too restless."

"I know what you mean." I followed as he headed for the far end of the long, shadowy chamber. "Like the clouds overhead, a feeling of impending doom. . . ."

"Stop that."

The beam of his flashlight darted frivolously around the room, glancing off ponderous stone pillars, illuminating a carved face or two bronze hands clasped around the hilt of a sword.

"What are you looking for?"

"There ought to be a door down here somewhere. For workmen, repair materials—they wouldn't drag lumber through the chapel. . . . Ah, I thought so."

The north end of the crypt was made of brick instead of the stone prevalent elsewhere. Set into the wall was a low door fashioned of heavy wooden beams bound with iron. One of the keys on the *Gräfin*'s ring fit the massive keyhole, but in addition there was a modern padlock and a series of bolts and chains. When these had been dealt with the door opened into a corridor with a number of rooms leading off it. The first was typical of all the others—a vaulted stone chamber, poorly lit by a grating high in the wall. It contained nothing but some scraps of wood and a broken pottery bowl.

"Storage room," said Tony, after an inspection had yielded nothing of interest. "We must be under the far end of our own wing now. My God, this place is big."

"Too big. All we need to do is miss one stone, in one wall or floor."

"It isn't as bad as that. These are public rooms—places the servants had access to. It's unlikely that the count would have a secret wall safe down here."

We gave the other storerooms only a cursory search. Finally we reached a big room lit by several windows at ground level, but still dark and dismal. On one wall was a flat stone slab like a table. In the corner was a hooded fireplace big enough to roast a couple of oxen.

"Kitchen," Tony announced unnecessarily. "How would you like to whip up a meal in this mausoleum? We're under the Great Hall—I'll bet that stair goes up to it. Here's where the banquets were cooked."

"We won't have to thump on these walls, then. I haven't got any skin left on my knuckles."

"Here's your well."

Tony tugged at a stone which was equipped with a rusted iron ring. The stone slid aside with a screech, leaving a gaping hole. Peering into it I saw, far below, the glimmer of water.

"Cover it up," I said suddenly, glancing over my shoulder.

Tony heaved the stone back into place.

"You can see," he said, "why I don't recommend solitary exploring. If something went down there, it wouldn't come up."

He led the way along the corridor outside the kitchen, dismissing a series of closed doors with the comment, "More storerooms."

At the end of the corridor we found something that couldn't be dismissed so casually.

Stairs led down into Stygian darkness, far below

ground level. Below was a short corridor with three doors opening onto it. The doors were of iron, with bolts as thick as Tony's arm. In the upper half of each door was a small barred opening that could be closed by a sliding iron plate.

We didn't need Tony's keys. The doors had not been locked for centuries, not since the last Count of Drachenstein had given up his seignorial privileges of imprisonment and execution to the state. But the doors looked functional, even now.

"They will squeak," Tony warned, and pushed on the first door.

Squeak was hardly the word. The hinges screamed like a wounded animal.

I was secretly relieved when the flashlight showed no heap of moldering bones, no grinning skeleton held erect by rusted chains. There was nothing in the cell, not even a bench or a shard from a broken water bowl. It was simply a square, windowless stone box about eight feet by eight. Yet there was an aura in that room which would have made human bones seem like meaningless stage props. The cell stank of fear and despair; a miasma of ancient agony shrouded the walls like fog. It required all the courage I possessed to step into that evil little room. From the sound of Tony's breathing I suspected he didn't like it either.

The walls and floors seemed to be solid. The second cell was a duplicate of the first, and the third, which was so small that neither of us could stand erect in it, was equally unproductive. Tony let me precede him in a retreat which closely resembled flight, and neither of us stopped running until we stood panting in the Great Hall, with a closed door between us and the grim medieval kitchen.

❀▱❀

I don't know how Tony passed the rest of the day; I spent quite a lot of time washing. I was gray with dust and sticky with perspiration, but I kept on washing long after my surface was clean. The stink of those cells had penetrated to the bone.

I had another errand to take care of. By the time I finished, I was good and hungry. The dining room was full when I arrived. Glancing around, I realized I had been so absorbed by the small group of guests who occupied my wing of the *Schloss* that I had lost track of the others. The family from Hamburg and the honeymooners were gone. Most of the tables were occupied by a party of German students, husky, tanned youngsters who made even Tony look elderly.

George was brash and cheery as ever.

"Where were you two?" he asked. "I went downtown later, but I couldn't find you."

"We drank beer," I said. "What did you do for amusement?"

"Went to church. I was breaking the Tenth Commandment—or is it the Ninth?"

"Coveting your neighbor's goods?" Tony was not amused. "The Riemenschneider altar?"

"Yes. I'd steal it if I could think of a way to get it out of Germany. There's another altar at Creglingen, across the valley. I think I'll drive up there tomorrow."

"It is considered his masterpiece by some," said Blankenhagen suddenly. "I myself prefer certain figures in the museum of Würzburg."

"We'll have to see Würzburg," George said. "Maybe after we leave here. How much longer do you plan to stay, Vicky?"

"I never make plans. I'm just a creature of impulse. Don't let me interfere with your arrangements."

Blankenhagen gave me an enigmatic look, and continued to be informative about Riemenschneider.

"He was one of the councillors of Würzburg. During the *Bauernkrieg*, he and eleven other councillors supported the peasants, and when the nobles captured the town he was imprisoned."

"So he picked the losers," George said. "He got his, I suppose."

Blankenhagen shifted in his chair.

"They pierced his hands," he said. "Never again did he do a work of sculpture."

"Artists shouldn't dabble in politics," George said. "He should have stuck to his last, or chisel, or whatever he used."

I wanted to hit him with something—something hard. I consider myself unsentimental, but I could not have joked about an atrocity like that. What made it worse was that George wasn't joking. He meant what he said.

"He had at least the knowledge," snapped Blankenhagen, "that he suffered for a cause he believed was right."

"I wonder," said George, "if that was any satisfaction to him."

❀▭❀

We spent the evening in the lounge, yawning at each other. Tony was silent and rather peaked-looking. For the first time in too long I remembered his injury. I hadn't even had the decency to ask how he felt. Feeling guilty, I let him escort me to my room when the witching hour of ten struck. If he had asked me nicely, I might even have agreed to stay there. But he didn't ask. He told me.

"Stay put tonight. That's an order."

I nodded. A reflexive movement is not binding legally.

The next two hours were difficult. I didn't want to leave my room until I was sure Tony had fallen asleep. It would be just like him to check up on me. But I had a hard time keeping awake. I was short on sleep and long on tiring adventures.

Finally I barred my door and shoved the heavy cupboard away from the wall. As I started down the hidden stairs I noticed that the beam of my flashlight was getting dim, and I retraced my steps. I had bought extra batteries and a can of oil in town earlier, and I was taking no chances on having my light fade out in the middle of some dark hole. Then I went back to the passage.

This time the door at the other end opened without difficulty. My errand that afternoon had taken me to Schmidt's room. His door was locked, but, as I had expected, my key opened it. Those locks were a joke. I assumed that the old ones had been ripped out and sold. If they were like the beautiful hand-made antique locks I had seen in museums, they had been valuable. The *Gräfin* hadn't missed much.

Naturally I couldn't give the Burckhardt-Schmidt apartment the careful search it demanded during the day, with people wandering the halls and servants popping in and out. My aim was to clear the secret entrance so I could come and go in the small hours.

Since I knew where the passage ended, it didn't take me long to locate the sliding panel and figure out how it worked. The mechanism was a variation of the carved rosette pattern in the Great Hall. It controlled a bolt instead of a handle; the door could be locked, but only from the inside.

I confess that bolt amused me. A tyrant, medieval or modern, needs all the locks and bolts he can get. But since one branch of the passageway ended in the bedchamber of the Countesses Drachenstein ... Marriage was as perilous in those days as it is today.

In the still hours of the night the unoccupied chamber had an uneasy atmosphere. It didn't feel abandoned. Too many Drachensteins had breathed their last in the carved, canopied bed. It may have been a trick of my imagination, but I almost fancied I could see a depression the size and shape of a human body in the smooth counterpane.

I wedged a chair under the door handle before I got to work. Schmidt was safely locked up in the local hospital, but that didn't make *me* feel safe. He might be the villain who had engineered some of the supernatural games, but he couldn't have played the star role of the Black Man. Some source of malice was still on the loose, and I didn't want it interrupting me.

By this time I was becoming an expert on secret panels. It took me only a few minutes to find another carved rosette. The old craftsman hadn't been very imaginative about that device, but maybe he had to select a design his dim-witted patrons could remember. The mechanisms controlled by the rosette were varied and ingenious; this one opened a panel rather than a door. It was only a couple of feet square, and its outlines were cleverly concealed by carved moldings that were part of the design of the paneling.

The count's wall safe was a single block of dressed stone that slid out of the wall like a drawer. I knew right away I hadn't found the shrine; the stone was only half a meter high. I lowered it to the floor and thrust my hand into the cavity in its top.

I touched some small brittle objects that felt like twigs. I shone my light down into the stone drawer and jerked my hand back with a snort of disgust. The brittle twigs were rodent bones—the remnants of a battalion of long-dead rats.

The bottom of the drawer was covered with scraps of chewed parchment and paper. I cursed the rat bones and selected a few scraps which were big enough to offer some hope of decipherment. Then I removed the only other object the drawer contained: a small chest, made of wood and bound with silver.

It had been a beautiful object—a rich man's prized possession. But the silver had turned black and the revolting rodents had ruined the box. One corner was completely gnawed away. I lifted the top with a quick twist that ripped out the decayed hasp and lock. The chest was beyond repair.

Most of the interior was filled with the remains of a linen bag, also gnawed by rodent teeth. When I tried to lift it, the rotted cloth dissolved, spilling a heap of coarse gray powder into the bottom of the box.

I touched it with a cautious finger, wondering what it had been. The centuries might have reduced any substance, solid or semisolid, to this state. My fingertip, penetrating more deeply, touched something hard. I extracted it and held it up to the light.

Not more than an inch in height, the small gold figure might have been an amulet; there was a rounded link at the top of it. After considering the object, I decided I would not care to wear it. It was meant to represent an animal of some kind. The wide, grinning jaws and pop eyes rather suggested a frog, but no frog I had ever met had such a wicked look. The Drachenstein crest had nothing to do with frogs. Whatever this monstrosity had been meant to be, it was not a dragon. It certainly wasn't one of Riemenschneider's pieces. He couldn't have produced an abortion like this if he had wanted to. In fact, the trinket had a look of antiquity far older than the sixteenth century.

I shrugged and dropped it into the pocket of my robe. Maybe it was a talisman or lucky piece belonging to an ancestor of Burckhardt's—that same crusading count who had brought the jewels back to Drachenstein. The amulet had an eastern look. . . .

And with that, a dark and elusive memory stirred unpleasantly in the back of my mind—stirred and subsided, like a slimy thing in a swamp.

TEN

❀▱❀▱❀

MY SLEEPLESS NIGHTS WERE BEGINNING TO CATCH UP with me. I didn't wake till almost noon next day. I had dreamed that some faceless intruder was tampering with the little chest, but when I stretched out an anxious hand, I found it on the nightstand where I had left it. That had been a stupid place to put it, but I had been too tired the night before to think straight. I tucked the chest into a corner of my suitcase and locked the case.

I didn't see Tony till lunchtime. I found him alone at our table. George had gone off to Creglingen to see the altar there. Tony seemed vexed by this. His mood was not improved when the *Gräfin* came in, a royal procession of one, and joined us at our table. I wondered what she was after this time.

"I wished to tell you again how sorry I am that your vacation has been so unpleasant," she began. "It is unaccountable. Never, until you came, have we known such violence."

"Is that right," I said. "You surprise me. I would think a place like this had seen a lot of violence over the years."

"Many years ago, perhaps. But this is ancient history now. There has not been a prisoner in those horrid cells since sixteen hundred and thirty. And on that occasion Graf Otto was severely reprimanded by the emperor."

I exchanged glances with Tony. Damn her, the woman knew every move we had made.

"You are well acquainted with the family history for someone who is not a Drachenstein by birth," I said.

"I was forced to amuse myself. To be buried in this provincial spot after Prague, Vienna, Budapest was not easy for a spoiled young girl. My husband loved his home and would not leave it. I painted, embroidered, studied music; but these soon pall."

"Especially when one has mastered them," Tony said. It was a reluctant compliment, and not an empty one. I too was sure the old lady could master anything she attempted. She acknowledged his courtesy with a chilly smile.

"So then I turned to a study of genealogy. As a professor of history, you will understand its fascination. Are you making progress with your research into the Peasants' Revolt, and Count Burckhardt?"

"I've been to the town archives." Tony eyed the woman with what he obviously thought was a look of fiendish cunning. "I imagine you've used them too."

"Oh, yes. I know the story of the Countess Konstanze's death."

"Does your niece know it?" I asked.

"She does not. She is already sufficiently unbalanced on that subject."

Tony was turning red—a sure sign that he was about to lose his temper.

"Irma must know the story," he said. "How else can you account for what she said in the séance?"

"Must I account for it? 'There are more things in heaven and earth,' as your poet so cleverly puts it."

"Rrrr," said Tony. He turned the growl into a cough. "I would be more willing to admit the supernatural if there were some quasi-logical reason for a haunting. Even a specter has to have a *raison d'être*. You surely know the classic explanations—unexpiated crime, for instance."

"How clever!" exclaimed the *Gräfin*. "But what of innocence abused and unavenged? Konstanze was falsely accused—"

"Naturally."

"Yes, we moderns know the folly of the witchcraft persecution. Yet her fate was not surprising. She was a learned woman who had been educated by a family priest in her home near Granada. His lessons apparently gave her ideas which were, in that day, dangerously heretical. It is said that she was in communication with Trithemius, at Würzburg."

"That must be apocryphal," Tony said. "Trithemius died in fifteen hundred sixteen. But that doesn't account for the lady's restlessness. She can't be worried about her reputation; we know she was innocent. And I'm afraid we're in no position to punish her persecutors, or give her Christian burial."

He looked at his hostess with the candid wide-eyed stare that had brought out the motherly instinct in many middle-aged ladies. I could have told him it wouldn't work; the *Gräfin* had about as much maternal instinct as a guppy. She smiled gently.

"It is very mysterious."

After she left, Tony and I discussed the interview. We agreed on one thing: the *Gräfin* almost certainly knew about the shrine. One of the most common motives assigned to restless spirits is their desire to tell their descendants where the gold is buried. The *Gräfin* must have been familiar with the whole corpus of supernatural literature; her failure to mention this point was significant.

"She knows," I summarized, "but she doesn't know where. If she had the shrine, she'd throw us out of here. She has every excuse; our snooping has been outrageous."

"I don't know." A visit from the *Gräfin* always depressed Tony. "She might let us stay on just for the fun of watching us stumble around. We must look pretty ridiculous, and her sense of humor is decidedly macabre."

"She couldn't risk it," I argued. "If we find the shrine, we'll turn it over to Irma—unless Elfrida can lift the loot before we make the discovery public. She'd have to silence us, in that case. Why should she take such a chance unless she had to? I'm sure she hasn't found it. Not yet."

Tony looked more cheerful.

"I guess you're right. Shall we have a look at Burckhardt's room?"

"Right now?"

"Right now. No more roaming by night. That's when all the kookie things happen."

"Okay," I said agreeably.

But when we reconnoitered, we found Schmidt's room occupied by a buxom chambermaid who was scrubbing the floor. It was clear that the process would take some time, so we retreated. I tried to console Tony—not, of course, by telling him I had already searched the room—but by pointing out an unpalatable fact that had just occurred to me.

If the *Gräfin* knew about the shrine, she had certainly searched Burckhardt's room and all the other obvious hiding places. She wasn't stupid; if she had not located the shrine, it must be concealed in a more obscure spot than we had anticipated.

The idea didn't cheer Tony much. It didn't cheer me either. My reasoning was not invalidated by the fact that I had found the secret drawer. Its contents held no useful clue, and the *Gräfin* would have no reason to remove them. Perhaps the scraps of parchment and the mutilated bag had not even belonged to Burckhardt, but to one of his many successors or predecessors.

Since there was nothing else to do, we went sightseeing. By Tony's definition, this activity includes frequent stops for liquid refreshment. The drinking places of Rothenburg are all charming; you can guzzle beer or drink tea in dark, raftered rooms or sit in a cobblestoned square admiring the view. We tried both, and since we couldn't decide which ambience was preferable, we tried both several times.

I suppose it was inevitable that we should end up at the Jakobskirche. With our chance of finding the shrine seeming even more remote, we were just torturing ourselves by visiting Riemenschneider's altar, but we couldn't keep away.

It is so beautiful that all the adjectives critics and art historians use seem inadequate. The dark wood glows. The bodies breathe, and are just about to move. The central carving depicts the Last Supper, at the moment when Christ makes the statement: "One of you shall betray me." You can see the effect of the words on every face.

I glanced at Tony, who was standing beside me. He never looked at *me* that way.

"Come on," I said gruffly. "Let's have another beer."

We had several more beers before we went back to the *Schloss*, but the beverage didn't have its usual effect on our spirits. I knew why I felt so uneasy. For the last thirty-six hours, there had been a strange absence of activity—not even a séance to disturb the peace. It was as if something were waiting for us to move. But it could not wait indefinitely.

I went to bed early that night. Tony gave me the usual lecture about staying in my room, but even that didn't stimulate me. I had no plans for the night. I was, to use a classic phrase, baffled.

Once in bed I found I couldn't sleep, or concentrate on the novel I had brought for light reading. The room was very quiet. The single lamp glimmered lonesomely in its restricted circle of light. But as I lay on the bed, smoking one cigarette after another in reckless defiance of every health regulation, I had never felt less sleepy. The sense of something waiting, a mounting pressure against my mind, grew steadily.

From where I lay I could hardly avoid staring straight into the painted eyes of the face that had become an unreasonable obsession. With just a little imagination I could sense a slender presence, just beyond the bounds of ordinary sight and sound, pressing on an invisible door, trying to come through, to tell me something. . . .

I sat upright with a profane remark. Going to my suitcase, I took out the crumbling wooden box. Maybe if I tried some logical research on the fragments of parchment, it would brush the cobwebs from my brain.

But the scraps were hopeless. Only a word here and there was legible, and they were common words such as "have" and "we." I couldn't even find a name.

Absently I reached into my pocket and took out the small golden frog. I sat staring into the empty pop eyes as if they held some knowledge. And as I stared, the memory stirred again—the dark memory, like fragments of a childish nightmare. . . .

My finger had dipped into the peculiar gray-black powder in the box. It was an odd substance, dusty but not dust. It was too coarse for dust, almost crystalline. . . .

The monstrous idea struck me like a fist in the stomach. For several seconds I sat gaping down into the box, my finger buried to the end of the nail in the gray powder. When I realized what I was doing, I jerked it out and wiped it against the skirt of my robe.

"It's impossible," I mumbled.

But the more I thought about it, the more sense it made. It distressed me horribly. It made me sick at my stomach. True or false, the bizarre theory should not have had such a strong emotional impact. It was only a side issue in any case, one which could never be settled.

That last thought was pure wishful thinking. Even as it formed in my mind, my inconvenient memory produced a paragraph from a book I had once read.

I must have stood by my door for almost five minutes, reaching for the handle and pulling my hand back, reaching, pulling back . . . It was a horrible idea. It was crazy.

I knew I would never sleep soundly again unless I found out.

The hour was later than I had realized. Tony was sound asleep. I beat on his door for quite a while before he answered.

"Come on," I said. "The game's afoot."

I didn't wait for him. The next victim was Blankenhagen. It took almost as long to rouse him. By the time he opened his door, Tony had joined me, which was just as well; Blankenhagen probably wouldn't have let me in without a chaperon. A chaperon for him, that is.

They were both furious. After I had talked a while they were still furious—but they were interested. I asked the doctor a question. His face was a sight to behold.

"*Heiliger Gott*—I do not know. I suppose it is possible. . . ."

"That's what I thought. Then . . ." I spoke softly but urgently. Several times Blankenhagen's mouth opened as if to interrupt, but he didn't. I think he was struck dumb. Tony kept making strange strangling sounds.

"But," said Blankenhagen when I had finished. "But—but—now, at this hour?"

"It has to be now. I know it sounds crazy, but I've got to find out. If I could do it alone, I would."

Blankenhagen sat twitching like a hen on a clutch of radioactive eggs. Finally his narrowed blue eyes moved to meet Tony's. They both turned to stare at me.

"I am insane," muttered Blankenhagen. "You understand, I have not the equipment, even if—"

"I know. But the first part has to be done now."

"Allow me then to assume my trousers."

Tony and I went out into the hall while the trousers were assumed. He was wide-awake now and so torn between anger and fascination that he was barely coherent.

"Why didn't you—why did you—I ought to kill you, you—you woman!"

"I woke you up," I pointed out. "I needn't have done that. I'm sorry I did, if you're just going to stand around and yell."

Blankenhagen emerged, with trousers, just in time to prevent an undignified scuffle. I led the way down the corridor, stopping in my room to get a coat and some other equipment. Our next stop was at the carpenters' shack in the south wing. Then we proceeded to the crypt.

As the work went on, I was convinced of one thing. This particular tomb had not been opened before. It was doubtful whether we could open it now. The mortar chipped away easily, but the stone slab on which lay the carved effigy of Count Burck-hardt von und zu Drachenstein behaved as if it were reluctant to leave its place. But it was a couple of inches thinner than the first slab we had raised, and this time nobody sat on the floor and watched. Finally we had the slab propped back, and Blankenha-gen climbed down into the vault.

The coffin was metal. Even after Blankenhagen had shot the bolts that held the lid in place, he had to score through the corroded joint. I had antici-pated this possibility; our tools included a couple of metal files. When Blankenhagen's hands gave out, Tony took his place in the vault. I followed Tony, ignoring male chauvinist complaints from Blanken-hagen. (There were no complaints from Tony, but not because he wasn't a chauvinist.) To reach the upper part of the coffin I had to sprawl across the lid, and some of my wilder fancies can be imagined. I got the lid loose at last. My hands were raw and so were my nerves.

Lying on the floor of the crypt, Blankenhagen reached down into the vault and grasped one of the coffin handles. Tony took the other. They heaved in unison; and we found ourselves looking down on the face of Graf Burckhardt, who had departed this life in the year of our Lord 1525.

Thanks to a well-sealed coffin, the Count's body was fantastically preserved, almost mummified. The features were not nice to look at. They had an expression of twisted agony which was the effect (I kept telling myself) of the shrinkage of the fa-cial tissue. The leathery lips were drawn back over yellowed teeth that looked predatory and vicious in spite of the long moustache that half veiled them. The body wore a gaudy court costume which had suffered more from the ravages of time than the flesh itself. The gold lace was black, and the velvet tore under Blankenhagen's careful hands.

The doctor appeared quite composed. After medical-school dissections, this probably looked like a relatively tidy specimen. He busied himself with the body. I found, to my disgust, that I didn't want to watch.

"We are all mad," he said finally. "But if madness has any method, I have what I require. Shall we . . ."

Tony helped him with the coffin lid. They got it, and the slab, back into place, though not without effort. Blankenhagen tucked his specimens into an envelope.

"I wonder under what law they will imprison me," he muttered, as we climbed the stairs into the chapel.

"If you get in trouble, we'll say we forced you," I said. "But I doubt if the *Gräfin* will make an issue of this."

Blankenhagen stopped under a trumpeting angel and looked at me.

"*Professorin* . . ."

I tried not to look pleased. I love that title.

"I am only flesh and blood," said Blankenhagen, thumping theatrically at his chest. "I am wild with curiosity. You must tell me the truth."

"I don't know the whole truth myself. How soon can you give me some test results?"

"If I give you these, you will in turn give me your confidence?"

"Well—okay. That's fair enough. I—what was that?"

Tony whirled around.

"Nothing. What did you see?"

"I could have sworn something moved behind the altar."

"Nerves," Tony said. "Mine are shot to hell."

Blankenhagen thought for a moment and then said decisively,

"*Also gut*. I will tell you results tonight. Come, we go to the town."

"Not the police," I said apprehensively.

"Ha, ha," said Blankenhagen, without humor. "I should go to the police with this story? No. I know slightly a man in Rothenburg, a chemist with whom I attended university. He has the equipment we need."

Blankenhagen's friend lived in a modern area outside the walls, on a street paralleling the Roedertor. He was a youngish man with quizzical eyebrows and nocturnal habits; there was a light in the upper window of the house, and our soft knock was promptly answered.

Blankenhagen's explanation of our errand was decidedly sketchy, but it was accepted with no more than a lift of the chemist's eccentric eyebrows. He ended up doing the experiment himself, after watching Blankenhagen fumble with his equipment for a while. He didn't even look surprised when the significant dark stain appeared in the test tube.

"You expected this?" he asked amiably.

Blankenhagen's eyes were popping.

"Amazing," he muttered. "Expected? It is what she expected."

Tony was staring at me as if I'd grown an extra head.

"I didn't think of it," he mumbled, as if denying an accusation of crime. "Only a real weirdo would think of a thing like this."

To tell the truth, I was pretty amazed myself. But in view of the general consternation it behooved me to be calm. I thanked the chemist, apologized for our intrusion at such an hour, and led my limp male acquaintances to the door.

The chemist waved my apologies aside.

"I do not ask questions. I do not ask if it is the Central Intelligence, the Federal Bureau, or perhaps Interpol. You will come for a beer, when it is over, and tell me what you can?"

"I may not be allowed to tell," I said. "You understand?"

"Yes, yes. Foolish, this secrecy; but I know how they are, these people."

I was tempted to linger; it was rather flattering to be taken for a lady spy.

The streets of the old town were silent under the moon. Shadows clung to the deep doorways and gathered under the eaves. I was in no mood to appreciate it. The past had come alive, but it had not brought the scent of romance or high adventure, only a dirty, ugly tragedy that would not die.

Nobody said anything till we got back to the *Schloss*. I was heading blindly for the door that would eventually lead to my beautiful bed when two hands caught at my arm. The hands belonged to two different people, but they moved with a unanimity that verged on ESP.

"Sit here," said Tony, indicating a bench in the garden.

"Talk," said Blankenhagen.

"I suppose it can't wait till morning?" I yawned.

"I can't wait till morning." Tony sat me down and took his seat beside me. Blankenhagen sat down on my other side. I hunched my shoulders, feeling closed in.

"Also dann, sprich." Blankenhagen was too absorbed to realize he had abandoned the formal third-person plural and was addressing me with the familiar form. "How did you know that a man dead for half a millennium had been poisoned with arsenic?"

I started out with a complete account of the story of the shrine, for the doctor's benefit. I was pretty sure by then of Blankenhagen's innocence, but it didn't really matter; if he was guilty, he already knew, and if he didn't know, it would not hurt to tell him.

Blankenhagen listened without comment. He didn't have to say anything; his reactions were mirrored in his face, which I could see fairly well in the moonlight. I stressed the fact that we had no leanings toward larceny. If and when we found the shrine, we intended to hand it over to Irma.

"But we got distracted," I went on. "From the first day I walked into this place, I kept losing track of the shrine in my preoccupation with the people who had been involved with it back in fifteen hundred twenty-five. Irma's uncanny resemblance to her ancestress was one reason for my interest, but it was more than that; as time went on, these people came alive for me. Konstanze and her tragic death; the steward, who had been foully murdered; and the count, Burckhardt.

"He was no worse than many of his peers, but he was not an appealing character. Nothing we learned about him made him any more attractive—his defense of the autocratic bishop, his participation in the torture of Riemenschneider, his murder of the steward. All these things were perfectly in character—as we saw his character. I was prejudiced against him from the start, and my prejudice kept me from seeing the truth."

Tony's face relaxed into a half smile as he listened. I knew what he was thinking. He was thinking that I was also prejudiced against Burckhardt because he was a lousy male. Konstanze was a woman—intelligent, repressed, and persecuted. I would automatically take her part.

It was quite true. But there was no need to say so.

"I was also biased," I continued, "by our modern view of the witchcraft persecution. We know witchcraft was nonsense. The countess's trial was a repetition of the classic features—the curse, the evil eye, the Black Man who came on cloven hooves to lie with his mistress. Bilge, all of it—familiar from dozens of historical cases, but still bilge.

"But in one sense the witchcraft trials were not nonsense. Many of the victims believed. Most were innocent, forced into false confessions by the agony of the torture. But enough of them went to the stake swearing eternal loyalty to their Dark Master to assure us that the belief was genuine. Witches and warlocks really did try to render cattle and people infertile, cause storms, kill and curse. They failed to do evil, not through lack of intent, but through lack of power. And when supernatural means proved ineffective, they might turn to practical methods. One element in the witchcraft cult was the use of poison."

Tony's breath caught.

"One of the oldest and most commonly used poisons is arsenic," I went on. "It's mentioned by Roman authors, if I remember correctly, and in the thirteenth century the properties of *arsenicum* were discussed by no other than Albertus Magnus. We found a copy of his well-known work in the library. I think I know now who owned it. . . ."

I turned to Blankenhagen.

"As a doctor, you know that there were no scientific tests for poison till the mid-nineteenth century. Maybe one of the reasons why arsenic was so popular is that the symptoms of arsenic poisoning are identical with those of certain gastrointestinal disorders. I read that in the same book that told me arsenic remains in the body—in the roots of the hair and under the nails—for an indefinite period of time. That's why I thought we might have luck tonight."

"I have never heard of it after so long a time," said Blankenhagen. "But perhaps no one ever tried. Murders several hundred years old are not generally of interest to criminologists."

"Get on with it," said Tony, nudging me.

"The other night I just happened to find myself in Burckhardt's room."

"I knew it," said Tony. "I knew it. . . . We'll discuss that later. I suppose you tripped and fell and accidentally, not meaning to do any real searching, discovered a secret panel?"

"I found a box," I said haughtily, "which contained a quantity of grayish powder. I didn't think of arsenic at first. The color put me off, for one thing. I think of arsenic, when I think of it at all, as white. Either the stuff was contaminated by dust and dirt, or it had been colored, as commercial arsenic is, to keep people from mistaking it for salt or sugar."

Blankenhagen interrupted.

"What you found may not be arsenious oxide, the 'white arsenic' of popular fiction. Elementary arsenic is gray, metallic in structure. Upon exposure to air it takes on a darker color and loses its luster."

"You can look at it later, if you want to. It's not important; most forms of arsenic are intensely toxic. It was not the color of the powder that alerted me. It was something else altogether.

"The hidden drawer where I found the box was littered with the bones of dead rats. They had gnawed their way into the box, and—curiosity killed a rat. Defunct rodents aren't unusual, but it was extraordinary that so many of them should have chosen the hidden drawer as a place in which to die.

"Dead rats . . . rat poison . . . arsenic . . . the witchcraft-poison complex. I guess that was the way my thoughts ran, but I wasn't aware of the progression; it just seemed to hit me all at once. And with that came another thought. What if we had been looking at the tragedy of Count Burckhardt and his wife backward? What if he was not the villain but the victim of a plot?

"My first reaction was a violent negative. But the more I thought about this new theory, the more things it explained. My assumption of Konstanze's innocence wasn't logical. It was based on a number of emotional prejudices which I needn't go into in detail."

Tony snickered. I took the golden amulet from my pocket and handed it to him.

"You weren't exactly logical about Konstanze either," I reminded him. "And your emotional prejudices in her favor aren't hard to understand. Take a look at this. I found it in the box with the arsenic. Then I remembered something you told me when we were discussing the witchcraft cult one time. I think it was the Burning Court affair, under Louis the Fourteenth, that set you off."

"Damn my big mouth all to hell and back," said Tony calmly. He handed the image to Blankenhagen, who was practically sprawled across my lap in his anxiety to see. "Probably of Moorish workmanship—possibly even older. I've seen something like it in an ethnological museum. So, when you saw the little frog god, you remembered the theory that the witchcraft cult was a survival of the old prehistoric nature religion."

"Right."

"Ingenious," said Blankenhagen. "But there is nothing in the amulet to suggest the countess rather than the count. You found it in his room. Why should he not be the one who worshipped devils?"

"Where I found it is irrelevant. The countess had the whole castle at her disposal after her husband died, and it would be smart of her to conceal such damning evidence outside her own room. I thought of her, instead of him, because of the suggestion of Eastern design. She came from Spain. The Moors were there for a long time, and cultural traits linger on. That's weak, though. You're overlooking the conclusive point."

"*Bitte?*"

"It was the count who died," said Tony.

"*Ach*, so." Blankenhagen grinned and rubbed his chin. "Yes, the symptoms described could well have been those of arsenic poisoning. In fact"—he looked startled—"we know now that they were. But the motive. Why did she kill him?"

"Maybe he found out about her unorthodox religious beliefs," Tony offered. "In that day and age it would have been a legitimate motive for murder—although Burckhardt would have called it execution. There's no reason to suppose he wasn't a proper son of Holy Church; our theories about his unwillingness to give up the shrine were based on nothing except the necessity to account for behavior which was otherwise unaccountable."

"That's right," I said. "But I suspect Burckhardt had a more personal reason for being annoyed with his wife.

"Remember the maid's hysterical story about the Black Man? It sounded like pure fantasy; the records of witchcraft trials are full of similar lies. But stripped of its supernatural interpretations, what did that story amount to? The maid saw a man, cloaked and booted, in traveling costume, sneak into the castle in the dead of night and embrace the countess."

"Booted?" said Blankenhagen dubiously.

"The wench heard his spurs clicking on the floor. That was what suggested cloven hooves."

"Du Gott allmächtig!"

"In short, what the maid gave us was a description of a midnight rendezvous. The count, as we know, was still in Würzburg. So the Black Man must have been—"

"Nicolas the steward," said Tony, with a groan. "Oh, my big swollen empty head!"

"It had to be Nicolas. The Black Man was wearing traveling costume, hence he was not living in the *Schloss*. Yet he must have been familiar with the place or he couldn't have entered it and reached the countess's room without being challenged. Who but the trusted steward would know the secret passages and hidden stairs? And—this is the most ironic thing, I think—Konstanze couldn't defend herself from the witchcraft charge by telling the truth. Adultery was a serious crime in those days. And there was the little matter of the arsenic."

"My God, yes," said Tony soberly. "She had to kill Burckhardt; sooner or later he was bound to learn about her and Nicolas. He must have found out the night he killed the steward. Then he went after his cheating wife. . . . She was trapped, all right. By the time she came to trial, maybe she didn't care any longer. Her lover was dead. . . ."

"You're a hopeless romantic," I said scathingly. "I

can't see our witch-poisoner-murderess wasting away for any man. The witches took drugs, you know; that was how they got their hallucinations of satanic orgies and visits to the Sabbath. The kindest thing you can hope for Konstanze is that she died believing—that in the fire she felt the embrace of her true lord and lover.

"I shouldn't have said that," I added, clutching at Tony. "I keep hearing things out there in the dark, rustling the bushes. Let's go in."

"But wait," said Blankenhagen methodically. "We have not finished our deductions. You have solved a mystery which no one so much as suspected for hundreds of years; but you have not yet solved the mystery that brought you here. This story is fascinating, but I fail to see its usefulness."

I wished he hadn't raised the point. Because, of course, our chemical experiment had not only solved a crime, it had solved the secondary mystery too. Now I knew what had happened to the shrine. There was only one place where it could be. And Tony, whose mind works the way mine does, saw the truth at once.

"I'll be damned," he exclaimed, bounding to his feet.

He almost was. Something streaked past his arm, chunked into the tree behind him, and hung there quivering.

I snatched at it—Count Burckhardt's dagger, which I had last seen lying among the dried ribs of the steward.

Tony was staring incredulously at his left arm.

His shirt was slit as neatly as if by scissors, and a thin dark trickle darkened the white cloth.

"That son of a gun tried to kill me!"

"What an ungrateful ghost," I said. "Here we are trying to clear Burckhardt's name, and he throws knives at us. He's a practical ghost, though. He must have sharpened this thing recently."

"Burckhardt, hell. Stop trying to distract me with spooks, Vicky, I'm already way ahead of you. Blankenhagen was in the crypt alone with the bones and the dagger for a good ten minutes. Hey—"

Blankenhagen was already gone, presumably in pursuit of the knife thrower. With a few well-chosen words, Tony took off after him.

I followed. I wasn't anxious to stay in that haunted garden alone. As I ran, I wasn't sure whom Tony was chasing; he surely didn't think the doctor could throw a knife like a boomerang. Too many people had had access to the steward's belongings—including the cloaked grave robber.

I reached the Hall in time to see Tony disappearing through the door which led to the cellars. When I got to the bottom of the stairs, I was relieved to see that Tony had had sense enough to bring a flashlight. By its glow I found the two men in the kitchen. Tony had apparently decided to keep his suspicions of the doctor to himself. The conference sounded reasonably amicable.

"I lost him when he descended here," said Blankenhagen. "Where do these doors go? I do not know this place."

"That's a dead end." Tony indicated the passage

leading to the dungeons. "I assume our quarry knows that; he knows this place too damned well. He must have gone the other way."

The trail was easy to follow—too easy, though this didn't occur to us till it was too late. One of the storeroom doors swung invitingly open. The room was empty. The only break in the walls was a ventilation slit too narrow to permit egress of a lizard, much less a man.

Tony swept the floor with his flashlight. One of the paving stones was out of line by a full inch.

Tony handed me the flashlight. Dropping to his knees, he tried to get the fingers of his right hand into the crack between the stones. Meanwhile, Blankenhagen picked up the crowbar which was lying conveniently in a corner and inserted its edge into the crack. He grunted as he put his weight behind the tool; and the stone flew up with a jaunty swing that threw Blankenhagen over on his back and almost decapitated Tony.

Balanced," said Tony, feeling his chin as if surprised to find it still there.

"Wait," said Blankenhagen, getting to his feet as Tony prepared to lower himself into the hole. "Should we not go for help?"

"And let this guy get away?" Tony was getting suspicious again. "You go first, Doc."

Blankenhagen shrugged, but complied. There was a streak of romanticism under that stolid exterior of his; by now he was as reluctant to abandon the chase as Tony was.

Tony lay flat, shining his light down into the hole.

"Vorsicht!" The doctor's voice came hollowly up. "Careful when you descend. The stairs are of wood, and shaky."

Tony turned around and prepared to follow. He glanced up at me. I could see his face; it wore a broad grin.

"Go call the cops, Vicky," he said, and started down.

From where I stand now—and even from where I was to be standing an hour later—I can see that this might have been the smartest thing to do. But at the time I had a number of objections to the idea. I was pretty sure of Blankenhagen, but I wasn't ready to risk Tony's neck on anything less than a hundred-percent certainty. If I left the two of them alone down there . . .

Also, Tony had the light. I was still thinking in percentages, and there was a fifty-fifty chance that the clearly defined trail was a decoy. I had no desire to meet the knifethrower in the dark cellar as I groped my way toward my room. I squatted by the opening, trying to make up my mind what to do.

I didn't have to make the choice. Matters were taken out of my hands.

Blankenhagen had reached the bottom of the shaft. I could hear him cautioning Tony, who was partway down. Tony had the light directed downward so he could pick his footing on the rickety stairs. It was very dark up there where I was. It got even darker. Somebody dropped a sack over my head, picked me up and—while I was still stiff with surprise—dropped me down the shaft feet first like a clothespin into a bottle.

I fell on Tony and swept him neatly off the staircase, which promptly collapsed. Blankenhagen, down below, had no chance to move. We both landed on him, as did the splintered pieces of the staircase. Oddly enough, I remember the noise as being the most hellish thing of all. In that narrow space the echoes of crashes and screams and yells and thuds were magnified into a roaring chaos.

Being on top, I came out best. I didn't even lose consciousness. I had my lumps; a strategic section of my anatomy had bounced off the wall as I fell, and my whole lower surface was full of splinters. But compared to the two men I was in good shape.

They were both out cold. I discovered that by feel; for all practical purposes I was blind. Tony's flashlight had gone with him. There was no light from up above. Nor was there any flow of air.

That realization stopped my humanitarian activities for a second or two. I should have suspected it; if someone had put me down the shaft it was because he wanted me there, and naturally he would make sure I stayed there. The stone up above had been closed and, no doubt, secured in some fashion.

I went back to my fumbling. There were arms and legs all over the place, and at first I couldn't figure out which belonged to whom. Then I found Tony's face, which my hands know as well as my eyes. He mumbled something when I touched his cheek. I was so relieved I might have cried, if I'd had the time. Instead I located his pockets and found what I was hoping to find—two packets of matches.

I lit one of the matches. While it burned I made a quick examination.

Tony was semiconscious and cursing. That was good. Blankenhagen, on whose chest Tony's head was pillowed, had a broken arm. It wasn't hard to diagnose, since I could see the bone sticking out. Both men were dirty and torn and bloody.

The match burned my fingers. I blew it out and went on examining in the dark. Blankenhagen's face was a bloody mess, but after running my fingers over his head I decided his skull had not been fractured.

At that point Tony woke up completely, and we had a rather emotional session for a minute or two. I lit another match, then, while Tony confirmed my diagnosis of the doctor's injuries.

"I don't dare move him," he said, as the match flickered out. "Something else could be broken."

"See if we can wake him up. Maybe he can diagnose himself."

We worked over the unconscious man until I started to get scared. Finally he stirred.

"Don't move yet, Blankenhagen," Tony ordered. "You've got a broken arm and God knows what else. Can you hear me?"

"Yes. . . . What has happened?"

"The stairs gave way," I said. "And the trapdoor above is closed."

The silence that followed this cheering summary was so prolonged that I began to think I had overestimated Blankenhagen's stamina and shocked him back into unconsciousness. Finally he said, in a gloomy voice,

"You are here too? I wish you were not."

"So do I."

"I will see what is wrong with me," said Blankenhagen.

"I'm glad somebody around here is a doctor," said Tony.

I offered to light a match, but Blankenhagen refused. Maybe he didn't want to see the damage. I didn't enjoy the following minutes; I could tell by Blankenhagen's grunts and gasps whenever he found a new bruise.

"Nothing has been broken," he announced, "except the arm. You cannot go for help?"

"I don't know," Tony said. "We haven't explored yet. But I have a feeling the guy who tricked us in here isn't going to leave an exit open."

"Perhaps you would care to look?" Blankenhagen suggested. I didn't blame him for sounding sarcastic.

"Okay," said Tony meekly. He stood up; and then sat down again, clutching his head.

"I am sorry," said Blankenhagen, feeling his weight descend. "I did not think . . . You are injured. If you will come here, I will try—"

"Oh, don't be so damned noble," said Tony grumpily. "I'm all right. I just had a thought. Maybe some of this wood might make a torch. We'd have an easier time with a little light."

"Without oil or petrol," Blankenhagen began.

I interrupted him with a hoot of triumph.

"I have some oil. I got it so I could oil the locks."

I fished the almost forgotten can out of my coat pocket and gave it to Tony. He wasted several matches experimenting, but finally a chunk of wood consented to burn.

We looked first at the shaft. One look was enough.

A few stairs remained, at the very top. The lowest tread was five feet above my upstretched fingertips.

Tony turned the light into the passage that led out of the shaft. It was faced with stones cemented together. We could see only a few feet of its length; it turned a corner not far from us.

Tony started down the passage, but he had taken only a couple of steps when he swayed dizzily and fell back against the wall. I grabbed the torch from his hand.

"Sit down till you get your strength back," I said. "I'll have a look."

He didn't argue. He looked sick.

The roof of the passage was so low that I had to stoop. I went on around the corner, but I didn't go far. Just behind the bend, the passage ended. It was not the original end. A mass of loose stones and dirt had spilled down from the roof, filling the tunnel from top to bottom. To me, it looked like a very recent cave-in.

ELEVEN

❀▱▱❀▱▱❀

I HAD NOT EXPECTED TO FIND AN OPEN DOOR WITH an EXIT sign beside it; but I hadn't anticipated anything quite as bad as this. My hands were shaking as I wedged my torch into a crack in the wall and started digging. It didn't take long to verify my pessimistic suspicions. The dirt and rubble continued for some distance. For all I knew, the rest of the tunnel might be filled. And I was here, in a neat airless trap, with two injured men.

I gave vent to my emotions briefly, but I did it without noise. Then I wiped my face on the sleeve of my coat and went back to the wounded.

Tony, squatting with his back up against the tunnel wall, looked a little better. I had put on a cheery smile, but it didn't deceive him.

"No way out?"

"It doesn't look good." I handed him the torch and knelt down by Blankenhagen, whose eyes were closed. "Doctor. If you can tell me what to do as I go along, I'll try to fix your arm."

"I will tell you first," said Blankenhagen, without opening his eyes. "I am about to lose consciousness."

And he did, too, as soon as I put my clumsy paws on his arm. Tony offered to take over, but I clamped my lower lip between my teeth and elbowed him away. Like mine, his knowledge was purely theoretical, derived from far-off memories of Scout manuals and Red Cross training. I did the job, with strips torn from my blouse and pieces of wood from the stairs; but I was covered with perspiration by the time I was through.

After a while, Blankenhagen opened one eye.

"Finished?" he inquired warily.

"Finished is right." I was sitting on the floor next to Tony.

"Then speak," ordered Blankenhagen, prone but positive. "What is our position?"

I told them. Neither of them liked it very much.

"Seems to me," I concluded, "that our best bet is to try to dig through the earth fall. Even if I could climb the shaft—which I can't—we can be sure that trapdoor is closed for good. The stone is a foot thick, and it's down in the cellars, where no one ever comes. But if the dirt is just a localized fall, we can dig through it. Maybe."

"I can climb the shaft," said Tony, squinting up at it. "It's a simple chimney job. But I agree with your other conclusions. I could hang up there yelling till I sprouted mushrooms before anyone would hear me."

"I didn't know you could climb," I said, distracted.

"I have many talents you don't know about." Tony tried to leer, but didn't do a very good job of it. "How far underground do you suppose we are?"

"You mean we might try to dig out through the ceiling of the tunnel? We must be twenty or thirty feet down; the land rises behind the *Schloss*. What would we do with the dirt? There's enough of it out there in the tunnel right now."

"But," said Blankenhagen, "if you dig through, and find the exit at the other end is also blocked?"

"Let's not cross bridges till we come to them," I said. "However, I don't think our friend would have created a landslide if the exit at the other end were easy to close."

"It was deliberate, you believe?"

"The dirt hasn't been there long. And the rest of this is deliberate. I can assure you I didn't dive feet first down that shaft on purpose. I'll bet the stairs were partially sawed through, too."

"Someone flung you down?" exclaimed Blankenhagen, as if the idea had just occurred to him. "You saw who it was?"

"I saw nothing. I still don't know who has been behind all the skulduggery. I suspect two people—"

"One of whom," said Tony, "could be you, Blankenhagen."

Blankenhagen surveyed his battered form in meaningful silence. Tony shook his head.

"That part could have been an accident—the stairs, I mean. You could have rapped me on the head and left me here if the stairs hadn't collapsed."

"That's silly," I said impatiently. "My money is still on the countess and Miss Burton. Good Lord, they are the only two left. And this argument isn't getting us out of here."

"And," said Blankenhagen, "we may not have so much time."

He didn't have that much time. My surgery had been crude, and we had no antiseptic. A couple of days down here in his condition and he wouldn't care about getting out. But that was not what he meant. The air in the tunnel had always been close and dry. Now, it seemed to me, it was already perceptibly warmer.

With Tony's help, Blankenhagen managed to drag himself along the tunnel to where the dirt blocked the way, but when he tried to dig he collapsed.

"I told you so," I said, helping Tony drag him out of the way. "I'll start digging. I am, if you will pardon the expression, in better shape than either of you. And put out that torch, it's just using air. This is going to be mostly by touch anyhow."

Then began a period of time which is the worst memory of a not wholly pleasant summer. I started with great energy, sending out a spray of dirt like a burrowing puppy. Despite my boast I wasn't feeling all that hot; I hadn't had any sleep and my bruises ached. But there is no incentive quite as persuasive as the fear of dying of asphyxiation.

It was slow, heartbreaking work. The dirt slid down from above almost as fast as I dug it out. Finally I went back and got some boards from the fallen staircase to shore up my miniature tunnel. It helped some.

When Tony tugged at my ankles, I let him pull me out and take my place. Utterly exhausted, I curled up on the stone floor and, incredibly, fell asleep.

I slept uneasily, dreaming there was a steel band around my chest. I awoke with a gasp to find Tony shaking me.

"The air is pretty bad, Vicky. We've got to get through soon, or we'll never make it. If you clear away the dirt I push out . . ."

"Blankenhagen?" I croaked, rubbing eyes that felt as if they were glued shut.

"He's still breathing, but he won't be for long. If we don't get out of here soon, none of us will be."

I insisted on taking his place in the hole. The air was foul in that narrow space, even worse than it was in the tunnel, and he had been breathing it for some time.

I felt as if I were working under water. Each movement had the languid deliberation of a swimmer's armstroke. I could see nothing. Eyes can adjust to a tiny amount of light, but there was no light at all in that stinking hole. My senses were foggy; I couldn't hear anything except the echo of my own hoarse breathing. After a time the only sense remaining to me was that of touch, the only reality the gritty yielding substance under my bleeding fingers. Occasionally I backed out of the hole to breathe the slightly less noxious mixture that passed for air out in the tunnel. I found Tony flat on the floor the second time I did this, and dragged him out of the way so the dirt wouldn't cover his face. Then I crawled back in, and worked till I started to see flames dance against the darkness.

Finally I waited too long. When I tried to back out, I couldn't move.

My hands went to my throat, as if to tear away the thing that was blocking my lungs. No use ... Blankenhagen and Tony were dying, maybe dead. And I was dying too. I would fall down in this awful dirty hole and never wake up. It was almost a relief to feel the pain of my laboring lungs fade as I fell forward into blackness no more absolute than that which already surrounded me.

When I came to, I was breathing. The shock of this discovery woke me completely.

I had been on the verge of breaking through the earth fall when my last convulsion threw me against the thin shell of soil remaining. I was lying with my head and shoulders on a downhill slope of dirt. The rest of my body was still in the hole. By a miracle, it hadn't caved in.

I went back through my little tunnel as fast as I dared. Tony was already stirring as the fresh air from beyond reached him. Ruthlessly I slapped him awake. We didn't waste time feeling Blankenhagen's pulse or handling him gently. I backed through the tunnel dragging him by the shoulder, with Tony pushing from the other end. Tony barely made it. The ceiling began to subside as his head came out of the hole, and he had to pull his legs through solid dirt.

The first thing I did was light a match. The feeble flame was a beautiful sight. I've had a slight phobia about darkness ever since that night.

To our surprise and relief, Blankenhagen was still breathing. That was all we bothered to find out. Tony was on his feet, swaying dizzily, but driven; I followed, lighting matches with reckless abandon.

The tunnel went straight on without bending. It ended in a flight of wooden stairs.

I let Tony go up. The stairs looked solid, but there was no point in risking a double weight. If only the stone I could see at the top was movable. . . .

When Tony came down, his face was gray. He didn't need to speak. He just shook his head.

The match went out. Holding hands, we stumbled back to where we had left Blankenhagen. He had not moved. We curled up, one on either side of him. Tony was mumbling about shock, and keeping the patient warm, and it all made very good sense to me at the time, but I didn't really care. All I wanted to do was rest.

When I finally awoke I knew I had slept for hours. All my bruises had solidified, and I was as stiff as Blankenhagen's splinted arm. Otherwise I didn't feel too bad. The first thing I did was take a deep breath. The air was still fresh. No problem there.

With that vital matter settled, I started to take stock. I could hear Tony snoring; it was loud enough to wake the dead. So I knew he was okay. Blankenhagen . . .

At least he was warm. I was in a good position to know. Somehow his one usable arm had gotten around me and my head was on his shoulder. His heart sounded a little fast.

I extricated myself, sat up, and lit a match. Blankenhagen's eyes were open.

The shreds of my blouse were wrapped around his left arm. I wasn't embarrassed. I wear less on the beach, and anyhow I was covered by a coating of dirt.

"Sorry for leaning on you," I said. "Did I hurt you?"

"Hurt me? You have saved my life—you and he." But he didn't look at Tony. "You are an amazing woman."

"And you," I said, returning his *du*, "are quite a guy. How do you feel?"

"Quite well." He smiled at me.

It was a silly question, and a ridiculous answer. He felt terrible. His face was flushed and his eyes had the glassy glitter of fever. The hand that reached for mine was dry and hot. But the smile was as attractive as ever. One thing you had to say about Blankenhagen: his emotions were wholehearted and consistent. When he disapproved of something, the very air turned icy. When he approved . . . Clearly he now approved of me. All of me.

The match went out. I felt sort of silly sitting there in the dark, so when he pulled at my hand, I lay down.

I'm not sure what would have happened next if Tony hadn't waked up.

Every time I heard him go through this process I decided that, if I was ever weak-minded enough to marry the guy, I would insist on separate bedrooms. He snorted, choked, gargled, and flailed around. By the time he was fully awake, Blankenhagen was clucking with alarm and I was sitting detached, wrapped in my dirt and my dignity.

Since we were undistracted by details such as breakfast and baths, we got right to work. I don't suppose Tony's hopes were any higher than mine; but we had been too tired to examine the exit closely, and after all—what else could we do but try? Sitting in peaceful silence waiting to die of starvation wasn't in keeping with any of our characters.

Blankenhagen could walk, but not much. Tony towed him to the foot of the stairs and propped him up, remarking,

"Sit and watch. Criticize, complain, cheer politely now and then to encourage us—"

"And think," I interrupted. "We could use a few ideas."

Tony went up the stairs. The first time he had banged and shoved and given up. This time he just looked. We were running low on matches, so he used pages from his notebook, twisted into tight little spills. Then he came down.

"There's a chance," he said. He was trying to sound matter-of-fact, but his voice shook slightly.

"You can lift the stone?"

"No." Tony dropped to the floor and took out his cigarettes. Those nice cancer-producing cigarettes . . . Without that vicious habit we wouldn't have had any matches. "No, there's something barring the trapdoor—metal, by the feel of it. I jabbed it with my pocketknife. But I've had an inspiration. Look at the way this place is built. We're sitting at the bottom of a narrow shaft. This tunnel, and the shaft, are faced with stones bonded with mortar. They're old. The mortar is crumbling."

He dug at a section with his knife blade and dislodged an impressive chunk of plaster.

"Gently," muttered Blankenhagen. "One landslide is enough."

"Okay, Okay. Now the stone that blocks the shaft is a monolith, must weigh hundreds of pounds, like the stones used to build the *Wachtturm*. I figure that's where we are—under the floor of the keep. The stones here in the shaft are much smaller. Behind them is—plain dirt. If I can remove part of the wall of the shaft, and dig out enough dirt to expose the floor slab next to the trapdoor, I can remove it. Either it will push up, or I can chisel out the mortar and let it drop down."

"Can't you let the trap drop down?" I asked.

"Stupid question. Trapdoors are designed not to drop down. This one is held up by a rim of stone and some solid metal hinges. We'd have seen it the other day, Vicky, if the floor of the keep weren't so overgrown. No, the side stone is the only chance."

The old mortar crumbled under Tony's vigorous knife. When the first wall stone came out, it was followed by a shower of dirt that got into our eyes and made me wonder whether he was about to start another avalanche. It trickled out, however, and he went on working. When four stones had been removed, there was enough space to allow a man's body to pass. Tony began to shovel out the dirt. He remarked,

"I have a feeling I'm never going to want a garden."

I didn't answer. My eyes were glued on that gap on the wall, which I was illuminating by means of another homemade torch. By this time we could see the end of the floor slab, and there was a considerable pile of dirt on the stairs.

In less than an hour Tony had cleared the lower surface of the stone. He began to chip out the mortar. This was the trickiest part of the job; we ended up replacing some of the dirt Tony had laboriously removed, in order to support one end of the slab so it wouldn't give way all at once and mash Tony. After a couple of heart-stopping scrapes, he finally managed to do what he had set out to do. There was an opening a couple of feet square in the wall of the shaft.

Tony turned.

"I think we can make it now."

But for several seconds none of us moved. We stared at one another with the white-faced incredulity of shipwrecked sailors who finally see a sail on the horizon.

"Better let me go first," I said. "I'm the thinnest."

At the expense of a few square inches of skin, I got through. A push from Tony and I was out, gooseflesh popping out on my bare arms as the heavenly coolness of the night air hit them. My coat was still down below, and so far as I was concerned, it could stay there. Nothing, not even the shrine, could have gotten me back into that hole.

At first I just lay there on the floor and admired the view through the open door. As Tony had predicted, I was on the ground floor of the keep, and the moonlight scene without was exquisite. A desert would have looked good to me just then if it had a sky over it.

The sight of the silvery moonlight reminded me of a minor discomfort that had been overridden by more pressing worries. Suddenly I was dying of thirst. Leaning over the hole I croaked out, "Put out the torch and come on."

Getting Blankenhagen out wasn't easy. Only fortitude and hope had kept him conscious; he was a dead weight, and even with Tony pushing from below and me pulling from above we had a hard time. When we finally extracted him, he collapsed at full length on the floor and lay there without moving.

Tony followed, breathing hard and looking as if he were going to be sick. We were both flat on the floor, just breathing, when the beautiful silver moonlight was blotted out by a shape in the doorway.

The figure crossed the room without a glance at the shadows where we were sprawled, and disappeared.

I applied grubby knuckles to my eyes. I knew the stairs leading up to the next floor had provided the means of exit for that incredible apparition, but I couldn't believe I had really seen it—a tall figure, cloaked and hooded, wearing boots that rang metallically on the stone floor—and carrying in its arms the white-robed figure of a woman.

Tony stared speechlessly. Blankenhagen sat up. He had no voice left; but the air came out of his lungs in an explosive whisper that broke my paralysis like a dash of cold water.

"Irma!"

TWELVE

I HAD NOT RECOGNIZED IRMA. I WOULDN'T HAVE known my own mother under those confusing conditions (especially my mother, under those conditions). But I was willing to take Blankenhagen's word for it. I couldn't figure out what Irma was doing there, but I decided maybe I had better go up and find out.

Tony beat me to the stairs. Blankenhagen was behind me, but not for long; I heard him stumble and fall after a few steps.

We kept going up—all the way up. I don't know what I expected to find up there. I wasn't thinking coherently. But I felt a mild shock when I came out of the opening onto the roofless top story, and saw what was happening.

The character in the cloak stood at the edge of the platform, with not even a ridge of stone between him and the ground some sixty feet below. Irma lay at his feet. She was drugged or unconscious—probably the former, because her face was quite peaceful and she was breathing heavily through her nose. If the poignancy of the moment had not raised my mind above ordinary cattiness, I would have said she was snoring.

The man who had brought her there was wearing riding breeches and boots. The hood of his dark-gray loden cloak was thrown back, so that his fiery head gleamed in the moonlight. His gun gleamed too. It was big and shiny and it was pointed straight at Tony's stomach.

"So it was you," I said unoriginally.

"In part. No, Tony, don't try anything. A bullet hole in you wouldn't spoil my plans at all. As soon as I'm finished here, you two go back where you came from. Where's Blankenhagen?"

Tony sat down, yawning. I couldn't help admiring his nonchalance. He didn't even look surprised. . . .

"You knew," I said to him. "You knew it was George."

"I knew George was one of the villains. Unfortunately, he isn't the only one." Tony looked at the villain. "Blankenhagen? He's down there someplace. Broke his arm when the staircase gave way."

"I admire your tenacity," George said, baring his teeth in one of those toothpaste-ad grins. "I didn't think you could get out."

"I'm a little tired," Tony admitted. He yawned again. "Can I sit over there, against the parapet, without your shooting me?"

"Just don't stand up."

Tony obeyed literally; and George raised his eyebrows politely at me. I shook my head. I didn't want to sit down. I had a feeling I would be lying down only too soon, and permanently.

"Found the shrine yet?" Tony asked.

"Oh, yes. I followed you last night and overheard Vicky telling Konstanze's life story. It wasn't hard to figure out what it meant, so far as the hiding place of the shrine was concerned. I had prepared the tunnel with no specific plan in mind—an emergency reserve, you might say—but I had to get you down there right away, before you could use your information. I had plenty of time after that to search."

"I hope you haven't told anyone else where it is," Tony said.

I wished George would stop grinning. He looked like an Aztec death mask—the kind that is half teeth.

"I'm not such a fool as that."

Tony wasn't as calm as he seemed. I could see the tension of bunched-up muscles in his legs and shoulders. I kept very still and watched him. He was leading up to something and I wanted to be ready to back him up, whatever he did.

"I don't know, Nolan," he said. "I find your position somewhat shaky. What are you going to do with Irma?"

"Somnambulists are accident-prone, old son. They even have fatal accidents."

"And you can always go down after you throw her off and make sure."

"What's one more?" said George.

It took me a couple of seconds to understand what he meant.

"Now, wait," I said energetically. "Let's not be hasty. You haven't killed anybody yet. We can't even accuse you of attempted murder; shutting us up in that hole was just a boyish prank, right? Why kill anybody? Just take the shrine and split. We haven't any proof."

"Wouldn't work," said George promptly. He waved the gun at Tony, who tried not to cringe. "He's been too nosy. Sending cables all over the place."

"You've been reading my mail!" Tony said angrily.

"Only the cables that arrived today. You know too much about the state of my finances, brother. And you were too inquisitive about Herr Schmidt."

"You crook," I said to Tony. "Were those the cables you sent that day it rained? How did you know where to inquire about Schmidt? Why didn't you tell me?"

"You have a lot of nerve talking about cheating," Tony shouted. "Squatting like a setting hen on all those little tidbits you dug up—"

"Sssh!" George danced irritably up and down. "Somebody will hear you!"

I expected Tony to jump him then; I braced myself, ready to move. There was a nasty cold lump at the pit of my stomach. I had never seen a gun from quite that angle. It is a disconcerting sight, and I had no desire to see it any closer. But we had to do something; I didn't intend to let myself be herded back into that hellish tunnel without putting up a fight. We would be in a better position to attack if we waited till George had us on the stairs. But we couldn't wait. He was going to kill Irma first.

Tony settled back.

"Does Schmidt really have a degree from Leipzig?"

he inquired conversationally. "I haven't had a chance to read my mail, you know."

George laughed.

"I think you'll be surprised when you find out who Schmidt is. He was using his own name. Not his fault if it's a common name."

"One thing I already know," said Tony. "He was the one who engineered the armor and the séance. What is he, an amateur hypnotist, or just a common garden-variety fortune teller?"

"Both. He hypnotized Irma with some crazy idea that she might have ancestral memories he could tap. Until the great séance he didn't realize that what he was doing could hurt the wench."

The gun barrel dropped, casually, to indicate the girl's motionless form, and my heart skipped a beat.

"Why don't you shoot her, if that's what you're going to do?" Tony said, between his teeth. "Get it over with."

"No bullet holes in Irma. That would spoil the illusion."

Tony was rapidly losing his calm. He glanced at me. Then, following his eyes, I finally realized what he was up to. He was trying not to look at the square opening of the stairwell, which was now, thanks to his maneuver, out of George's direct line of vision. I didn't share his optimism. Blankenhagen might come, but I doubted it. The man wasn't superhuman.

"So Schmidt hypnotized Irma," I said. "He was the one who prompted her with all that stuff about fires and possession."

"He had help. The old lady has been working on the kid for years."

"She would," Tony muttered. "Just for fun."

"It came in handy, after Schmidt appeared at the *Schloss* with his questions about the shrine. He didn't realize Irma was the heiress. He went straight to Elfrida and they started searching. He was no match for the old witch; he did just what she told him to."

"How did he find out about the shrine?" I asked curiously.

"He read the same book you all found, and reached the same conclusion. When you arrived he got panicky. He wanted the shrine and he was afraid you'd beat him to it. I met him prowling the corridors one night and persuaded him to join forces with me to discourage you. But he didn't realize how far I was prepared to go. The night we staged the armor episode, I had to use the dagger myself, after I tapped Tony on the head. The sight of blood sent the old fool into a tailspin. I had to keep him from yelling, and in the struggle he passed out. I thought I was going to have an attack myself before I got him out of that armor and into his room, so I could rush down to take my part in the drama."

"And the second attack? Staring eyes, look of horror?"

"Baffling, wasn't it?" George grinned. "I only meant to scare him. He was threatening to confess all."

"Then the *Gräfin* is in with you," I said.

"It's not fair," Tony said wildly. "Everybody's guilty. There's only supposed to be one criminal. What about Miss Burton?"

"She is innocent, if that consoles you any. Arrogant, stupid, and innocent."

"Nolan, don't you see you're being used?" Tony demanded. "That old bitch is in the clear. She'll end up with the shrine, after you've killed Irma, and you'll end up in the chair, or whatever they use in this country. You're a stooge, buddy; a lousy cat's-paw."

For the first—and last—time in his life, he hit George where it hurt. The big white grin disappeared. George took a step forward, almost stumbling over Irma, and Tony braced himself. I got ready to jump. Then I saw two things.

One was a hand, whose whitened fingers were curled gruesomely over the edge of the topmost step. The other was Irma's eyes—wide open.

"No," I said hysterically. "No, don't! Don't kill us!" I threw myself onto my knees, yelped as the gritty stone bit into my lacerated skin, and wriggled gracefully forward until my body was between George and the stairwell.

It was no use. George's gun stayed smack on Tony's liver, and Blankenhagen followed his hand out onto the roof.

He looked like death walking—tattered, bloody, smeared with dust and cobwebs. He was an automaton, moving by pure will. It was so awful it was fascinating; I half expected to see him walk stiff-legged into a hail of bullets, like the monster out of Frankenstein.

Everybody has his limits, though, and Blankenhagen reached his. He fell to his knees, his eyes crossed and his mouth half open.

"What do I have to do, use a meat cleaver?" George demanded irritably. "All right; you'll be out of your misery in just a few seconds."

I didn't see exactly what happened. My eyes, like those of the others, were fixed on Blankenhagen. I saw enough, though, to keep my dreams uneasy for some time to come. Suddenly Irma was up on her hands and knees. George's arms were in the air, flailing frantically. I'll never forget the expression on his face. The sudden change from triumph to failure, and his awareness of it, were blended with the most ghastly terror. For a moment he tottered on the edge of oblivion. Then he was gone. His scream came up like a shriek of anguish from some bodiless ghost borne through the air by the scudding clouds. It ended in another sound. Then there was silence.

I looked at Irma. She had risen to one knee. Her arm was lifted in the gesture that had just sent a man to a messy death. Her black hair was whipped about her face by the wind, and her eyes were enormous.

"Well," said Tony weakly, "well, well, well . . ."

He might have gone on like that indefinitely if Irma had not interrupted.

"He would have killed you," she cried, gesturing from Tony to the prostrate form of the doctor. "Should I lie still and see him kill you?"

She didn't mention me. I was in no position to complain; I don't mind having my life saved as an afterthought.

I cleared my throat. Nobody looked at me. Irma had decided the doctor was the more pathetic of her two heroes, and had taken his bloody head onto her lap. She was crooning over him, and I thought I detected a slight smirk on his face. One of his eyes was open; when he saw me staring, it quickly closed. Tony was trying to look pitiful too, but he couldn't match Blankenhagen's performance.

"Somebody should go for help," I said. "Hey, Tony—"

"*Aber nicht!*" Irma gave me a cold look. "He cannot go, he is bleeding, in pain—near death, in saving our lives. Run! Go at once!"

"Run?" I said. "Me?"

Tony moaned and let his head fall back against the parapet.

"You creep," I said to him. I looked at Blankenhagen. "The same to you," I said. With great dignity I crawled to the stairs and started down them.

I covered about half the distance to the *Schloss* before my legs gave out. Shivering with shock and reaction, I squatted in a patch of nettles and let my mind wander.

The outlines of the castle wall wavered like fog in front of my half-closed eyes. I was sick. I was thirsty. I was all covered with dirt, and nobody loved me.

After a while my head cleared a little, and I tried to think. Maybe I should go directly to the police. The idea made me giggle wildly. They would take one look at me and send for a doctor. Meanwhile the *Gräfin* would be on the loose. What if she took a notion to go out and see how George was coming along with his murder? Tony's groans weren't altogether phony, he wasn't in shape to fight anybody, and the *Gräfin* had always scared the hell out of him. She wouldn't have to shoot him; she would just stare at him. He would shrivel up and blow away. So would I, if I ran into the old lady now. She could demolish me with a breath.

"What I need," I said aloud, "is an army. Right now."

Then I remembered a fact out of a past that seemed years away. I hauled myself to my feet and headed for the front door of the castle.

My entrance was public, and as spectacular as any ham actress could have prayed for. In the hall I met one of the blond waitresses on her way to the lounge with a big tray of steins. I grimaced into her horrified face and went on my way, hearing the crash of glassware behind me. In the lounge was the group I had hoped to see—the university kids, brimming over with beer and song and youthful *joie de vivre*. I was incapable of counting them, but the general effect was just what I wanted.

"*Guten Abend*," I said politely; and saw four . . . eight . . . sixteen—good heavens, how many were there?—all those eyes focus in glazed stares. I'm sure they expected me to bend over and extract a knife from my stocking. Only I wasn't wearing stockings.

"There has been an accident," I said, in my best German. "We must have the police. And a doctor. And on the top of the keep, behind this place, you will find several people who need to be transported to the *Schloss*. And—could I have a drink?"

I fell flat on my face, but they wouldn't let me pass out; dozens of enthusiastic arms bore me to a couch and another arm poured the dregs of a glass of beer down my throat. I lapped it up like a dog, and somebody brought a full glass, and somebody else held my head . . . I have some unpleasant memories about my sojourn at the *Schloss*, but the heavenly coldness of that beer trickling down my dusty gullet compensated for all of them.

I shouldn't have had it, though; on an empty stomach it was almost disastrous. After a while I found myself lying flat on the couch with my head floating up somewhere near the ceiling and a handsome tanned boy bending over me with a glass of brandy.

"Oy," I said, pushing it away. "That I don't need. Will you please—"

"I am a student of medicine," said the boy grandly. "Rest quietly, *Fräulein*, all has been done as you directed. But what in God's name has happened?"

"Look at my face," I said hysterically. "I know I'm drunk, but I can't help looking like this, I didn't do it on purpose; and I don't know why all you men can't stop looking at my—"

He had been patting me—absentmindedly, I'm sure. He got quite red and leaped to his feet.

"I apologize! No disrespect was intended—"

"I know," I said sadly.

I had not forgotten the *Gräfin*, but I was no longer worried about her; with all those husky witnesses running around, it was unlikely that she could do any more damage. She must have heard all the activity and come down to see what was going on. When I saw her standing in the doorway, I struggled to a sitting position.

She dismissed the student with an autocratic wave of her hand. Her faint smile, as she studied my unkempt person, told me more clearly than any mirror how terrible I must look. It stung me into relative coherence.

"Grin all you want," I said. "You still lose. All is known."

Her smile didn't change.

"Poor girl, you are delirious after all you have suffered. But if you will insist on prying into places where you have no right to be—"

"It won't work," I said. "George is dead."

That did it. Her smile vanished.

"I'm going to let you go," I said. "I hate to do it, but without George I'm not sure how much we can prove. In your position, though, I wouldn't risk it."

"You would turn an old woman from her home?"

"You can go live with Miss Burton. I'll bet she's loaded; you wouldn't cultivate her for her gracious personality. And you probably have plenty stashed away. You've been milking this place of its salable antiques for years."

She stood there looking at me with the Medusa stare that had paralyzed so many luckless victims. It didn't affect me. She had no power, except over weak minds like Irma's and Miss Burton's.

"The police will be here any minute," I said.

She left.

The local constabulary of Rothenburg, accustomed to drunken brawls and traffic jams, were out of their depth at the *Schloss*. The case was closed. There was nothing for them to do but gather up the wounded. However, they were understandably confounded by the train of events. Finally one of them settled the matter.

"Mad," he said, tapping his forehead. "The man was mad, no doubt."

Everyone agreed. Then, at long last, they led me to my room, and with a groan of voluptuous satisfaction I fell full length on the bed, dirty and half naked as I was, and let my poor old eyes close.

❂━❂

It was late the following afternoon when we all assembled in my room for the denouement. I had slept till noon. Then I washed. That took quite a while. I spent the rest of the time at the hospital with Schmidt, who was coming along nicely. We had a fascinating talk. I was giddy with the implications when I joined the others.

Tony and Blankenhagen were still acting like wounded heroes. I thought Tony had overdone the bandages just a bit, but the effect was impressive.

Irma looked beautiful. She hadn't dug through forty feet of dirt or fallen down a shaft or crawled through a couple of miles of brambles. She had simply rested peacefully for a few hours. She was safe, rich, beautiful, and surrounded by men who had risked all for her sake—at least that was how she thought of it. No wonder she looked gorgeous. She could even afford to be nice to me. She made me a pretty little speech thanking me for my help.

I looked at my bare arms, which were covered with a network of scratches, and squinted at the tip of my nose, which had a scab on it, and I said dispiritedly, "Oh, no problem. I had a talk with your aunt last night. I was dignified, but convincing."

"You should not have let her escape," said Blankenhagen critically.

"It would be hard to prove her guilty of anything except poisoning Irma's mind. That kind of crime is hard to describe in a court of law."

"It was a nightmare." Irma shivered prettily. "To think that the soul of that dead woman could seize my body . . ."

All of us looked at that astounding portrait.

"Damn it," Tony muttered. "The resemblance is uncanny."

"Not really." I lifted the portrait off the wall. I had had plenty of time to study it, and I wasn't proud of myself for seeing the truth. It should not have taken me so long. "The *Gräfin* didn't miss a trick. See how faded the rest of the picture is, compared to the face? Someone has touched it up."

"You mean—that is not how she looked?" Irma gasped.

"No one will ever know what she looked like." I tossed the portrait carelessly onto the bed. "When your aunt mentioned that she had studied painting . . ." I shrugged. "If you doubt me, have an expert examine this thing. Even I can see that it is modern work."

"It started so long ago," Irma said, pressing her hands to her face in another of those pretty, fragile gestures. "Even before my uncle died, she hated me. Then, later, she started to tell me stories—terrible stories about the crimes of the Drachensteins and the burning of Konstanze. I had not noticed the portrait till she showed it to me; there are so many faded pictures here."

"She had to keep you off balance so she could steal your belongings," Tony said.

"She sold even the locks from the doors. She said there was no money from my uncle, that we had to live."

"Forget it," I said. "Everybody has a few rotten apples on the family tree. We all have the same family tree, if you go back far enough. I have a little surprise for you that should take your mind off your troubles."

"I hope," said Blankenhagen apprehensively, "that you do not want any stones moved?"

"I'm no more anxious to move stones than you are. George has already been here, so it shouldn't be necessary."

❀▱❀

Mortar had been cleared from around four stones that formed a door. It yielded easily to the pressure of my hand, exposing a dark cavity in the wall. The space was almost filled by a big wooden box. Everyone rushed forward to help me get it out onto the table. I brushed off some of the encrusted dirt and broke the corroded hasp with a twist of my hands. The front of the box fell away.

Against a Gothic tracery of carved vines and flowers sat the Virgin, her unbound hair flowing over her blue robe, her hands lightly touching the Child on her knee. Above them, cunningly supported by sections of the vine, hovered two angels, slender youths with austere young faces and lifted golden wings. One of the wings was missing.

The three kings knelt at Mary's feet, and for a disgraceful interlude my eyes forgot the beauty of the carving and lingered greedily on the stones set in the sculptured forms. Balthasar was dressed in crimson; on his head, framed in gold, was an emerald whose depths caught the sunlight and flung it back in a thousand green reflections. Melchoir, behind him, wore a turban set with a great baroque pearl. The third king, balancing the group on the right, lifted his gift in both hands: a golden bowl, holding a globe of scarlet fire.

Irma's eyes were as round as saucers.

"Mine?" she said, in a childish squeak.

"Yep," I said.

She was staring at the stones, not the figures. Her open mouth was pink and pretty and wet and greedy. And then, just as I was enjoying my contempt for her, she did something that cut the ground out from under my feet.

"No, it is yours," she said suddenly. "Three gems, for the three who saved my life. Do they measure any value compared to that?"

"Certainly not," said Blankenhagen; and "My God, no," said Tony.

They could afford to be noble. Whoever married Irma—and I figured they had an equal chance, she was ready to fall into the arms of any man who asked her—got all three stones. I felt old and wise and rather sad. She was corny, but she was a good kid. I think she really meant it—for about a minute and a half.

"Aw," I said, "shucks. Forget it, Irma."

"But I mean it!"

"Sure you do. But we can't accept anything like that."

"But—but what can I do with it?" Irma asked helplessly.

"The National museum, I think," said Blankenhagen. "It is the richest in Germany; it will offer a fair price."

"The Met, or some foreign museum, might offer more," said Tony. Irma looked at him.

"No," said Blankenhagen firmly. Irma looked at him. "It is fitting that such a treasure should remain in Germany."

"Hmmm," I said. "Tell you one thing. If I were you, I'd take those jewels out and sell them separately. Nobody can afford to buy the shrine as it is; and the jewels will attract every crook on two continents. You can substitute paste copies without affecting the beauty of the workmanship; and isn't that the important thing?"

"Are you always right?" asked Blankenhagen, looking at me severely. "You are too clever. That is a very annoying quality. How did you know the shrine was here, in this room?"

"Oh, well," I said modestly, "that was easy. You told Irma about the arsenic, and Burckhardt's murder? But don't you see, that was the clue we were looking for. Many of the details will never be known; but I think I can reconstruct the outlines of the story now.

"Konstanze was young, seventeen or eighteen, when Burckhardt married her and brought her here. Yet even then she must have been deeply involved in the witch cult; they started young, usually at puberty.

It isn't surprising that she should have learned to despise her oafish husband. Maybe she turned to Nicolas because he was available, and corrupted him. Maybe he didn't need corrupting. A man of his ability must have hated the social system that labeled him inferior, and the ignorant clod who exemplified that system.

"Anyhow, I'm sure the two became lovers before the Revolt broke out. Konstanze had been poisoning her husband for some time; it takes several months for arsenic to work its way through the body and show up in the hair and nails. And there were all those references to Burckhardt's queasy stomach, remember?

"Burckhardt's call to arms must have pleased her. She wouldn't have shed any tears if he had been killed in battle. Then the matter of the shrine came up, and that was a real bonus. I can see Konstanze drooling over those jewels and cursing the old count for giving them to the church.

"At first, everything seemed to be working out for the lovers. Burckhardt practically handed the shrine over to them by sending it to Rothenburg in Nicolas' charge. Nicolas murdered or bribed the guards and brought the shrine to the *Schloss* alone. He and Konstanze hid it in the tomb of the old count. Then Konstanze wrote that letter to her husband saying that the expedition had never arrived."

"He kept her letters," Tony muttered. "Carried them around with him, brought them here. . . ."

"He was a stupid sentimentalist," said Blankenhagen, looking contemptuously at Tony. "Stupid not to suspect such a story . . ."

"We didn't suspect it," I said wryly. "And he was deeply in love with her; love has a very dulling effect on the brain. There was no reason why anyone should have been suspicious. Even when we found Nicolas' body, and the wing that had been broken off the shrine, there was no evidence to show that Konstanze knew anything about it.

"After that night, when Nicolas appeared as the Black Man, he went into hiding. He couldn't be seen hanging about; Konstanze meant to kill her husband, if he wan't killed in battle, but until he was dead she couldn't let him get suspicious. And he wasn't the only one who had to be deceived. The bishop was after the shrine and he was giving Konstanze a hard time. I'll bet her reputation was already shaky. The mere fact that she read authors like Albertus Magnus and Trithemius would be enough to start nasty gossip.

"So Burckhardt came home from the wars, hale and hearty, and delighted to see his loving wife. She didn't waste any time. He was taken ill the day after his return.

"On the crucial night, the night of the steward's murder, the conspirators decided to move the shrine. We'll never know why; Burckhardt was dying, so maybe they thought it was safe to proceed with their plans. At any rate, there they were, down in the crypt; I can see Konstanze holding the lamp and Nicolas working on the tombstone. He raised it. The shrine was lifted out, losing a wing in the process. And then . . .

"Then they looked up and saw, in the lamplight, the face of the man they had robbed and cheated and tried to murder. God knows what aroused him, or how he got the strength to come looking for them. But he was there. He must have been there. He saw the lovers, with the shrine between them, and he knew the truth. You can't blame him for turning berserk. The theft of the shrine was bad enough, but the knowledge that his servant and his beloved wife had cuckolded him . . . he went mad. By the time he finished Nicolas, who must have put up a fight, Konstanze was gone—with the shrine. I suppose she had someone with her, a servant maybe, who had helped with the heavy work. She could quietly bump him off at any time with her handy store of arsenic. Nobody asked questions in those days about the death of a serf.

"After stabbing Nicolas and throwing him down at Harald's feet, like a dead dog, Burckhardt piously closed his father's tomb. What I can't get out of my mind is a suspicion that Nicolas wasn't dead when the stone was lowered. If you remember the position of the body . . . Well, enough of that. It certainly wouldn't have worried Burckhardt. Having disposed of one traitor, he went after his wife. He would have killed her too, if it hadn't been for the nurse, who thought he was delirious. She testified to his insane strength and mentioned that his dagger was not at his belt. But Burckhardt was half dead from arsenic poisoning. They wrestled him back into bed, and Konstanze finished him off in the next cup of gruel.

"Maybe he had time, before he died, to whisper an accusation to a servant or priest. Maybe not; she would have watched him closely, and arsenic doesn't leave a man particularly coherent. In any case, the bishop got suspicious. He disliked Konstanze anyhow. So she got her just deserts, by an ironic miscarriage of justice—though I think the punishment was worse than the crime."

"Death by arsenic poisoning is exceedingly painful," said Blankenhagen.

"I know. But the count had helped torture Riemenschneider and had bashed in the skulls of a lot of miserable peasants who were only trying to get their rights . . . I guess they were all rotten."

"So we figured," Tony said sweepingly, "that the shrine had to be in the countess's room. The count had the whole castle at his disposal, but she was limited to her own room."

"We," I said. "Yes."

"One more thing," Tony said, ignoring me. "I don't think anyone else caught this. Remember Irma's cry at the séance—'das Feuer'? That was the result of Schmidt's hypnotic talents and the *Gräfin*'s gruesome stories; but what I didn't think of until later was that Konstanze *didn't know German*. She was a Spaniard, and she and Burckhardt probably communicated by means of the Latin spoken by the noble classes in those days. So if she had given a last frantic scream, as she may well have done, it would have been in Latin or Spanish. In other words—no ghost."

"Obviously," I said.

"Sooo clever," murmured Irma.

"That's about it," I said briskly. "No more questions?"

"Only my heart's gratitude," said Irma mistily.

"Now I go to see that we have a celebration dinner. I cook it with my own hands, and we dine together, yes? And a bottle of *Sekt*."

"*Sekt*," I said glumly. *Sekt* is German champagne. It is terrible stuff.

Irma departed, to cook her way into somebody's heart. I wondered whose heart she was aiming for.

I looked from one man to the other. Neither of them moved.

"Well," I said.

"I want to talk to you," said Tony to me, glaring at Blankenhagen.

"And so do I," said the doctor, staying put.

"Go ahead," I said.

"If we could have some privacy . . ." said Tony, still glaring.

"I do not mind speaking in your presence," said Blankenhagen. "I have nothing to hide."

Tony said several things, all of them rude. Blankenhagen continued to sit.

"Oh, hell," said Tony. "Why should I care? All right, Vicky, the game is over. It wasn't as much fun as we expected, but it had its moments. So—speaking quite impartially, and without bias—who won?"

"Me," I said. "Oh, all right, Tony, I'm kidding. Speaking quite impartially, I'd say we came out about even. It was partly a matter of luck. You would have fingered George sooner or later—if he hadn't fingered us first. I solved the murder of Burckhardt, but primarily because I was the one who found the arsenic. Shall we call it a tie?"

"That's all I ever wanted to prove," said Tony smugly.

"You're a damned liar," I said, stung to the quick. "You were trying to prove your superiority to *me*. And you did not. I didn't need you at all. I could have figured out the whole thing—"

"Oh, you cheating little crook," said Tony. "You said you would marry me if I could prove you weren't my intellectual superior. I proved it. I didn't need you, either. I could have handled this business much better if you hadn't been around getting in my way and falling over your own feet—"

"Liar, liar," I yelled. "I never said any such thing! And even if I did, you haven't—" I stopped. My mouth dropped open. "I thought you wanted to marry Irma," I said in a small voice.

"Irma is a nice girl," said Tony. "And I admit there were moments when the thought of a soft, docile, female-type woman was attractive. But now she's rich. . . . Let Blankenhagen marry Irma."

"No, thank you," said Blankenhagen, who had been an interested spectator. He looked severely at Tony. "You use the wrong tactics, my friend. You do not know this woman. You do not know how to handle any woman. Under her competence, her intelligence, this woman wishes to be mastered. It requires an extraordinary man to do this, I admit. But—"

"Really?" said Tony. "You think if I—"

"Not you," said Blankenhagen. "I. I will marry this woman. She needs me to master her."

"You!" Tony leaped out of his chair. "So help me, if you weren't crippled, I'd—"

"You," said Blankenhagen, sneering, "and who else?"

"You can't marry her." Tony added, unforgivably, "You're shorter than she is."

"What does that matter?"

"Right," I said, interested. "That's irrelevant. I can always go around barefoot."

"Shut up," said Tony to me. To Blankenhagen he said, "She doesn't know you. You could be a crook. You could be a bigamist!"

"But I am not."

"How do I know you're not?"

"My life is open to all." Blankenhagen had kept his composure which put him one up on Tony. Turning a dispassionate eye on me, he remarked, "You are somewhat concerned, after all. Perhaps we should hear your views."

"Thank you," I said. "I don't feel that I ought to interfere . . ."

"Well," Tony said grudgingly. "I guess you are entitled to an opinion."

He was flushed and bright-eyed, and he looked awfully cute with his hair tumbling down over the romantic bandages on his undamaged brow. In the heat of argument, or for other reasons, he had risen to his feet. Blankenhagen cannily remained seated, but he was right about his height. That was unimportant. If it didn't bother him, why should it bother me?

I sighed. Turning to Tony, I said, "Have you had a chance to read the answers to your cables yet?"

"My God, how can you ask at a time like—"

"Do you know who Schmidt really is?"

Tony sat down with a thud.

"You're going to marry Schmidt?"

"Schmidt," I said, "is the top historian at the National museum. I had a long talk with him this afternoon."

"Anton Zachariah Schmidt?" Tony gasped. "That Schmidt?"

"That Schmidt. One of the foremost historians in the world. At the moment he is a sad and sorry Schmidt . . ."

"He should be," said Blankenhagen, unimpressed. "Such disgraceful behavior for a grown man and a scholar."

"He's a nut," I said. "What's wrong with that? Why, the nuts found the New World and discovered the walls of windy Troy! Where would we be without the nuts? Schmidt has dabbled in parlor magic and spiritualism since he was a kid. He's in good company. Businessmen and politicians consult astrologers; many scientists have been suckers for spiritualism. When he got on the trail of the shrine, Schmidt went a little haywire. It was his dream come true—sneaking around the halls of an ancient castle, finding a treasure, and presenting it to his precious museum. When Tony and I arrived, he had horrible visions of rich Americans stealing his prize—it had become 'his' by then."

"Even so," said Blankenhagen coldly. "Even so . . ."

"You're a fine one to talk. You're a secret nut yourself. If you were as sensible as you think you are, when I came around in the middle of the night babbling of arsenic you'd have sent me away and gone back to bed. You would have gone for the police when the knife missed Tony, instead of chasing George into the tunnel."

"Umph," said Blankenhagen, turning red.

"Schmidt didn't mean any harm," I said. "He's a sweet little man. I always liked him."

Blankenhagen's face got even redder.

"You are going to marry Schmidt!"

"I'm not going to marry anybody," I said. "I'm going to take the job Herr Schmidt has offered me, at the Museum, and write a book about Riemenschneider, and also a best-selling historical novel based on the Drachenstein story. Maybe I'll call it 'The Drachenstein Story.' The plot has everything—murder, witchcraft, blood, adultery. . . . I'll make a fortune. Of course I'll publish it under a pseudonym so the scholarly reputation I intend to build in the next five years won't be impaired. Then—"

"You aren't going to marry anyone?" Tony asked, having found his voice at last.

"Why do I have to marry anyone?" I asked reasonably. "It's only in simpleminded novels that the heroine has to get married. I'm not even the heroine. You told me that once. Irma is the heroine. Go marry her."

"I don't want to," Tony said sulkily.

"Then don't. But stop hassling me." I smiled impartially at both of them. "You're very sweet," I said kindly. "The trouble is, *neither* of you has the faintest idea of how to handle women—not women like me, anyhow. But you're both young, and fairly bright; you can learn. . . . Who knows, I might decide to get married someday. I'll be around; if, in the meantime, you feel like—"

Blankenhagen's expression changed ominously, and I said, with dignity,

"If you feel like taking a girl out now and then, I am open to persuasion."

I smiled guilessly at him.

After a long moment he smiled back.

"*Also*," he said coolly. "I will be here. I will continue to be here. I do not give up easily."

There was a knock at the door, followed by the voice of one of the maids telling us dinner was ready. I started for the door.

Tony got there ahead of me.

"It wouldn't help Schmidt's reputation if this affair were made public," he said meditatively. "I don't suppose you intimated—"

"Why, Tony," I said, with virtuous indignation. "That would be blackmail! Would I resort to such a low trick?"

"Of course not. Schmidt offered you a job because of your brilliance. I'm brilliant too," said Tony. "I imagine Herr Schmidt could find another job at the Museum, if I asked him nicely. . . ."

Blankenhagen stood up.

"You talk to me of rascals!" he exclaimed. "You are an unprincipled, dishonest—"

I left the two of them jostling each other in the doorway and went humming down the corridor. The next five years were going to be fun.

Coming soon in hardcover

THE LAUGHTER OF DEAD KINGS

by Elizabeth Peters

The heist of the century has taken place in Egypt's Valley of the Kings, and Vicky Bliss's boyfriend, "Sir John Smythe," is a prime suspect. Even Vicky isn't sure that John hasn't fallen back into his old bad ways. Pursued by Interpol, the Egyptian police, rival gangs of thieves, and Vicky's inquisitive boss, Anton Z. Schmidt, she and John set off on a wild chase to find the real culprits—and retrieve an extraordinary treasure.

Turn the page for a sneak peek at the long-awaited final installment in the beloved series featuring art historian Vicky Bliss—back for the first time in more than a decade.

❀═❀═❀

JOHN SAT WATCHING ME WHILE I BUSTLED AROUND the living room, plumping pillows and trying to scrape Clara's hairs off the sofa cushions.

"Why this sudden burst of domesticity?" he asked. "Schmidt will sprinkle cigar ashes and spill beer over everything as soon as he settles in."

"He's bringing a guest."

Another of those slight but meaningful pauses. "Oh? Who?"

"He didn't say. From the frequency of his chuckles I suspect it's a lady. A female, anyhow."

I paused for a quick look in the mirror over the couch. Some of my guests have complained that it is a trifle high for them, but I'm almost six feet tall and whose mirror is it, anyhow? Actually, I hate being tall. It's okay if you want to be a fashion model or a basketball pro, but being tall and blond and well-rounded (as I like to put it) can be detrimental to an academic career. Some people still cling to the delusion that a female-shaped female can't possibly have a functioning brain.

I tucked a few loose strands of hair into the bun at the nape of my neck, checked to make sure my makeup was on straight and grimaced at my reflection. For whom was I primping, anyhow? Schmidt's postulated lady friend?

John glanced casually at his watch. "I think I'll take Caesar out for a quick run before they arrive."

"It's still raining."

"Misting. Normal weather where I come from."

Moving with his deceptively casual stride, he almost made it to the door before I caught hold of him.

"All right, that's enough. Sit down in that chair and tell me what's wrong."

Caesar began barking indignantly. He's not awfully bright but he was smart enough to put two and two together: somebody had been about to take him for a walk and somebody else had interfered. The sheer volume of his protest almost drowned out another sound. The doorbell.

"That can't be Schmidt yet," I exclaimed. "He's never on time."

The doorbell went on ringing. It sounded almost as frantic as Caesar. John put his head in his hands.

"Too late," he moaned.

"Who is it?" I shouted over the cacophony. A longish list of dangerous names unrolled in my head. "Max? Blenkiron? Interpol? Scotland Yard?"

"Worse," said John, in a voice of doom. "Shut up, Caesar."

Caesar did. In the comparative silence the sound of the doorbell was replaced by rhythmic pounding. John got up and went to the door.

The forty-watt bulb on the porch illumined the form of a man, his black hair shining with damp.

Shadows obscured his features, but I saw enough to identify him. Relief left me limp.

"Feisal? Is that you? Why didn't John tell me you were coming?" And why, I thought, was he so appalled at the idea of your coming? Feisal wasn't an enemy, he was a friend, a really good friend, who had risked life, limb and reputation to keep me safe during our latest escapade in Egypt.

John caught Caesar by the collar and dragged him out of the way so that Feisal could come in. Now that I saw his face clearly I knew this was not a social call, a happy surprise for Vicky. He is a handsome guy, with those hawklike classic Arab features, long fuzzy eyelashes, and a complexion the color of caffe latte. Only now it was more latte than coffee, and the lines that framed his mouth looked as if they had been carved by a chisel. I didn't ask any more questions. Why bother, I wasn't getting answers anyhow. Wordlessly I gestured Feisal to a chair.

"I'd offer you a drink," I began, groping for a steadying cliché. "But you don't. Drink. Alcohol."

"I do," said John, "thank God."

He filled three glasses—vodka and tonic for me and for him and plain tonic for Feisal.

"Start talking," he said curtly.

I stared at him. "You mean you don't know what this is about either?"

"No. Dire hints, hysterical groans, a demand that I meet him here—immediately, if not sooner. Talk fast, Feisal. Schmidt will be here before long."

"Schmidt!" Galvanized, Feisal sprang to his feet. "Oh, Lord, no. Not Schmidt. Why didn't you tell me he was coming? I've got to get out of here!"

"I didn't know until it was too late," John said. "You've got approximately three quarters of an hour to put us in the picture and then make a run for it, or compose yourself and behave normally. If I'd been able I'd have headed you off, but alas, it was not to be. Do we want Vicky in on this?"

"She's in on it," I said, folding my arms in a decisive manner.

Feisal nodded gloomily. "May I smoke?"

I shoved an ashtray at him. "I thought you'd quit."

"I had. Until day before yesterday."

"Get on with it," John said.

"I'm going to tell you what happened, as it was told to me by the man on the spot. I wasn't there. As Inspector of Antiquities for all Upper Egypt I have a huge territory to cover, and I'm short on personnel, and—"

"We know all that," John said impatiently. "Don't make excuses until you've told us what you're accused of doing."

❁═❁

Ali looked up at the sun, glanced at his watch for verification, and sighed. Over an hour before he and the other guards could kick the tourists out of the Valley of the Kings and go home. He unscrewed the top of his water bottle and drank. It was a day like any other day, hot and dusty and dry. The fabled burial ground of the great pharaohs of ancient

Egypt held no charm for him; it was just a job, one he had held for more than ten years.

The mobs of visitors had diminished somewhat, but there were still hundreds of them crowding the pathways of the Valley, kicking up dust, chattering in a dozen languages. A group of Japanese visitors passed him, clustering round the flag held high by their guide. Like little chickens, Ali thought, scampering after the mother hen, afraid to leave her side. He didn't know which was worse, the little chickens or the Germans, who kept wandering off and poking into places where they weren't supposed to go, or the French, who went around with their hairy legs bare and their bodies indecently exposed. He didn't hate any of them. He just didn't like them much, any of them. At least the Americans tipped well. Better than the British, who haggled over every pound.

The tomb he guarded was locked, as it often was, but that hadn't prevented people from trying to bribe him to let them in. One fat-faced American had offered him a hundred Egyptian pounds—two months' pay for him, the price of an inexpensive dinner for the American. God knew he could have used the money. But it would have cost him his job to break the rules, especially with this tomb. It was too conspicuous, right on the main path, the most famous tomb in the Valley.

He leaned back and closed his eyes. The babble of voices faded; and then a sound brought him wide awake. He sat up and stared.

Coming toward him was a black SUV, horn blaring, warning pedestrians off the road. It had to be an official vehicle, no others were allowed in the Valley. It was followed by two other cars, and behind them was an object that made Ali's eyes open even wider. It was as big as a tour bus; but it wasn't a bus, it was a van, painted white and covered with writing in some language that definitely wasn't Arabic. Memory stirred and Ali invoked his god. He'd seen a van like that before. What was it doing here now? Why hadn't he been told?

The cavalcade pulled to a stop in front of the tomb. Men in black uniforms got out of the sedans and fanned out, forming a cordon around the entrance. The doors of the SUV opened. A man got out and strode briskly toward Ali. He was bearded and wore horn-rimmed glasses. Another, younger, man followed him. He carried a worn briefcase.

"You the fellow in charge?" the older man barked. "Jump to it. Get that gate open. We haven't much time."

"But," Ali stuttered. "But—"

"Oh, for God's sake. Weren't you notified we would be here?"

Ali's blank stare was apparently answer enough; the man turned to his younger companion and said something in an undertone. Ali caught the words "typical Egyptian efficiency."

"Well, we're here now," the bearded man went on. "I am Dr. Henry Manchester of the British Institute of Technoarchaeology. I presume you would like to see my authorization. Yes, yes, quite proper."

He snapped his fingers. The younger man fumbled in his briefcase and pulled out a paper, which he handed to Manchester, who handed it to Ali. "I don't suppose you read English, but you should recognize the signature."

Ali prided himself on his knowledge of English but knew better than to express his resentment. The document looked impressive. The Supreme Council of Antiquities, Office of the Secretary General. It was signed by the Great Man himself. Not that Ali had ever received a letter from the Great Man, but he had met him once, just after his appointment to the post, when he made a tour of the major sites. Perhaps "met" wasn't the precise word; but the Great Man had nodded graciously in his general direction.

"Yes, I see," he said slowly. "But I cannot—"

"Put in a call to the Supreme Council, then," the Englishman said impatiently. "Only make it fast."

Oh, yes, Ali thought. Telephone the Supreme Council. This is Ali, you remember me, the guard from the Valley of the Kings. Put me through to Dr. Khifaya right away . . .

"No," he said. "The paper is in order."

"I should think so. Now don't delay me any longer, we were held up at the bridge and are short on time. Never mind the key, I have one."

He pushed past Ali and went down the stairs.

From that point on things moved so fast Ali couldn't have stopped them if he had wanted to. The back doors of the van opened. Inside was a bewildering medley of machinery—cables, tubes, shapes of plastic and metal. Several men in crisp white dungarees jumped out and followed the two Englishmen down the stairs. Ali looked around for help—advice—reassurance. A small crowd had gathered, tourists gaping and speculating, and several of his fellow guards, kept at a distance by the men in black uniforms. After a moment he went down the stairs and along the corridor into the tomb chamber. He let out a faint cry of protest when he saw that the glass covering the stone sarcophagus had been set aside. The white-garbed men were in the process of lifting the lid of the gilded coffin inside the big stone box. From the coffin base they removed a long, rigid platform covered by dusty fabric. Moving quickly but with care, the bearers maneuvered their burden through the narrow space and out of the room.

By this time interest and curiosity had replaced Ali's initial concern. Yes, it was like the last time. The van wasn't the same—the other one had been larger—but from what he could tell, the equipment inside was similar. Only this time there were no journalists or television crews. He'd seen himself on television when they showed the program—just a fleeting glimpse, but he'd bought a tape and played that part over and over. Maybe they had got it wrong the first time and had to come back and do it again? That made sense. They wouldn't want to admit a mistake, so they had arranged for this to be done without publicity and advance notice.

Finding himself alone in the burial chamber, he went back along the corridor and up the stairs. They had put the litter and its contents into the van and closed the doors. Machinery was humming and sputtering. There were beeping noises and people talking. He squatted down and lit a cigarette and waited and thought about . . . him. How did he like being dragged out of what he had hoped would be his final resting place, stared at by impious strangers, discussed as if he were a piece of wood? He had been an infidel, a pagan, but once he had been human and he had been faithful to his own gods in his time.

The sun was low above the cliffs when the doors at the back of the van opened again. The shrouded shape was lifted out and carried back into the tomb.

"You have been very helpful," the Englishman said. He smiled for the first time, and Ali saw the glint of a gold tooth or filling. "I shall mention you to Dr. Khifaya. Here."

Ali took the folded paper but he didn't look at it until after the men had piled back into their vehicles and driven off. Then he unfolded the banknote. His lip curled. Ten miserable Egyptian pounds.

Englishmen.

❀▭❀

"I don't get it," I said. "Why the consternation? Nobody told you in advance, but maybe this was a sudden decision and they tried to get in touch with you and couldn't because you were out in the desert or something. Or maybe . . ."

My voice trailed off. The two of them sat there staring fixedly at me. "Oh, Lord," I said.

"She's a little slow this evening," John explained, nodding at Feisal. "Be patient with her. What did you do after Ali informed you of the—er—visit?"

"Went into the tomb." Feisal removed a crumpled white handkerchief from his pocket and mopped his brow. "At first sight everything looked normal. But I had a feeling . . . One of *those* feelings. It was unlikely, verging on impossible, that I wouldn't have been notified in advance. I'd have ordered Ali to leave, but I couldn't lift the coffin lid by myself, it's too heavy. We managed to shift it just enough to get a look inside. The poor devil is in pieces, you know, they've got the various parts laid out on a sand table, padded all round with cotton wool and covered with a sort of heavy blanket. At first glance it looked normal. But when I folded the blanket back from where his head was supposed to be, it wasn't there. He was gone. Not so much as a stray bone left."

Available in mass market—
the first five novels in the
Vicky Bliss Mystery Series
by *New York Times* bestselling author

ELIZABETH PETERS

Borrower of the Night

❀▭❀

A missing masterwork in wood may be hidden in a medieval German castle in the town of Rothenburg. The prize has called to Vicky Bliss—the beautiful and brainy art historian—drawing her into the forbidding citadel and its dark secrets. But the treasure hunt soon turns deadly. Here, where the blood of the long-dead stains ancient stones, Vicky must face two equally perilous possibilities: either a powerful supernatural evil inhabits this place . . . or someone frighteningly real is willing to kill for what Vicky is determined to find.

It was not until we heard the creak of hinges that we realized what was going on. Even then things might have worked out if Tony had kept his head. Instead of moving slowly and quietly, he leaped to his feet, planting a knee in my stomach in the process. I grunted.

The scuffle was warning enough for the grave robber. I had only a glimpse of a dark form leaving the grounds at impressive speed. Tony started in pursuit and lost valuable time by falling into the hole that had been excavated. When he realized where he was, he got out with considerable alacrity. The moon was still hidden, and he cursed it fluently, without noticeable results.

I had caught up with him by that time, having recovered my breath while he was floundering around in the open grave.

"Hurry," I yelled. "Street outside is lighted . . . we can see . . ."

We couldn't see our quarry, but we could hear him. Cemeteries are notoriously quiet places, especially in the middle of the night. From the sounds, the man seemed to be heading for the gate on Ansbacher Strasse.

As we had already ascertained, the gate was locked. I didn't expect it to detain our agile adversary for long, however. He was over the gate before we reached the spot. Our progress had been frustratingly slow; even if I had had no qualms about stepping on graves, the stones were close together and the paths were winding. We got over the gate, in our turn, leaving a piece of my slacks on the spikes.

The street outside curves and is lined with trees. There was no one in sight. Assuming that the grave robber would head for the inner city, and the *Schloss*, we took that direction. As we neared the open area in front of the city gate, we were finally rewarded by a glimpse of the man we were after. One glimpse was enough for Tony, who staggered and stopped, for a vital couple of seconds, before he got a grip on his nerves and began running again.

I couldn't blame him for hesitating. The figure was that of a tall Black Man, enveloped in a cloak that swooped out around his body like giant dark wings. The head appeared to be a featureless lump.

The monstrosity disappeared under the stone arch of the Roedertor. I admit, without shame, that I felt a healthy reluctance as we followed, running into darkness and into the enclosing walls that had been designed to hold back entire armies.

If you have never seen a medieval city gate you may picture it as a pair of wooden doors, plus a portcullis or two. Not so. This particular gate, which is more properly called a bastion, consists of a series of massive walls and narrow passages, designed so that a defending force could clobber the attackers at several points. Once past the first gate, an invader found himself in a circular area hemmed in by high stone walls with enclosed galleries, from which various missiles could be propelled onto his head. The only way out of this area was over a moat, whose drawbridge could of course be raised. Beyond the drawbridge a high tower defended the inner part of the bastion.

The gates are gone nowadays, and the drawbridge has been replaced by solid pavement. All the same, my shoulders hunched apprehensively as we entered the circular court. Pounding along the brick-paved street that crosses the moat and goes through the narrow tunnel under the tower, I felt a wave of sympathy for the soldier who had had to attack the place—not for the arrogant knight, safely encased in steel, but for the conscripted peasant in his leather jerkin, clutching his pike in a sweaty hand and hoping to God he'd never have to use it. I half expected an arrow to whistle over my head and rattle on the pavement. It was the sort of humorous gesture our adversary seemed to enjoy.

We got through the tunnel without incident, however, and came to a baffled halt in the street beyond the bastion. The tall houses of the old city loomed dark and silent on either side. We hadn't made enough noise to awaken the inhabitants, since we were both wearing rubber-soled sneakers. The loudest sound was Tony's heavy breathing.

I was pretty sure we had lost our man. There were a dozen hiding places in that crowded, narrow way, half a dozen alleyways and side streets he might have taken. Yet I still felt vulnerable and exposed, as if someone were watching me.

I glanced up over my shoulder. The town walls were shadowy bulwarks, cutting off the sky. A single lonely streetlight did little to lighten their darkness. Up above, on the balustraded walkway, something moved. It looked like a black sleeve, flapping.

I clutched at Tony, who was starting stupidly down the Schmeidgasse. He let out a yelp.

"For God's sake, don't do that!"

"He's up there," I gasped. "On the wall. Tony—I think he waved at me."

Street of the Five Moons

❀⚍❀

When it comes to medieval history, Vicky Bliss knows her stuff, and this blonde beauty is a master at solving mysteries that turn the art world upside-down. When an exquisite gold pendant is found stitched into the suit pocket of an unidentified man found dead in an alley, Vicky vows to find the craftsman who created it. It's a daring chase that takes her all the way from Munich to Rome, through the dusty antique centers and moonlit streets of the most romantic city in the world. But soon she's trapped in a treacherous game of intrigue that could cost her life—or her heart.

"Get to a phone," John snapped. "Call Schmidt. Tell him everything."

I started to say something, but before I could speak he transferred his grip to my knees and heaved me up. I saw his face go dead white as his arms took my full weight. Then my elbows were over the edge of the roof. From then on it was a piece of cake. John's hands on the sole of my shoes gave me one last push that took me onto the flat roof.

He had time to close the window and move away from it before the bedroom door gave way. When I peered down, I saw the window was closed, and I heard the sounds from inside the room. He put up quite a fight.

He could never have climbed onto the roof. I kept telling myself that as I scuttled across the steaming, tarred surface. Without his pushing me from below I couldn't have made it myself, and he only had one good arm. I also kept telling myself that he was safe now, in the hands of the police, and that as soon as I could reach Schmidt he would be all right. At least he wouldn't be charged with murder. I wondered if the Italian police used the third degree on suspects.

I knew he hadn't killed Helena. I couldn't think of a reason why anyone would want to kill her. Pietro wasn't the type to fly into a jealous passion, even if he had discovered she was unfaithful to him; he would just curse and shrug and dump her. There was, of course, the possibility that she had stumbled on some information that made her dangerous to the gang. But what? She wasn't awfully bright, poor girl, and I doubted that she could have learned more than John and I knew. The gang had imprisoned us when they decided we were dangerous. Perhaps they had meant to kill us. But why kill her? A handful of diamonds would have shut her mouth quite effectively—and they needn't have been real diamonds. One of Luigi's pretty copies would have fooled her nicely. No, there was no need to commit murder—unless the streak of hidden violence I had already sensed beneath the seeming harmlessness of the original plot had finally surfaced.

These ideas were swimming around in my mind, not quite as coherently as I have expressed them, as

I went loping across the roofs of Trastevere like Zorro or the Scarlet Pimpernel or somebody of that ilk. Those fictitious heroes weren't as fool-hardy as they appeared; they always had a stooge down below, with a wagon filled with hay or with a snorting white stallion, so that they could drop dramatically onto the animal's back and go riding off into the sunset shouting "Vengeance," or "I will return."

I stopped and took a look around. Nobody had climbed the wall after me. Either John had convinced the policemen that he was alone, or they had concluded I had made my getaway. I felt horribly conspicuous up there, though. The apartment building was of moderate height; some of the neighboring structures were higher, some were lower, and there were balconies and windows all around. I sat down in the shade of the parapet that ran around the roof and tried to catch my breath.

I wasn't going to have any problem getting down from the roof. The old buildings of Trastevere don't boast modern luxuries like fire escapes, but they have other features that could make cat burglary a cinch. There are no yards or gardens in that quarter, so the people use roofs for out-of-doors living. Some of them were prettily arranged, with furniture and awnings and potted palm trees. Obviously there was access to the roofs from the lower floors. All I had to do was select a building at a safe distance from the one where I was sitting, and descend.

I was about to rise and go on my way when I heard noises from the street below. A car stopped with a faint squeak of tires and someone called out. I stood up and peeked over the parapet.

The car was big enough to fill the street from side to side. It was parked in front of John's apartment building, and as I watched I saw three men emerge from the courtyard. All I could see from up there were the tops of their heads and odd, foreshortened views of shoulders, but it wasn't hard to identify John. He had lost his hat, and his head flopped forward as the other two pulled him along between them. They looked like big men, but that may have been because John wasn't standing up straight. His feet dragged helplessly along the pavement as they threw him into the car. They got in after him and drove off.

Silhouette in Scarlet

❀▭❀

*One perfect red rose, a one-way ticket to Stockholm,
and a cryptic message consisting of two Latin words
intrigue art historian Vicky Bliss—precisely as they
were intended to do. Beautiful, brilliant, and always dangerously inquisitive, Vicky recognizes the
handiwork of her former lover—the daring jewel
thief John Smythe. But the hunt for lost treasure
threatens to turn deadly on a remote island, where a
captive Vicky Bliss must lead an excavation into the
distant past—and where digging too deep for the
truth could mean digging her own grave.*

We could make a run for it, or we could call for help
and hold the gang at bay until said help arrived.
Holding the gang at bay meant hiding; I wasn't
about to consider anything more adventurous. Gus
must know some good hiding places. The burning
question was: Could I contact the mainland?

Just for the hell of it, I tried the telephone. As I
had expected, it was dead. Gus probably had an
emergency means or communication laid on—a
shortwave or CB radio or something of that
sort—and if I ever found Gus I would ask him. I
decided not to waste time searching, though. Unless
it was well concealed, Max had probably dealt with
it already.

Smoke signals, setting the barn on fire, flashing SOS's with my pocket mirror ... Too chancy. So much for the idea of communicating with the mainland. The alternative, running for our lives, presented one minor difficulty. We couldn't run. We were surrounded by water.

The silence of the house was getting to me. I headed for the door. It was a relief to be in the sunlight and fresh air. The rain had left everything looking fresh and clean. The wind stung my face. I assumed the thugs were all in the pasture, digging for treasure, but I kept a wary eye peeled as I descended the stairs to the dock. When the boathouse door opened, I got ready to duck. But it was only Leif.

"I have looked," he said. "Nothing we can use."

I was prepared for that discouraging statement; the fact that Max hadn't bothered to set a guard on the boats was proof positive that they had been put out of commission. Hope dies hard, though. When I advanced, Leif grinned and stood aside to let me see for myself.

The more I looked, the madder I got. Max hadn't just destroyed the boats, he had smashed the dreams and memories they symbolized. In his younger days Gus must have been a first-class mariner. Now the canoe and the kayak and the neat little sailboat lay deep underwater, held only by their mooring ropes. The rowboat was a utility craft, big enough to hold several people and a tidy amount of cargo. At least it could have held them if someone hadn't chopped a hole in the bottom. The cruiser appeared to be undamaged, except for the shortwave, which had been demolished.

I sat in the cockpit and swore.

Leif peered in at me. "The key is missing."

"I know."

"Perhaps there is another key."

"If we ever find Gus, we can ask him." I took Leif's proffered hand and climbed out. "Isn't there some way of starting her up without a key? I've done it with cars, but I'm not familiar with this type of engine."

Leif shrugged, looking almost as bland and stupid as Hans, and I snapped, "I thought you were an engineer."

"I am not a mechanic," Leif said in an offended voice. "But I do know there are many things one can do to an engine to make sure it will not start."

"They can't have done anything drastic," I argued. "This must be the craft they plan to use when they leave."

"Unless they have arranged for a boat or helicopter to pick them up," Leif said.

I hadn't thought of that. It didn't make me feel very good.

"In any case, it would take hours to check the cruiser," Leif said. "The ignition system, the fuel lines, and so on. Do you suppose Max will stand back and allow us to do that?"

"How did you get here?" I asked.

Leif blinked. "I swam."

Through the open doors I could see the distant shore and the waves that rose and fell in brisk cadence. The water was a deep, rich blue; it looked as cold as a freezer. No wonder Leif's calf muscles looked like the hawsers of the *Q.E. II*.

Trojan Gold

◎ ▭ ◎

A picture is worth a thousand words. But the photograph that art historian Vicky Bliss has just received gives rise to a thousand questions instead. A quick glance at the blood-stained envelope is all the proof she needs that something is horribly wrong. Inside, a picture of a woman adorned in the ancient gold of Troy—gold, as Vicky and her fellow academics know, that disappeared at the end of World War II. Now as this circle of experts gathers for a festive Bavarian Christmas, a very determined killer is in their midst.

It was at that point in my cool, deliberate reasoning that I heard something that was not the wind moaning in the branches. The wind wouldn't call my name.

The voice came from behind me—between me and the car. Did I panic? Of course I did. I started forward, my progress agonizingly slowed by the depth of the snow. Get behind something—that was my only thought. A snow bank, a wall—how about a tombstone? Plenty of them around.

"Vicky!" Unmistakably my name, though the wind snatched the syllables and played with them. High-pitched and distorted by emotion, it could have been the voice of a man or a woman.

I reached an area where the snow was slightly less deep—only about to my knees. The black square framed in whiteness was Hoffman's tombstone. The snow lay deep and untouched over the graves. One of my wreaths had toppled forward, only a black half-circle showed, partially veiled by the drifting snow.

I could hear him now, thrashing after me. I reached into my bag and found the gun. My hands were stiff with cold, despite my gloves. I realized I'd have to remove one of them to get my finger around the trigger.

"Vicky!" Then, at last, I knew the voice.

He was a dark featureless shadow against the paler blanket of snow, but I would have known that shape anywhere. His voice was rough and uneven, barely recognizable. "What the hell are you doing? It's thirty degrees below freezing; are you trying to turn yourself into an ice cube?"

I said, "Friedl is dead. Murdered. Strangled."

"Ah." His breath formed a ghostly plume against the darkness. After a moment he said, "It's here. I should have known. The bulb."

"The wrong time of year, you said." My lips were numb with cold. "Bulbs are planted in the fall, before the ground freezes. I expect he put the chrysanthemums in at the same time. Even if anyone noticed, in this remote place, the signs of digging would be explained."

"And what more appropriate spot than the grave of his Helen," John murmured.

Had he read Hoffman's love letters? Not necessarily. His quick, intuitive mind was capable of appreciating the poetry of real life, even if he couldn't feel it himself.

When he spoke again his voice cracked with anger. "So you came rushing up here in the dead of night, with a blizzard forecast, to catch a killer. Are you out of your mind? Even if he knows—"

"She's safe until he finds out, you said."

"I said a lot of things. What am I, the voice of God? He may have had other reasons for murdering her."

I said, "I have a gun."

"How nice." He had regained control of his breathing; his voice broke, in a long in-drawn breath. Then he said quietly, almost reverently, "My God."

Even the great John Smythe couldn't have feigned that emotion. I glanced behind me.

It was almost upon us. I caught only one flashing glimpse before it engulfed me, but the sight burned the image into my eyes.

Snow. A solid, opaque wall of whiteness, silent, deadly, moving down from the mountain heights.

Night Train to Memphis

◉━━◉

An assistant curator of Munich's National museum, Vicky Bliss may not be an expert on Egypt, but she does have a PhD in solving crimes. So when an intelligence agency offers her a luxury Nile cruise if she'll help solve a murder and help stop a heist of Egyptian antiquities, all 5'11" of her takes the plunge. But when she spots her missing lover—the art thief known only as "Sir John Smythe"—with his new bride in the shadow of the Sphinx, Vicky is so furious at the romantic stab-in-the-back that she may overlook a danger as old and unchanging as the pharaohs . . . a criminal who hides behind a mask of charm.

As I approached the side entrance I heard voices. The movers were working late, but one look told me this clever idea wasn't going to work a second time. The man who stood by the open door watching them pass in and out was wearing European clothes. Though darkness was not yet complete, the floodlights illumining the entrance had been turned on, enabling him to see their faces clearly. They also enabled me to see his features clearly. I had known him as Bright. I had a hunch that wasn't his real name.

The floodlights served me well, half-blinding him to anything that was going on outside their glare. I sidled through the landscaping until I reached the terrace. As I crawled on hands and knees in the dubious shelter of the low walls, one of my sandals fell off. Instead of replacing it I kicked the other one off. Once I was inside the house, bare feet would be quieter and quicker than those clumsy sandals.

I had come prepared to break the glass if I had to; one of the useful objects Schmidt had pressed upon me was a roll of tape. However, the French doors weren't locked. The parlor was lighted but empty. After I had closed the door behind me I relaxed a little, though I knew the feeling of greater safety was mostly wishful thinking. There were places to hide, behind draperies and furniture, but several of the pieces I had seen before were gone—into one of the moving vans, I supposed.

I wished I were more familiar with the plan of the house. Somewhere, I felt certain, there were rooms not open to the general public, and I wasn't thinking of the kitchen and service areas. But if they were as secret as they had to be—underground, protected by every possible security device—access wouldn't be easy. I had decided I would investigate the bedrooms first.

My turban had come unhitched and my hands were too unsteady to deal with the damned thing. I tied it around my neck in a neat Girl Scout knot and paddled toward the hall and the front stairs.

If the man who came down the stairs had been barefoot I would have walked right into him. He was wearing boots and his step was firm and confident; I heard him coming and ducked back into the parlor, praying that room wasn't his destination. He went the other way, heading for Larry's study. The door opened and I heard voices before it closed again.

Evidently a business meeting was in progress. There had been several voices, including a woman's soprano, considerably louder and shriller than her usual soft tones. I hadn't dared look to see who the latest arrival had been—Max? Larry?—but at least four of them were now in the office.

Lifting my skirts, I ran up the stairs. All the doors along the corridor were closed; lights in antique bronze sconces shone brightly.

A methodical searcher would have tried each door in turn. That procedure had its risks, however. It was too much to expect that all of them would be in Larry's study. If I opened the door of an occupied room the search would end then and there. I tried the door of Schmidt's former room first, and then that of my own. Both were dark. I had to turn on the lights to make certain nobody was there. It was not a very smart move, but I hadn't thought of bringing a flashlight. There were a lot of things I hadn't thought of.

Time was getting on. The meeting could break up at any moment. It occurred to me that maybe I ought to find a place where I could hide in case someone came upstairs. If I couldn't find him right away, if he wasn't in this part of the house, I would have to wait till after they had gone to bed before I resumed the search. Maybe I would be lucky enough to overhear a snatch of conversation: "Let us go to the cellar, which is reached by a flight of stairs next to the kitchen, and see how our guest (sneering laugher) is getting on."

Fat chance. I had been associating with Schmidt too long even to imagine such a thing.

It was likely that he was in the cellar (if there was a cellar) or in one of the other buildings. Checking the bedrooms was probably a waste of time, but it had to be done and now was the best time, before the occupants of the house retired for the night. First, though, I needed to find a place where I could hide temporarily. The narrow unadorned door at the back of a shallow recess looked as if it led to another broom closet or linen closets, so I tried it first. No one would be there.

Someone was, though.